PUBLISHING

D0067205

ONCE UPON

A

Royal

CHRISTMAS

USA TODAY BESTSELLING AUTHOR

TERI WILSON

For everyone who dreams of a Hallmark Christmas. xoxo

CHAPTER ONE

Girl-Boss Princess

"Y̲OUR PAPERWORK SAYS YOU'RE HERE about a small business loan." The bank manager looked up from the file folder on his desk, and his gaze flitted immediately to the tiara sitting atop Gracie Clark's head—the ridiculous, rhinestone-bedecked elephant in the room. "Your, um, Majesty?"

Nervous laughter bubbled up Gracie's throat. Of all the days to get stuck at work for over an hour past the time she was supposed to leave, *why* did it have to happen today?

"Again, I'm so sorry. I fully planned to go home and change before this appointment." Gracie was beginning to sweat beneath the velvet and lace bodice of her costume, and she was pretty sure she had a dollop of pink buttercream frosting in her hair. Occupational hazard and all that. "Children's birthday parties don't always go according to plan."

The bank manager, who had introduced himself as Benjamin Curtis, was a befuddled, grandfatherly-type man

1

dressed in suspenders and a tweed suit. Although, admittedly, Gracie's attire might have been the source of his befuddlement. Somehow she doubted his other customers showed up for their loan interviews dressed as fairy tale characters.

Mr. Curtis's gaze traveled slowly from Gracie's glittering crown to her big, dangling earrings and down the length of her thick, cinnamon-brown braid. The pattern on the heavily bedazzled bodice of Gracie's ballgown reflected back at her from the lenses of his bifocals, glittering like an icy winter kaleidoscope. This meeting was getting more awkward by the second.

"It's Your Royal Highness, actually," Gracie said in an attempt to lighten the mood with a bit of regal humor.

Mr. Curtis's brow furrowed. "I beg your pardon?"

"Kings and queens are addressed as Your Majesty. I'm not a queen." Gracie felt her smile begin to falter. Maybe playing along hadn't been the best idea. This man was one of the few remaining bank officers in Denver who had the power to change Gracie's life. Not just hers, but the lives of her employees as well. "I'm a princess."

"Indeed you are." Mr. Curtis's eyes darted to the paperwork and back again. "Princess Snowflake."

"I'm kidding, obviously. I'm a businesswoman and a performer, not an actual princess. You definitely don't need to call me Your Royal Highness." Gracie squirmed beneath the weight of endless yards of snowy white tulle.

Mr. Curtis nodded, but the lines in his forehead seemed to grow deeper. Gracie could practically see the future she'd envisioned for her company vanishing into thin air.

She straightened in her chair. "Perfect Party Princesses is a costume character business. We provide a variety of fairy tale princess characters for children's birthday parties, school events, weddings, tea parties, and corporate gigs. Pretty much any sort of occasion where guests would appreciate a dash of royal fairy tale magic."

The bank manager tilted his head. "Weddings? Brides and grooms actually want princesses at their marriage ceremonies?"

"Sometimes they do, yes," Gracie said.

She wondered if he'd ever seen an episode of *Fairy Tale I Do*, the popular reality show about couples getting married at theme parks around the world. Gracie and Clara—her best friend, roommate, and business partner—loved it. They watched it every Thursday night with pepperoni pizza from their favorite delivery place in Cherry Creek. Last week, the show had featured a couple who'd gotten married at Cinderella's castle in Disneyland Paris. On Christmas Eve. It had been *très* magical, but somehow Gracie doubted Mr. Curtis was a fan.

The loan officer didn't have a single holiday decoration in his office, and Christmas was less than a month away. For a girl who made her living as a snow princess, that seemed like a giant, Scroogey red flag.

"Anyway." Gracie cleared her throat. "I started the business a little over four years ago. At first, it was just me, as Princess Snowflake. Then my partner Clara came on board. She works on publicity, social media, and scheduling. As the headline performer, I'm the face of the company, and I train all of our other princess characters as well."

Clara had been Gracie's best friend since elementary school. The first successful business they'd started together had been their lemonade stand in second grade. Gracie had been responsible for creating the product, and Clara had taken charge of their marketing, mostly in the form of colorful handmade posters and securing a prime location near the entrance to the subdivision where both their families lived. Their business partnership followed pretty much the same dynamic to this day.

"Our gross income has quadrupled in the past two

years." Gracie sat up a little straighter. She was proud of how far she'd come, proud of the fact that she provided a great hourly wage for princesses who were mostly struggling college students and young single moms. She'd worn out *three* bedazzling tools in the process of affixing crystals to the dress she was wearing. She'd started out as a twenty-two-year-old in a frothy princess gown, and in the span of just four years, she'd built a successful business. No Fairy Godmother required, thank you very much. "We currently support eight part-time staff members in addition to Clara and myself."

"That's quite impressive," Mr. Curtis said.

Gracie relaxed ever so slightly. Maybe being forced to show up in her Princess Snowflake costume hadn't been as disastrous as she'd feared it would be. At least the bank manager who possibly held the future of her business in his hands was getting a chance to see her handiwork up close and personal. Gracie made all the costumes for Perfect Party Princesses herself, on the same Singer sewing machine she'd been using since her mom taught her how to sew back in high school.

"We're in the perfect position to expand. A small business loan would allow us to move our business operations to a more professional office environment." Translation: they were running out of room in the small mountain cabin they rented from Clara's aunt and uncle. The dining room was beginning to look like a tiara museum. But that wasn't even the biggest issue. "As you'll see from my business plan, another of my goals is to transition my part-time staff to full-time employees with benefits. I believe Perfect Party Princesses can make a positive impact on the community and empower young women along the way."

She loved the girls who worked for her, and she wanted to do right by them. Pasting a smile on your face and doing your best to make children happy wasn't easy when you were worried about health insurance or what might happen if you fell off your glass slippers and got injured. Gracie knew what those struggles were like, and she didn't want to pass them along to other young women, simply because she was their boss.

She beamed at Benjamin Curtis, willing him to approve her application. If she'd thought the plastic magic wand her Fairy Godmother character used had any real power whatsoever, she would've gladly brought it along and sprinkled the bank manager's office with a generous dose of Perfect Party Princess pixie dust—which was actually just a combination of fine silver glitter and baby powder that Gracie and Clara mixed together in their cabin bathroom.

Then again, if Gracie had been in possession of actual fairy dust, she wouldn't need a business loan, would she?

Mr. Curtis's gaze strayed once again to her ballgown, billowing beyond the confines of her chair and threatening to take over the small office in all of its shimmery glory. Then he sighed.

Gracie crumbled inside.

No. Please, no.

"I'm sorry, but unfortunately, you're not an ideal candidate for a loan at this time," he said.

Gracie shook her head. "I don't understand. I know I'm only in my twenties, but I have a proven track record. Surely there's something I can do to get you to reconsider. Is it the costume? Because I can come back tomorrow in a business suit, *sans* tiara, if that helps."

Had she really thought she could walk into a bank with buttercream frosting in her hair and five pounds of rhinestones pinned to her head and walk out with twenty-five thousand dollars? She should have rescheduled this meeting the instant little Susie Golding blew out the candles on her cake and accidentally set the tablecloth on fire. The subsequent chaos had postponed Gracie's big entrance by over an hour, and now the rest of her day seemed to be going up in flames too.

"That won't be necessary." Mr. Curtis stood and offered Gracie his hand. The meeting was over, apparently.

She'd blown it...again. She'd entered this office hoping she might be able to give her princesses modest Christmas bonuses, apply for a group health plan, and still have the resources to start looking for office space after the first of the year. But this was the fifth bank she'd visited in the past three days. The fifth polite rejection she'd received. Gracie was beginning to think Santa Claus himself wouldn't be willing to write her a check.

The beads on Gracie's costume tinkled like tiny sleigh bells as she rose from her seat and shook the banker's hand. Her vision blurred. The effort it took not to cry was monumental, but there was no way Gracie was going to break down—not until she was home with a pint of peppermint ice cream in her hand. "Thank you for your time."

"Thank you for considering Denver First Bank." Mr. Curtis gave her a bow and an exaggerated wink. "Your Royal Highness."

Gracie's face went warm. Was this guy for real? He'd just turned her down for a business loan, and now he was sending her off with a metaphorical pat on the head like she was a little girl instead of a grown adult. She counted to ten in her head so she wouldn't say something she might regret later and repeated a favorite mantra—the one she always relied on for times like this. *Chin up, princess, or the crown slips.*

Buttercream in her braid aside, she looked like she'd walked straight out of a fairy tale, from the sparkling snowflake crown all the way down to her glass slippers, embellished with bits of silver glitter to look like ice.

But she'd never felt less regal in her life.

An hour later, Gracie slinked home with her glittery train trailing behind her to find Clara sitting at the kitchen bar glued to her computer screen. Their little tabletop Christmas tree stood just to the right of it, dripping with tiny pearl garland, pink velvet bows, and satin-covered ornaments the approximate size of marbles.

One of these days, their living room wouldn't be crammed with rolling racks of princess gowns and plastic bins filled with tiaras and glass slippers, and they'd have room for a real, full-sized Christmas tree. Maybe even a flocked evergreen decorated with vintage mercury glass baubles and white twinkle lights. But alas, that day wouldn't come during the current holiday season.

"How did it go?" Clara asked without bothering to tear her gaze away from the screen.

"Not great." Gracie grabbed her favorite polka dot Kate Spade mug from the cabinet, popped a single-serve hot chocolate pod into the coffee maker, and cleared her throat.

Clara finally looked up. She took in the sight of Gracie still dressed as Princess Snowflake instead of wearing her tailored red girl-boss suit and her eyes went wide. "Oh. Wow. I'm guessing the Golding party ran over."

"Indeed it did. I had to go straight to the bank from the event, and let's just say that the loan officer didn't seem overly eager to write a big check to a fairy tale character. No one does."

Clara's eyes narrowed. "You have frosting in your hair."

"I'm aware." Gracie's stomach growled. She would've sold her soul for a slice of Susie Golding's lavish pink prin-cess cake right about now. "I have to say, you're taking the news really well. Aren't you getting worried? We've tried five banks. *Five*. How many financial institutions does Denver even have?"

"Ninety-six." A lock of auburn hair fell from Clara's messy bun and she tucked it behind her ear. "Plus seventy-five credit unions. Give or take."

Of course she had that frighteningly specific information tucked away in her brain, ready to rattle off at the drop of a hat.

"You scare me sometimes, you know that?" Gracie said, tossing a generous helping of marshmallows into her cocoa.

"But you love me." Clara's eyes sparkled the way they always did when she was about to try and talk Gracie into something. The last time she'd aimed that particular look in Gracie's direction, Clara had tried to get her to audition for the Denver Playhouse's production of *Anastasia*.

No. Way.

Gracie wasn't a singer. Period.

"Forget the bank loan. I've found the perfect way to get the capital we need to expand the business." Clara did a little dance on her barstool and swiveled her laptop so Gracie could see the screen.

Tiny, animated snowflakes twirled over fancy calligraphy script that spelled out the words *Royal Winter Wonderland Contest*. The midnight blue lettering looked as formal as a wedding invitation. Below the headline was a photograph of a castle nestled among jagged, snow-capped mountains and surrounded by a lush forest of spruce trees, glittering with frosty white. The castle itself was a pale dove-gray and boasted at least twelve turrets, topped with tile in a shade that could only be described as Cinderella-blue. An ice-covered pond shimmered in front of the castle—a perfect, frozen mirror.

Gracie leaned in for a closer look. "What is this? Did *Once Upon a Time* open up another location?" Visiting that amusement park in Fort Lauderdale was on Gracie's bucket list. "How has this place not been on *Fairy Tale I Do?*"

Clara shook her head. "Because it's not a theme park. That, my friend, is a real castle in an actual kingdom near the Swiss Alps."

Gracie blinked. Everything about the picture appeared too perfect to be real, from the swirl of frosty mist that surrounded the base of the castle to the soft watercolor hues of the sky overhead. "It looks almost magical. Can you imagine living somewhere like this?"

"That's the best part." Clara waggled her eyebrows. "Someone does live there—a real royal family. And they're going to finance the expansion of Perfect Party Princesses."

Gracie's heart sank all the way down to her faux glass slippers. For a minute there, she'd actually let herself believe Clara had come up with a solid plan. "Have you lost your mind? Wishing for a fairy godmother seems like a more realistic scenario."

Clara rolled her eyes. "I'm serious. Look right here. Didn't you read the full caption?" She jabbed her pointer finger toward the script at the bottom of the screen.

"'Royal Winter Wonderland Contest,'" Gracie said flatly. She'd been so enamored by the picture that she'd forgotten about that part for a second. "'Spend this Christmas with San Glacera's royal family.' What does that even mean?"

"The royal family of San Glacera is holding a contest to promote tourism. Apparently, the kingdom has a big holiday market and ice village every year during the holidays. You're a shoo-in to win. I just know it." Clara was talking so fast that Gracie could barely keep up.

"San Glacera? I've never even heard of it."

"It's a kingdom near the Swiss Alps. I already told you that," Clara said.

"This is just a lot to take in." Gracie waved a hand toward the laptop, where Clara was busy scrolling through a collage of more scenic photographs of San Glacera, which looked as charming as a porcelain Christmas village, complete with a Gothic cathedral, a medieval village square, and Swiss-style chalets with fanciful gingerbread trim.

A towering blue spruce stood in the center of the frozen pond, its boughs laden with snow. The tip of each branch held a Dickensian candle holder with a slender flameless torch. Mittened children and couples holding hands skated around the tree in graceful circles, the blades of their skates as shiny and silver as jingle bells.

Elaborate ice sculptures surrounded the skating pond, lit in pastel shades of lavender, pink, and blue. They were like nothing Gracie had ever seen before—a graceful swan with a filigree crown and downy wings, Father Christmas in a flowing robe with an owl perched on his shoulder, a grand sleigh pulled by an icy white stallion.

And that breathtaking castle loomed over it all, frosted with so much snow and ice that it almost looked as if it had been crafted from a frothy mountain of whipping cream.

Wherever San Glacera might be, it seemed like a Christmas fairy tale come to life.

"Tell me more about this contest," Gracie heard herself say.

"It's part of the kingdom's Christmas Ice Festival." Clara angled the laptop so it was situated between them and banged away at the keyboard. "On Christmas Eve, they unveil a ballroom made completely of ice and they have a big theatrical performance."

"So kind of like the Ice Capades?" Nostalgia tugged Gracie's lips into a smile. Her parents had taken her to an Ice Capades performance back when she was ten years old. She'd been besotted by the princesses. But at the end of the night, when the characters skated to the edge of the rink to shake hands and talk to the children up-close, Gracie had been too terrified of the evil queen to go meet Sleeping Beauty, her favorite character.

And here she was, all these years later, wearing a glittery

crown and approximately twenty yards of tulle and velvet. No wonder there wasn't a banker in town who would take her seriously.

Being a party princess hadn't exactly been her Plan A. No, Plan A had involved recital halls, auditions for musicals, maybe even a part in a Broadway show someday. But after those lofty aspirations had fallen so spectacularly apart, Gracie had dusted herself off and made a Plan B.

And maybe with Plan B, she was *still* dreaming too big. This was her life, not a fairy tale. With Clara's help, she'd taken Perfect Party Princesses further than she'd ever expected. Maybe it was time to give up on being a girl boss of epic proportions.

Clara made a *pfft* sound, dragging Gracie's attention back to the computer screen. "This is a way bigger deal than the Ice Capades. The king and queen are real, remember?"

Gracie narrowed her gaze at the castle. People actually *lived* there?

"The winner of the contest plays a part in the Ice Village and participates in a weeklong junket of holiday traditions and Christmas activities alongside members of the royal family," Clara said.

"Why would they want to do something like that?"

"To increase tourism. The place is magical, but I never knew it existed until today. Neither did you. Clearly, they needed some better PR. Mission accomplished—the contest is all over social media right now." Clara's forehead scrunched. Her head was probably spinning with ideas for Instagram posts. "Anyway, like I said, you would be perfect for this. They're choosing a winner in less than a week. You have a passport, right?"

Gracie did, in fact, have a passport. Not that she'd ever gotten the chance to use it, but still. It existed.

"There's no way I can leave the country. We have Christmas parties booked, and the holidays are the busiest time of year for Princess Snowflake." Why were they having this conversation? She couldn't even get a local bank officer to take her seriously, and Clara somehow thought that people clear on the other side of the world—people who wore crowns in a serious way, not just for playing dress-up—would jump at the chance to invite her to appear at their event at their actual *castle*.

"Most of your bookings are for school parties and children's functions. Denver schools close for the holidays ten full days before Christmas. Worst case scenario, you'd only miss a handful of small family parties. You could train one of the other girls to take your place," Clara said.

Gracie wasn't in a position to argue. As the person in charge of booking, Clara knew Gracie's schedule better than she did.

"I don't know. This seems like it could be a total internet scam. How do we know this contest is even real?" Gracie reached to start the complicated and lengthy process of unpinning her snowflake tiara from her elaborately braided up-do. She was ready to crawl into her Nutcracker pajamas and call it a day.

Clara arched a brow. "Thirty thousand dollars says it's legit."

Gracie's fingertips paused. A lone bobby pin fell onto the countertop with a tiny clatter.

"That's the cash prize," Clara said. "Thirty thousand dollars, plus travel and accommodations for two. Plus, just imagine all the publicity you'll get for the business on top of the prize money." She shot Gracie a smug grin. "Now are you ready to enter?"

With that sort of prize money on the table, it was a no-brainer. It was also probably the biggest long shot since Santa chose Rudolph to guide his sleigh onc legendary, foggy Christmas Eve.

"There's no way I'm going to win. Not with that kind of

prize package. I'm a party princess. Real performers are going to enter this thing—professional actors, dancers, and singers." Her voice broke a little bit on that last word, so she busied herself with finishing unpinning her crown in the hopes that Clara hadn't noticed.

"You *are* a real performer, or have you forgotten about your music degree from Juilliard?"

Gracie set the tiara down on the counter. A stone had gone missing from the central snowflake, and sure enough, bits of pink frosting clung to parts of the filigree. From a distance, it was all glitter and sparkle, but up close and personal, it wouldn't have fooled a soul. It was just a cheap imitation of the real deal.

And so was Gracie. The little girls at her events thought she hung the moon, but she had no business whatsoever spending the Christmas holidays with real royals.

"College was a million years ago," she said, throat going thick.

"Five." Clara held up a hand, fingers spread wide like a starfish. "It was five years ago. That's hardly a lifetime, and you still sing to some of the kids as Princess Snowflake."

"Not officially, and definitely not publicly. You know that." Gracie's eyes flew to the laptop. "You're not typing that on the contest application, are you?"

"I'm not filling out the application right now. I'm answering an email from a preschool that wants to plan a Christmas party for next week." Clara kept typing, studiously avoiding Gracie's gaze. "And besides, the contest requires a video submission."

"Good." Gracie nodded. They had dozens of video clips from parties where she'd played Princess Snowflake, and not one of them featured a vocal performance. Because she didn't do that sort of thing anymore. "Do you really think we should apply?"

Clara finally looked her in the eye, biting her lip as she

did so. "I sort of already did."

Gracie's chest went tight. "You did *what?*"

She was going to need more than a simple pint of peppermint ice cream to get over this day. Clara never made unilateral decisions like this. Sure, they were partners, but Perfect Party Princesses was Gracie's baby. It always had been.

"I know." Clara pressed her hands to her heart. "I'm sorry. I really am, but this is a huge opportunity. Plus, I wanted to be able to offer you a little hope in case the meeting at the bank didn't go well. We're running out of ice cream... and so is the market down the street. I'm just saying."

Gracie couldn't really argue, considering her track record with loan officers thus far. It was sweet, in a way. And Clara had always been great at thinking outside of the box.

This is as far out of the box as you can get. The box isn't anywhere to be seen.

"What video did you send?" Gracie asked.

"The one from the birthday party at the ballet school. *So* adorable. Remember?" Clara shot her a hopeful grin.

Of course Gracie remembered. "There was that sweet little girl who fell out of her curtsey."

"Major heart-tugging moment. Those royals won't know what hit them." Clara nodded. The matter was settled, whether Gracie was ready or not. "You know we can't win if we don't enter, right?"

"Point taken," Gracie said.

But Princess Snowflake knew better than to hold her breath.

CHAPTER TWO

The Abominable Snow Prince

CROWN PRINCE NICOLAS LUCA MONTAVAN had been back in San Glacera for less than twenty-four hours, and already his face was plastered on the cover of every newspaper and tabloid in the kingdom he called home.

The photographs, taken at Hornlihutte, the base camp of the Matterhorn, weren't the most flattering. Nick's eyebrows were frosted over, icicles dripped from his dark beard, and his face shone red from a serious case of windburn. But he'd been fresh off the peak where he'd been mountaineering and snow camping for over a month. He'd been sleeping in a glorified igloo for five weeks alongside the veterans he'd accompanied to the summit.

"The Abominable Snow Prince? That's what the press is calling me now?" He looked up from the news app on his iPad to find his eighteen-year-old sister Emilie biting back a smile. "They realize I've been away on a climbing expedition with wounded war veterans, don't they?"

The trip had been an annual event since the inaugural expedition nearly sixty years ago, organized by his grandfather, the late, great King Noël. Nick had taken over as leader of the climbing trek in his early twenties, eager to continue his grandfather's meaningful work supporting the citizens of San Glacera who'd served in the armed forces. The goal of the trip was to show that no matter what emotional or physical challenges the veterans faced, they could still accomplish remarkable things. If they could conquer the mountain, they could face whatever waited for them back in the real world. Nick looked forward to the expedition every year.

He looked down at the iPad screen again and shook his head. "How could that possibly make me 'abominable?'"

"I think you're reading too much into that headline," Emilie said as she dragged him away from the entrance of his palace quarters toward the castle's massive central hallway, where rows of silver Christmas trees flanked them on either side.

Mittens, his three-year-old Cavalier King Charles spaniel mix, had been snoozing at the foot of Nick's four-poster bed, but now he lifted his head from his paws and shot Nick a forlorn look. The pup was in full pout mode over Nick's recent absence, despite getting the literal royal treatment while Nick had been away. He didn't need to ask Mittens where he stood on the abominable issue. His sister was another story. Nick could usually count on her to be somewhat objective.

Emilie tucked her arm through Nick's and dropped her head onto his shoulder as they made their way to the palace press office in the more public area of the castle, where they'd both been summoned for a family meeting.

"*Am* I reading too much into it, though?" Nick narrowed his gaze at the iPad's screen. "Abominable is hardly a compliment."

"They're not talking about your personality...even though everyone knows you can be a bit of a grump at times."

"Thanks." Was that supposed to make him feel better? "I think."

Just because he didn't particularly enjoy frivolous things like royal balls or hanging out in cafés for hours on end talking about nothing, it didn't mean he was a *grump*. He was just focused. He had big shoes to fill one day. Enormous ones. No one else in the palace seemed worried about that very significant fact, but Nick certainly was. King Noël had done his best to prepare Nick for his destiny since the day he'd been born. He'd taken Nick under his wing, and when he'd fallen ill a year ago, Nick had been splashed all over the headlines—and not in a good way.

Now here he was, still trying to shake off the shame of disappointing his grandfather during the beloved king's last days...and the press was calling him more unflattering names.

"It probably doesn't help that you have the household staff iron your boxer briefs," Emilie said with a smile in her voice.

Nick's jaw clenched. Were people ever going to forget the details of that interview with his ex-girlfriend Sarah Jane? "That is categorically untrue. Even if it were, it's more an example of fastidiousness—not crankiness. Just to be clear."

"You sound super laid-back right now," Emilie said. "Not cranky in the slightest."

Nick offered her a stiff smile. "Duly noted."

"Relax, would you? I'm pretty sure they just mean you look like a Yeti." Emilie gave his unkempt beard a sideways glance. "I can't imagine why."

A *Yeti*? Had the reporters expected him to look like a picture-perfect Crown Prince with gold epaulettes on his shoulders and a sash across his chest?

Probably. He was the future king, after all.

"I think Yeti is a slight exaggeration," he said under his breath.

Emilie laughed. "Suit yourself. But three of my friends have already texted me animated gifs of Bumble, the abominable snowman in that old Rudolph film. With a crown emoji pasted onto his head."

"Your generation spends far too much time on electronic devices," Nick said, mildly aware that he sounded a decade or three older than his thirty-two years. Five weeks away without cell service had been blissful. If thinking so made him a grump, so be it.

"Says the man whose face is currently buried in his iPad." Emilie snatched the tablet out of his hand and powered it down as they reached the press office.

Even the business area of the palace was dripping in holiday decor, as it always was this time of year. Swags of silver garland intertwined with sparkling Swarovski crystals hung from the crown molding, and jingle bell wreaths tied with icy blue velvet ribbons decorated every door.

"Stop obsessing," Emilie said. "The Bumble thing will blow over."

Let's hope so. Nick had his doubts. He'd been down this road before.

With a swift motion, he smoothed his tie. He hadn't had a chance to tackle the beard yet, but at least his attire was a bit more regal than the climbing gear he'd been wearing in the photos currently making the rounds in San Glacera. Emilie flashed him one last smile as he held the door open for her.

The press office was made up of a large conference room with windows overlooking the village square. A corridor to the right led to the smaller, individual offices for the staff. In the main room, a long conference table stretched from wall to wall, surrounded by a dozen leather chairs embossed with the family's royal crest. A fire roared in a hearth at the far end of the space, and a portrait of King Noël hung above the mantle. Nick paused, his gaze fixed on his grandfather's kind face, before unbuttoning his suit jacket and preparing to take a seat.

"Well, there you two are." Queen Livia sashayed toward them from the window.

Dressed in her unofficial uniform of a pastel tweed Chanel skirt suit, large pearl earrings, and a spritz of Creed Fleurissimo perfume, Nick's mother was as effortlessly regal as a person could possibly be. He'd never seen her with so much as a lock of her sleek platinum bob out of place. No one in the kingdom would dare refer to her as abominable.

Ever.

"Good morning, dear," she said to Emilie and then paused to give Nick's shoulders a squeeze while she kissed his right cheek and then his left one. "My darling snow prince. Welcome home."

Nick arched a brow. "*Et tu*, Mother?"

She waved a hand at him. "I'm just teasing you, as is the press, I'm sure. After all, you did look a fright in those photographs. Rest assured, everyone in San Glacera is delighted you're back. And just in time for the holidays."

"I'd never miss Christmas in San Glacera," Nick said. The very idea was unthinkable. "I know how important this time of year is for the kingdom."

"Indeed, it is. And that's precisely what we've called a meeting to discuss, now that you've returned." King Felix rose from his chair at the head of the conference table to give Nick's hand a hearty shake. Even after a year, it was still strange to see his dad sitting in the chair his grandfather had always occupied. King Noël's presence loomed large, from the painting on the wall to the memories ingrained in every part of the palace.

"Good to see you, son." King Felix's face cracked into an easy smile as he appraised Nick's appearance over the top of his round, tortoiseshell glasses. His neatly clipped salt-and-pepper hair seemed to have started leaning more toward the salty side in Nick's absence.

"You as well, Dad." Nick smiled.

His father's gaze narrowed. "Your beard isn't *quite* as bad as it looks in the papers."

"Shall I keep it then?"

"You look like a younger, stodgier Father Christmas," Emilie said.

Ah, teenage princesses were such a joy. "I'll take that as a no."

The king and queen both laughed and made their way back to the conference table, where Jaron Lutz, the palace's senior press advisor was busy setting up a laptop and projector. Tall and lean, with his trademark Viking-gold hair and a killer backhand, Jaron still resembled the tennis champ he'd been back when he and Nick had been in boarding school together. He glanced up from the equipment and gave Nick a slight bow when their eyes met.

"Good morning, Your Royal Highness," he said. In any other setting, he probably would've greeted Nick with a one-armed man hug.

Roommates since their first year at Le Rosey—the boarding school in Switzerland where every monarch to sit on San Glacera's throne had been educated, dating back to its inception in 1880—Nick and Jaron had been friends for more years than Jaron had worked for the royal family. He was more of a brother than an employee. When Nick had a nasty fall and broke his arm on a ski trip to Gstaad when they'd been teenagers, Jaron had been the one to help him down the mountain so he could get help. He probably knew Nick better than his own family did, and not once had he ever spoken to the press about his royal friend. Never betrayed a confidence or sold him out for a fleeting moment of fame. Nick wished he could say that same about everyone he'd once trusted.

"Good morning, Jaron." Nick pulled out a chair and sat down beside his father. It had been a while since someone had bowed to him. Royal protocol hadn't applied up on the mountain. There, Nick had been just an ordinary guy.

As ordinary as a prince could ever be, he supposed.

"Shall we proceed?" Jaron asked, tapping a key on his laptop until a photograph of San Glacera's Ice Village flashed on the white projector screen situated at the head of the table.

"Yes, let's." The queen folded her hands neatly in her lap.

Jaron nodded. "Certainly. While you were away, sir, we put our heads together to discuss ways to give San Glacera's tourism industry a boost this December. As I'm sure you're aware, Christmas visitors to the kingdom have become increasingly fewer and farther between in recent years."

"Might that be an exaggeration?" Nick frowned, but then an image of an ominous-looking bar graph appeared on the screen.

"Vendors have reported a steady downward trend in sales over the past five years." Jaron cleared his throat. "Last year, tourism was down thirty-five percent. Two shops in the village square closed while you were away, sir."

Nick's stare bore into the bar graph as a sinking feeling settled in his gut. Why was he just now hearing about this? As heir, he should be privy to this sort of information.

He took a deep breath and swiveled his gaze toward the king. "Father..."

His dad held up a hand. "I know, son. You expect to have been included in discussions about this months ago."

You think?

Nick bit his tongue. His father knew good and well that he wanted to be more involved with the kingdom's day-to-day operations. There was no need to repeat himself, especially now that he was front page news again.

The king smiled. "Not to worry, though. We've already come up with a brilliant solution."

If only they hadn't done so while Nick had been away...

You're here now, though. And you're part of the conversation. Things could be worse. Indeed. This meeting could have been about his less-than-jolly reputation. It could have been a repeat of the crisis talks that had taken place in this very room a year ago when the not-so-flattering details about his personal life had been splashed across every front page in Europe.

But another personal embarrassment would have been far preferable to shopkeepers being forced to shut down and people losing their livelihoods. Nick was already worried that the "abominable" headlines might have an impact on the charity where he served as patron. They were already struggling for donations.

Nick sat a little straighter in his chair. But then Jaron advanced his PowerPoint presentation to the next slide, and the words *Royal Winter Wonderland Contest* appeared, surrounded by whirling, twirling snowflakes. Nick was so distracted by the animated graphics that he almost missed the finer print near the bottom of the screen.

Spend this Christmas with San Glacera's royal family!

A bark of laughter escaped him. What was he looking at? An ad for some inane reality television-style competition? "Is this a joke?"

Nick glanced around the table and, to his horror, no one else cracked a smile.

Emilie glared at him. "You hate the concept already, and you don't know a thing about it. Seriously?"

"I gather this was your idea." Nick said, speaking with exaggerated calm, even though the thought of his family Christmas being someone's "prize" in a global contest was enough to make him want to climb into a parka and move back to his igloo.

Emilie lifted her chin. "Yes, and it's a good one. Everyone thinks so."

Nick waited for someone…*anyone*…to politely object. No one did, not even his dad, who never wanted to let Nick or Emilie make any real decisions.

They couldn't be serious about this. Nick had already made a mockery of the royal name once—and had failed his grandfather in doing it. As King Noël lay dying, it hadn't been his good deeds or social policies that had been in the news. It had been Nick.

How had his ex-girlfriend described him, exactly?

Cold.

Distant.

Unable to utter the word "love."

None of it had been true. Nick had definitely uttered the word *love* before. Plenty of times, in fact. He'd just never used it in conjunction with this particular ex-girlfriend; hence, the problem. The truth hadn't mattered, though. Nick hadn't been about to defend himself—not when his grandpa was so sick. Instead, he'd taken the hits and let everyone believe he was the year-round equivalent of Ebenezer Scrooge. It didn't matter what people said about him, but his grandfather's legacy *did* matter. And Nick's newfound frosty reputation had overshadowed even that.

Nick had been trying to restore dignity and honor to the House of Montavan ever since those dark days. He hadn't just lost a grandpa. He'd lost his mentor…his king. The least he could do was make sure that everything King Noël had worked so hard for wouldn't crumble in his absence.

A contest, of all things, didn't seem like the path to dignity. Frankly, it sounded the opposite.

The queen smiled. "Nick, you're always saying that your father and I should include you and Emilie in more of the monarchy's day-to-day affairs. You both do a wonderful job with your charitable endeavors, but you're right. Someday, you'll be the one sitting on the throne. Emilie will be among your most trusted advisors. Perhaps you've been right. Maybe it's time for the two of you to take a more active role in the business of running the kingdom."

Her comment should have been music to Nick's ears. It *was*, actually. He just hadn't realized that more involvement might come with some very dubious strings attached. Nor had he realized that of all the times for his concerns to finally be taken seriously, it would occur while he'd been fourteen thousand feet above sea level with icicles forming in his facial hair.

"When it became clear just how much local shopkeepers were struggling, we included Emilie in the discussion," his father said. "You would have had a seat at the table as well, of course, but you were away on your climbing adventure, which was equally important. However, with Christmas coming up, the issue was rather time-sensitive. We didn't want to wait until next year to make a change."

"I understand." Nick nodded, forcing his mouth into some semblance of a smile.

He was probably being a grump, as Emilie had so bluntly put it. Surely they could come up with some sort of respectful compromise and he wouldn't wake up on Christmas morning to find himself dressed in matching pajamas with his family and a complete and total stranger.

"The contest has already begun, sir," Jaron said, fumbling with his laptop and studiously avoiding Nick's gaze.

Right. So no compromise, then.

"Why don't you catch Nick up on the details, Jaron?" The king leaned back in his chair.

"The object of the contest is to increase awareness of all that our kingdom has to offer during the Christmas season. One winner will be chosen to appear in San Glacera's Ice Village and participate in some of our traditional holiday activities alongside members of the royal family. The contest closed two days ago, and the entries numbered in the thousands." Jaron advanced the presentation to a slide with a bar graph that looked like an exact mirror image of the dismal chart from earlier. The numbers increased as steadily as the previous chart's figures had bottomed out. "As you can see, we've already experienced a slight uptick in tourism. Most local hotels and bed and breakfasts are reporting a ten percent increase over reservations from last year at this time."

"Still think the contest is a joke of an idea?" Emilie gave him a swift kick under the table—maturity at its finest.

Nick's shin throbbed.

"I never called it a joke," he said. Hadn't he, though? "The numbers are...hopeful."

Ten percent wasn't even a dent, and there was no real evidence that the contest had anything to do with the uptick. At least not any that Nick had seen.

He rested his hands on the table. Surely there was a way to make the others see reason. "I'm simply concerned that the idea of a contest sends the wrong message. San Glacera is steeped in centuries of history and tradition, and this seems to have the potential to become a..."

Train wreck.

Nick bit his tongue and wracked his brain for another word—one that wouldn't get him kicked, labeled a grump, or otherwise land him on Santa's naughty list.

He swallowed. "Spectacle."

"Hashtag #ChristmasInSanGlacera is already trending on Instagram," Emilie said haughtily.

Nick's head was beginning to hurt. "My point exactly."

"Did you hear that?" The king's face cracked into a wide smile. "We're trending."

King Noël was probably rolling over in his grave. Nick shot an apologetic glance at his grandfather's portrait.

"That's good, right?" the queen asked.

"It's outstanding, ma'am." Jaron puffed out his chest a little, clearly thrilled to be the bearer of such good news.

Emilie beamed. "Wait until you see the winner we've selected. She's perfect."

Nick glanced around the table. "You've already chosen the winner?"

"She's the *preliminary* winner. Of course we're interested in hearing your opinion. Why do you think we called a meeting as soon as you returned?" the queen asked.

Nick was beginning to wonder. It sounded like his family had things completely under control. Perhaps he shouldn't have come down from the mountain at all.

"Her name is Gracie Clark, and she's from America." Jaron nodded toward the projector screen, where a picture of a woman who looked more like a cartoon character than an actual human flicked into view.

She wore a ballgown trimmed in white fur with a ridiculously oversized train and what had to be the gaudiest crown Nick had ever seen. It was tipped with crystal snowflakes as big as his fist.

And was that *glitter* on her face?

Nick's head pounded with renewed intensity. If the press had been so quick to give him an insulting nickname in the wake of his snow prince pictures, they were going to have a field day with this ridiculous person. "Please tell me there's a reason she's dressed like a royal caricature."

Emily's nostrils flared. "It's her *job* to dress that way. She's a party princess."

"That clears things right up," Nick deadpanned. What on earth was a party princess?

"She performs in character at children's birthday parties and such." Jaron advanced the slide show until a video of this so-called party princess began to play.

Dressed once again like Cinderella on her way to a blizzard, she was surrounded by a group of adoring children in pink tutus and leotards. Faces upturned, with plastic crowns on their heads, the little girls were positively rapt by the princess, who spoke to them in a singsong voice and held her hands in an exaggeratedly graceful position, like someone sipping tea with an extended pinkie finger.

"Good morning, my snowflakes," she gushed. "I was ever so happy to leave my frosted forest and come visit your ballet class today."

Nick fought back a mighty eye roll. She was so over-the-top sweet, he was certain that cavities were forming in his teeth at this very moment.

One of the children held up a hand and started jumping up and down in her tiny ballet slippers. "How did you get here from so deep in the forest, princess?"

The princess pressed a hand to the lacy bodice of her gown and tilted her head just so. Rich, chestnut curls spilled over her shoulder and down her back. "My pet reindeer brought me here in my magic sleigh."

The children onscreen collapsed into giggles, and Nick somehow refrained from asking if anyone knew whether she would be bringing said reindeer with her to San Glacera.

The silver glitter on Gracie Clark's cheekbones twinkled as she dropped into a deep royal curtsey. Then the children mirrored the gesture, wobbling into shaky curtsies of their own. When a little girl who looked to be around five or six years old tipped over and fell to the ground, the "princess" dashed toward her in a flurry of sequins and tulle to scoop her up and offer a hug.

"I'm not a good ballerina. I want to be, but I'm not as good as the other girls. I fall down a lot," the child said with a sniff and then buried her face in the princess's poufy ballgown.

"Do you want to know a secret?" Gracie's blue eyes glittered like icy sapphires as she spoke in a mock whisper so all the children could hear, even though she was directing her words to the distraught little girl. "It's good to be different.

Being your own special someone is what makes you wonderful and unique. No two snowflakes are the same, either. That's what makes them beautiful."

Nick shifted in his chair. *I suppose some people might find her charming.*

The child looked up at the princess with eyes as wide as saucers as Gracie opened a hand and gently blew into her palm. Fine silver glitter and iridescent blue confetti shaped like snow flurries twirled in the air.

The screen went ballet-pink as the tiny dancers dove to try and catch the falling snow. While the giggly chaos ensued, Gracie held a finger to her lips, winked, and then pressed a single piece of the sparkling confetti into the hand of the girl with the wobbly curtsey. The child smiled wide, displaying a gap where she'd obviously recently lost a tooth, her tumble quickly forgotten.

If the winner was being chosen based purely on cuteness factor, Nick couldn't imagine anyone outdoing Gracie Clark. But surely that wasn't their sole criteria.

Being in the public eye wasn't easy. Did she have any actual experience, outside of children's birthday parties?

"Her character name is Princess Snowflake," Emilie said.

Of course it is, Nick mused.

"We think Princess Snowflake would be a lovely addition to the Ice Village, don't you, Nick?" The queen rested a hand on his forearm. "Jaron has suggested that we hire a local actor to play the part of Prince Charming. As the contest winner, Princess Snowflake can do photo ops during the week leading up to Christmas, and then Prince Charming can accompany her on Christmas Eve at the opening of the ice ballroom. We think this Princess Snowflake character will attract new visitors to the Christmas market. Younger tourists."

This was the part where Nick was supposed to be a team player and agree. After all, the decision had already been made. What difference would it make if he dissented? He'd been outvoted before he'd even set foot in the room.

But all those times Nick had asked for a greater role in the business of running the kingdom, he'd been steadfast in his intentions. He didn't want to rubber-stamp things. He wanted to contribute. To make San Glacera a better place for everyone who lived there.

"She fits the theme," he begrudgingly admitted. *But she's a Rent-A-Royal dress-up character.* "With such a generous prize package, I would think we'd attract entrants who have more to offer than simply showing up in costume and acting sweet enough to make everyone's teeth ache. Didn't we get any entries from people with genuine acting experience? Real performers?"

"There's nothing wrong with being sweet, dear," his mother said.

"You actually might want to try it sometime," Emilie said through gritted teeth. "Besides, you haven't seen the best part. Keep watching."

Nick forced his attention back to the video just as the screen went dark.

"Riveting," he muttered.

"Just wait," Emilie said.

As silly as Nick found this entire proposition, it warmed his heart to see his sister so excited about something—just not quite enough to melt away his doubts about the proposed winner. Or the contest as a whole.

Long seconds passed, and just when Nick was about to ask Jaron to speed up the video so they could get to the alleged good part, more footage flickered to life onscreen. This part of the recording was blurry and out of focus, tilted almost sideways, as if the camera had been turned on accidentally. The walls and ceiling of the room where Princess Snowflake stood were painted an industrial gray color, and at first, Nick thought the video had been shot at an elementary school. But then an IV pole came into view... and the corner of a child-sized hospital bed.

Nick leaned forward in his chair, despite his lingering reservations. The slight tingle at the base of his neck told him he might be on the verge of witnessing something he shouldn't.

Onscreen, Princess Snowflake talked to the little girl whose petite head rested on the pillow. She brushed the child's cheek with a tender swipe of her graceful fingertips and then crouched down so they were eye-to-eye.

Was there anything sadder than a child in a hospital bed? Nick's throat went tight. He'd visited sick children himself. It was one of the toughest parts of his job. He suddenly had a new respect for the party princess as her voluminous, snow-white gown puffed around her like dandelion fluff. Then Princess Snowflake began to sing a Christmas carol. *Silent Night.*

Nick suddenly couldn't seem to remember how to breathe.

She had the voice of an angel—dulcet and lyrical. So hauntingly beautiful that a chill ran up and down Nick's spine. Every so often, her lyrics went breathy, giving the song an aching vulnerability that seemed to scrape his insides. He almost felt like a boy again—innocent and full of the sort of hope that had become so much harder to believe in now that he was a world-weary adult.

"Thoughts?" Jaron asked as the film abruptly cut off.

Nick blinked. What had he just watched? Certainly not a performance or an audition, but something special. Something real.

Still, he was a prince. He had a responsibility to make decisions for the kingdom with his head, not his heart. And intellectually, Nick knew this whole affair was a terrible idea. Not that anyone really cared what he thought at the moment.

"She'll do, I suppose," he said, acquiescing at last. As if

he had any real choice in the matter.

"Very well." The king nodded. "Jaron, you'll reach out and make the necessary arrangements, then?"

"Of course, sir." Jaron closed the laptop, signaling the end of the meeting. "And just so you know, plans are also underway for the Vernina royals to attend the Christmas festivities."

Nick shook off the last vestiges of the trance he'd fallen into and stood. Five weeks of sleeping on hard, frozen ground had clearly left him bone weary and too tired to think clearly. Had he really just come home to find the esteemed House of Montavan joining forces with a *parody* of itself? "Pardon?"

"The king and queen of Vernina will be visiting San Glacera for the start of the Christmas market and Ice Village, along with their daughter Princess Alana. The princess has just returned from getting her advanced degree in America."

"At Georgetown University. Right, I remember," Nick said. He hadn't seen Alana since they were small children, but the European royal circle was a small one. Word got around.

"We extended an invitation, and the family has graciously accepted," the queen said.

Vernina and San Glacera shared a border and had long been allies, but the Vernina royals hadn't embarked on an official royal tour of San Glacera in years. Not since Nick had been a boy. Wouldn't they be delighted to arrive and find themselves mingling with a woman playing dress-up?

Again, Nick bit his tongue. If this meeting didn't end soon, he might bite it off entirely.

He managed a curt nod. "Good, a real royal visit."

As opposed to the absurdity of bringing a pretend princess all the way from America in the hopes that a glorified cartoon character could breathe new life into San Glacera's most treasured holiday traditions.

Impossible, was it not? Things had been fine when King Noël was still alive. They should be trying to bring back that same sense of grace and nobility to the holidays—the way things used to be before the kingdom was reading about Nick's imaginary, neatly pressed boxer briefs. Tossing a make-believe royal into the mix hardly seemed like the way to go about doing so.

Nick was far from convinced, despite the hopeful bar graphs, but he didn't want to fully rain on his sister's parade. The matter had already been decided, anyway. It no longer mattered if he thought the idea was, in a word...

Abominable.

CHAPTER THREE

Santa Would Never

"**W**E'RE *SO GLAD YOU COULD* fill in at the last minute." A zookeeper clad in head-to-toe khaki grinned as he looked Gracie up and down. His smile widened as he shook hands with both Gracie and Clara. "I'm Brian, senior deer keeper. We didn't know what we were going to do when Santa cancelled this morning. But you're perfect. The kids are going to love you."

Twinkle lights formed a colorful halo around Brian's khaki baseball cap. The massive wooden giraffe sculptures standing just inside the Denver Zoo's entrance glowed in shimmering shades of neon pink and green, as they always did during the holidays.

Every December, the Denver Zoo transformed into a glittering world of whimsical light installations that ran along the paths between animal habitats. The trees overhead sparkled with so many tiny gold bulbs that it looked like all the stars in the sky had fallen and settled among their branches. The annual Zoolights never failed to take Gracie's breath away, and today, she was officially going to be a part of it.

Thanks to Santa Claus's head cold.

"Thank you. I'm happy we could help." Gracie picked up her billowing skirt to keep it from dragging on the ground as she walked alongside the zookeeper and Clara.

When she'd gotten the call from the zoo, she'd been stepping out to the parking lot of yet another bank. Since her disastrous meeting with Mr. Curtis at Denver First, she'd gone to her three subsequent appointments like she was on autopilot. So long as she didn't get her hopes up, she couldn't be crushed again. The rejections had come as no surprise whatsoever.

At least she'd been wearing a suit this time. And at least one loan officer had said she'd sleep on things and get back to Gracie.

A tiger made from hundreds of orange and pink holiday lights peered at them from behind a tree trunk as they passed. Two little girls standing near the tiger, their faces lit rosy pink, went wide-eyed when they noticed Gracie. She waved at the children with a flourish, and the rhinestone snowflake rings on her fingers glittered like tiny, wintry kaleidoscopes in the glow of the lights. Both little girls squealed.

The days were notoriously short in Colorado during December. It wasn't quite four o'clock in the afternoon yet, and already the sky had grown dark enough for the Christmas lights to be flicked on. Gracie—rather, Princess Snowflake—would be on duty until the zoo closed at ten o'clock, wrapped snugly in her heavy velvet princess cape, while Santa stayed home, presumably eating chicken soup and watching Hallmark Christmas movies.

"These gals are going to love you too," the zookeeper said as they rounded a corner and a three-sided, red mini-barn came into view. Alternating red and white lights lined the roof in a candy cane pattern. "Princess Snowflake, meet Jingle and Belle."

"Oh my gosh, look how sweet they are." Clara whipped her phone out of her pocket and immediately began snapping pictures of the two reindeer huddled near the back of the structure.

The animals turned their heads in unison and trotted toward the railing on the open side of the barn. When they reached the fenceposts, they poked their heads over the railing with their huge brown eyes trained on the red plastic bucket in the zookeeper's hand.

"Brian, they're precious. I've never worked with real live reindeer before," Gracie said.

"They're surprisingly laid-back. We do twenty-minute reindeer encounters for small groups of kids during Zoolights. I'll teach the kids some facts about the animals, and then they'll get a chance to hand-feed the reindeer some grain." Brian jiggled the bucket, and Jingle pawed at the ground with one of her large hooves.

Gracie held out a hand. "Can I try?"

"Of course." Brian scooped a handful of grain from the bucket and spilled it into Gracie's hand. "Just hold it out to them with a flat palm, and they'll eat it right up."

Gracie laughed. "It tickles." Clara snapped photo after photo.

"At the end of each encounter, we'll give the kids a chance to pose for pictures with you and the reindeer. Then we'll take a ten-minute break and invite the next group in." Brian glanced back and forth between Gracie and Clara. "Does that sound good?"

"Sounds great." Gracie felt something brush against her cheek and tipped her face toward the sky. "And look—it's starting to snow! Perfect timing."

Brian opened the gate and the two of them stepped inside the little barn while Clara stayed on the other side, ready to capture snapshots and video.

The zookeeper attached leads to Jingle and Belle's harnesses and then handed the lead ropes to Gracie. "If you want to start things off by greeting the children, that would be super. Sometimes they're nervous around the animals, so an icebreaker is helpful."

"No problem at all. I've got this," Gracie said as Belle poked at her tulle skirt with a quivering nose.

Princessing never failed to be an adventure. Gracie wondered if Kate Middleton had ever needed to navigate a royal engagement while simultaneously avoiding curious reindeer. Somehow, she doubted it.

Brian shot her a thumbs-up and then ushered a group of five small children toward the barn. Their faces lit up the moment they spotted Gracie, flanked on either side by the reindeer—one of which kept trying to nibble at the rhinestones on the bodice of her gown. She smiled so hard that her face hurt as she artfully dodged Jingle's snout.

"Boys and girls, welcome to the Denver Zoo." The zookeeper gestured toward Gracie. "We'd like you to meet Princess Snowflake."

The kids went starry-eyed. Gracie's heart swelled like it always did when a child gazed up at her as if she were real royalty. Someone special.

And even though she knew better—even though she was really just a regular girl who couldn't even get a bank loan—Gracie almost believed. She couldn't help it. Playing a princess was serious business where the children were concerned. She felt a responsibility to make the moment as magical as she possibly could.

"Hello there, my special snowflakes." She glanced from one reindeer to the other. "These are my reindeer friends, Jingle and Belle." Belle paused from attempting to eat Gracie's gown and blinked her comically huge eyelashes at the children.

"Is it true that you're made of snow, Princess Snowflake?" one of the little girls said.

Gracie turned her face and tilted her head so that the glittery silver snowflakes she'd painted on her cheekbones sparkled beneath the twinkle lights. Then she winked.

The children oohed and ahhed.

"And look! I brought the snow with me tonight from my frosted forest," Gracie said.

She shifted Belle's lead rope to the opposite hand with Jingle's, then twirled her fingertips in the air and held out her palm. Snow flurries danced from the sky and landed on her outstretched hand. Even the reindeer seemed mesmerized.

"Does anyone have questions about snow?" Gracie fluttered her eyelash extensions. A little girl near the front of the crowd emulated her, blinking rapidly.

"Why is snow white?" a young boy called out. He tilted his head and the pompon atop his red knitted hat bobbed.

"It's actually isn't. Snow is made up of ice crystals that reflect light, just like the Christmas lights above." She gestured toward the twinkle lights with a graceful flick of her wrist. Belle and Jingle both rose their heads in unison—probably because they thought she might have more grain in her hand, but the effect was awfully adorable, all the same. Like they were listening to her snow lesson, as rapt as the children.

"Since snowflakes are tiny, the light scatters in so many directions that they look white, even though they really aren't." Gracie twirled her fingers and pointed at her audience as if casting an enchanted ice spell. "Which just goes to show that tiny things—and tiny people—are more special and powerful than they appear."

The children beamed. This was normally the point when Gracie might toss a little glitter or make a snowflake appear like magic, but she doubted glitter and live reindeer mixed well.

The zookeeper shot her a wide grin and a thumbs-up. Then he held up a finger, indicating she had about a minute to wrap things up so he could give his reindeer talk.

Suddenly, a Christmas carol chimed out of nowhere—*Jingle Bells*. Gracie recognized the tinny rendition immediately as the ringtone from Clara's phone.

Odd. Clara was usually so good about putting her cell on vibrate during a princess appearance. She winced and fumbled with the phone, answering it in lieu of trying to turn down the ringer. The speedier option, probably.

Gracie ignored the interruption and began winding down her snow lesson. "Every snowflake that falls to the ground has its own special journey. That journey eventually determines what they look like. Every snowflake follows its own path, just like people do." Gracie tipped head toward Jingle. "Reindeer too."

Clara was probably loving this. The reindeer definitely added something special. Gracie wouldn't have been surprised if Clara had the entire interaction uploaded to Instagram before Brian ushered in the next group of kids to meet the reindeer.

But when Gracie cast a quick glance in Clara's direction, she spotted her business partner still talking on the phone. She wasn't exactly speaking, though. Her mouth seemed to be frozen in a perfect, astonished O, and her face had gone as white as Frosty the Snowman's. Gracie's throat instantly constricted. What could possibly be wrong?

She blinked and switched back into Princess Snowflake mode. "Now who wants to hear more about my friends Jingle and Belle?"

The children's hands flew up, and she transferred the leap ropes over to the zookeeper. The reindeer both pawed at the ground and snorted puffs of frosted breath. The snow was coming down harder now, coating their fur with a fine layer of white. As Brian began his reindeer spiel, Clara waved frantically from behind the group of kids.

Gracie's smile froze in place. Clara knew better. Gracie was still in character; she couldn't just excuse herself and walk away. Santa would *never*.

Gracie stood off to the side and responded with princess-appropriate glee to Brian's presentation, while Clara pointed at her cell phone and continued to cast pleading glances in her direction.

She was still on the phone? What in the world could possibly be going on?

Then, just like magic, hope stirred in Gracie's chest. Could it be the loan officer who said she'd get back to them?

Gracie posed for photos alongside Jingle and Belle after Brian finished his reindeer talk. The seconds seemed to stretch on forever, but at long last, the kids filed out of the barn and Brian told her to relax until the next group entered in ten or fifteen minutes.

"Finally," Clara mouthed and thrust her phone toward Gracie.

Gracie bustled toward her as quickly as multiple pounds of velvet, tulle, and rhinestones would allow.

"What's going on?" she whispered.

"Just take it." Clara let out a shriek. "It's the *palace*."

Gracie's heart drummed as she fumbled for the phone. The palace?

What palace?

Surely this wasn't about that fancy royal contest Clara had entered. Gracie had written that off as a pipe dream days ago. But the maniacal grin on Clara's face told her otherwise.

Gracie's stomach took a nosedive, as if she were perched atop the Swiss Alps in one of the glass gondolas that Clara had shown her on the palace's website. The phone slipped from her fingers, and as she scrambled to catch it, she accidentally pushed the FaceTime button.

A man's face came into view. He had striking gold hair, razor-sharp, Nordic features and—from what Gracie could tell—he was wearing a business suit, like he was a regular person at a regular job. Not that Gracie expected kings and queens to wear their crowns to work every day. She had no idea what royals did Monday through Friday. The man appeared to be sitting at a conference table in a room with lavish, not-so-regular gold accents. Swags of blue spruce intertwined with silver garland hung from the crown molding behind him.

Great. Gracie was already messing this up. *Please don't let him be the king. Or the prince. Or even a duke...*

Were dukes still a thing in San Glacera? Had they *ever* been a thing there?

"Hello? Gracie Clark?" The man smoothed down his tie. "This is Jaron Lutz from the royal press office in San Glacera calling on behalf of His Majesty, King Felix."

Not an actual royal, then. Gracie breathed the smallest possible sigh of relief. Was he calling because she'd won? Surely the palace wouldn't personally call to *reject* her—although after the recent meetings at more banks than Gracie cared to think about, she wouldn't have been surprised.

"So sorry. I didn't mean to force you into a video chat. I was in the middle of a performance and then I dropped the phone, and—" She shook her head. She was babbling. To a man sitting in a castle. "Anyway, it's a pleasure to meet you, Mr. Lutz."

He offered her a polite smile. "Please call me Jaron."

"Oh." A rush of warm air tickled the back of Gracie's neck, and she did her best not to fidget, seeing as she was on a video call with a royal representative. "Okay then, Jaron."

He frowned and leaned closer to the camera. "Is that a, er, live reindeer standing behind you?"

Gracie turned to find Jingle quite literally breathing down her neck. Her face went hotter than a flaming Yule log. "Yes, actually. It is. I'm afraid you've caught me in the middle of something."

Jaron's gaze narrowed. "I hadn't realized reindeer were quite so large. Or friendly, apparently."

Gracie ducked her head as Jingle poked at her tiara with her nose.

"I'm so sorry for the distraction. Santa has a head cold," she said, as if that made any sense whatsoever. *Ugh.* What if she *had* won, but she was being so awkward, they changed their minds?

"Well, then. Please give Santa my regards." Jaron gave the collar of his dress shirt a slight tug. Gracie could sense the poor man's discomfort clear across the globe. "I'll make the rest of the call brief, as it appears I've caught you at a bad time. I'm pleased to inform you that you've been chosen as the winner of San Glacera's Winter Wonderland Contest."

Gracie's knees buckled.

She'd known it was coming. But hearing the words come out of Jaron Lutz's mouth and seeing even a tiny glimpse of the castle's interior in the background were just too much.

"This is such a surprise." She shook her head. Was this really happening? "I don't know what to say."

"Say you'll accept our offer to come tour our kingdom and perform as Princess Snowflake at the Christmas Ice Festival." He gave her another polite, regal smile. "The royal family is very much looking forward to welcoming you to San Glacera and hearing you sing."

"I..."

Wait.

What?

Gracie's heart pounded so hard and fast that it felt like a hummingbird was trapped inside her ribcage. She pressed a hand to her chest. The bedazzled snowflakes on the velvet bodice of her princess gown dug into her palm, but she barely noticed.

Surely she'd misheard. He hadn't just said that he expected her to *sing*, had he? In front of an audience? An audience that would include a *real* royal family?

No possible way. The presence of a king, queen, prince, and princess wasn't even relevant. Gracie couldn't do it—not even if she was a legit fairy tale princess and her audience was made up of mice friends, a la Cinderella.

But before she could make that abundantly clear to this royal footman or whoever he technically was, Jingle made another move for Gracie's tiara. And this time, the animal wasn't merely playing reindeer games. She was on a mission.

Oof.

Gracie teetered in her glass slippers, and the phone once again slipped from her hand. Then all she heard was the unmistakable crunch of a reindeer hoof coming into contact with Clara's iPhone.

Jingle. All the way.

CHAPTER FOUR

Barber and the Beast

"PLEASE OPEN UP, EM. I said I was sorry." Nick tapped lightly on the door to his sister's bedroom. *Again.*

Four days had passed since the ill-fated meeting in the press office about the Royal Winter Wonderland Contest, and in those four days, Emilie had barely uttered a word to Nick. She made polite, clipped conversation with him at dinner every night, but when their parents weren't around, he may as well have been invisible.

Nick's kid sister was giving him the royal cold shoulder. He was beginning to wish she'd kick him in the shin again. Anything was preferable to stony silence.

"Emilie?" Nick knocked a few more times.

At his feet, Mittens turned three circles and let out a resigned sigh before curling into a snug ball against Nick's foot. His little eyes drifted shut.

"I'm proud of you. You really took some initiative, and you actually got Dad to listen to you," Nick said, raising his voice an octave or three.

Mittens cracked one eye open and gave Nick a look that said *really?*

He was talking to a *door*. He knew Emilie was on the other side, but there was no guarantee she heard a word he said. For all Nick knew, she could be plugged into her headphones or lounging in a bubble bath, happily ignoring his existence.

And now Nick's jaw hurt from clenching his teeth so much.

He glanced down at Mittens. "What do you think it's going to take to get her to thaw?"

The dog's furry little paws twitched. Emilie always said he must be chasing rabbits in his dreams when he moved like that in his sleep.

"Glad to see one of us isn't losing any sleep over this sibling drama," Nick muttered.

Then Emilie's door flew open and he nearly stumbled backward over the dog. Mittens jolted awake and launched himself at Emilie, tail wagging like mad. The little traitor.

"Would you stop banging on my door? It's really annoying." Emilie gazed impassively at him before bending to scoop Mittens in her arms and pressing a kiss to the little copper spot on the top of the dog's head.

In purebreds, such a spot on a Cavalier's head was known as "The Duchess's Thumbprint," named after the Duchess of Marlborough, who reportedly found comfort in stroking the tiny head of her beloved Cavalier when her husband was away at war in the 1700s. Mittens was a rescue, and not quite purebred. Nick was pretty sure there was a little cocker spaniel in there somewhere. Maybe even a dash of some other breed prone to disloyalty in the face of family strife.

"Not trying to be annoying," Nick said through gritted teeth. "I just..."

"What? You wanted to congratulate me on my first big idea?" Emilie shot him a saccharine smile.

Nick opened his mouth, fully intent on saying something complimentary about the party princess. And then...

Nothing. He couldn't seem to find the words. No matter how touching he'd found the hospital footage, he couldn't get past the costume. And the glitter. And the doe-eyed princess act.

Had everyone in this palace lost their minds? Was that how they wanted the public at large to see them—as cartoon characters?

"Ugh. You're the worst." Emilie thrust Mittens toward him and slammed the door in his face.

Nick's jaw clenched so hard he could have cut coal into diamonds with his molars. Mittens licked the side of his face, and even that didn't relax him like it usually did. He stalked back toward his quarters, holding the pup close. They'd simply have to try again later.

Back in his room, Nick deposited Mittens on the bed, and the dog immediately started snoring. Nick just stared down at him, wondering what it must be like to possess such a clear conscience.

Then a knock sounded on his door, and relief flowed through him. *Finally.* Emilie was the one knocking this time, and not him. At least they were speaking. That was progress, right?

"Em." He flung the door open, but it wasn't his sister at all.

Instead, Nick found Jaron standing on the threshold with his hands up in a gesture of surrender. "Just so you know, this wasn't my idea."

Nick's gaze flitted from Jaron to the unfamiliar man standing next to him and did his best to keep his outward expression neutral. Internally, he scowled.

He'd been doing a lot of that in the days since his return

from the mountaineering trip—scowling. He was becoming more famous for it with each passing day.

The strange man, dressed in a plain black suit and carrying a black leather case in his left hand, bowed. Beside him sat a sleek barber's chair on wheels.

"Your Royal Highness," the barber said stiffly.

Nick's attention shifted back toward Jaron. "You've got to be kidding me."

What was this? Haircut by ambush?

Jaron nodded at the barber. "Go ahead and get set up inside. We'll be right with you."

The barber wheeled his chair past Nick and began making himself at home.

Nick held the door open wide and motioned for Jaron to enter. "Join us. By all means, the more, the merrier."

"I told you I had nothing to do with this." Jaron nodded toward the barber. "I'm just the messenger, by request of Her Majesty, the Queen."

Nick's mother. Of course.

"Does the queen really think a haircut might put a stop to the articles?" Nick's parents still hadn't sat him down to talk about the snow prince pictures. He knew they'd been talking about them, though. Wasn't everyone?

Jaron's gaze flitted toward Nick's beard. "Perhaps a haircut *and* a shave?"

Nick crossed his arms. "Anything to make me a bit less abominable, eh?"

What difference did it make? Nick had fully planned on getting rid of the beard and getting a trim before the opening of the Ice Festival. But it would have been nice if he'd been able to do it of his own free will instead of being strong-armed by the royal press officer.

Even if that royal press officer doubled as a friend. Probably Nick's *closest* friend, aside from Emilie.

"I could always send out a statement. Just give me the

word and I'll get something drafted," Jaron said.

Nick shook his head. "No. If we respond, it will look like we're taking the matter seriously."

"Which we aren't." Jaron nodded. "Got it."

Mittens woofed and took a flying leap from the foot of Nick's grand canopy bed, anxious to greet their new visitors. The dog sat politely at the barber's feet and once he'd been petted, he scurried toward Jaron with a mad wiggle of his entire back end.

Jaron slipped a dog biscuit from his pocket and offered it to Mittens, who crunched at it with unabashed glee. Tiny crumbs fell onto the toe of Nick's polished loafer.

Nick eyed the barber chair and sighed. His mother had a point. A shave and a haircut couldn't hurt.

"Thank you for coming," Nick said to the barber, belatedly remembering his manners. He shook the barber's hand, sat down, and leaned back as a steaming hot towel was placed over his face. Mittens jumped in his lap and curled into a warm ball of fur as Nick tried his best to relax.

He'd known the *Abominable Snow Prince* nickname was going to cause trouble. Sure enough, within days, the tabloids had dredged up the articles from a year prior, as if the presence of icicles in his beard had somehow confirmed everything his ex-girlfriend had said about him in the press all those months ago.

"You do realize that not every woman you date will sell you out to the press, don't you?" Jaron said as he loomed above him.

"I do." But Nick wasn't taking his chances. Not anytime soon, anyway.

This is precisely why arranged royal marriages used to be in fashion, he thought.

Dating with a royal title was complicated, at best. Still, he'd never expected Sarah Jane to accept money in exchange for a tell-all interview. Especially when said interview had painted him in a less than flattering light.

Was he really cold and distant? Nick didn't think so. Not back then, anyway. He'd been careful. Guarded. But that had been necessary. He was a future king who would one day rule San Glacera. He couldn't simply give his heart away on a whim.

Irony of ironies, being painted as cold had made him even less inclined to let someone get close to him. Yet again, he thought about going back to his igloo on the mountain. At least it had been peaceful there.

Until he'd reemerged looking like a snow monster.

"The nickname will blow over," Jaron said for the tenth time in as many days. "As soon as the press has something else to talk about, they'll drop it."

"You're right," Nick said.

He'd just somehow thought that the Sarah Jane mess was behind him. *Far* behind. He'd never imagined her interview would be front page news a full year later.

"How are things going with the Winter Wonderland contest?" he asked, eager for a change of subject.

"You're seriously asking me about the contest?" Jaron said with more than a hint of irony sneaking into his tone.

"I'm trying to be a supportive brother, even if Emilie thinks otherwise."

"Ah, of course." Jaron's voice seemed to be coming from the opposite direction, which meant he was pacing. A nervous habit he'd picked up back when Nick and Jaron had been in boarding school together.

This couldn't be good.

"Don't tell me there's a problem with the cartoon princess," Nick murmured into the towel.

"There's not. No problem whatsoever." Jaron cleared his throat. "In fact, I've video chatted with her. And she's a party princess, not a cartoon character."

"Was she dressed in that over-the-top getup when you

video chatted?"

Jaron didn't answer.

"I'll take that as a yes," Nick said.

"She was at an appearance. It was perfectly normal."
Jaron's tone dropped an octave. "Except for the reindeer."

"Did you just say..." Nick peeled the towel back from
his face so he could look Jaron in the eye. "*Reindeer?* Like
someone dressed up in a plush Rudolph suit?" He could
just imagine the woman showing up in San Glacera with
a sidekick like that. His grandfather would turn over in
his grave.

"A live one," Jaron said, which somehow didn't make
Nick feel better at all. "Because Santa had a cold. I think
that's what she said."

Nick arched an eyebrow. *Bite your tongue. You're being
supportive now, remember?*

"Anyway, the point is that everything's fine." Jaron's
gaze darted elsewhere.

"What aren't you saying?" Nick said.

The barber stood motionless, glancing back and forth
between the two men. Mittens shifted into a sit position in
Nick's lap and did the same.

"She hasn't exactly agreed to come to San Glacera."
Jaron winced. "Not yet, anyway."

"*What?*" Nick sat up straighter, and Mittens hopped off
his lap to hunt down one of his numerous squeak toys.
"Does Emilie know? Do the king and queen?"

Jaron shook his head. "No. No one does. Princess Snowflake's business manager assures me it's a go."

Nick should have been hoping the fake princess would
say no. After all, he still wasn't convinced that bringing her
to the kingdom was a good idea. If she didn't turn up, his
family could have a normal holiday without playing tour
guide to a glorified storybook character.

But Emilie would be crushed.

Also...who did this so-called princess think she was? The palace was paying her an enormous sum of money to travel to San Glacera. If she didn't want to come, why had she entered the contest to begin with?

The more Nick thought about it, the more he seethed. Princess Snowball—or whatever her silly name was—had been issued a royal invitation, which she definitely didn't deserve, and now she was waffling about accepting it? The Vernina royals were actual heads of state and they'd accepted the invitation to San Glacera for Christmas *immediately*.

She wasn't even here yet, and already things were turning into a circus. If and when she did decide to turn up, what would happen if she decided to talk to the press? Nick could see the headlines now. *Fake princess spills tea on San Glacera's real royal family! Dress-up character takes the crown!*

Nick's gut churned. How far could they possibly fall?

"Do I need to call her myself and convince her to come?" Nick heard himself say. This entire situation was getting more absurd by the minute.

"No," Jaron said a little too quickly, as if Nick's abominable reputation had made its way clear across the globe. Perhaps it had. "I'm handling it. She'll be here, right on schedule."

The barber shot Nick a questioning glance, and he leaned back in the chair. At this rate, his makeover would take all day.

"Anything else I should be aware of?" Nick asked.

Jaron raised a finger. "Just one more thing. The king would like you to escort Princess Alana of Vernina to the opening evening of the Ice Village. He's asked me to reserve side-by-side seats for the two of you in the royal box."

Just what Nick needed—a royal blind date. As if this Christmas wasn't going to be awkward and uncomfortable enough already, now dating was being added to the agenda, even though he'd already proven himself a spectacular failure in that department.

"It's purely for diplomatic purposes," Jaron added.

Right...because no one would actually choose to be romanced by the Abominable Snow Prince. Not that Nick would blame them.

Mittens dropped a dog toy shaped like a snowman near the foot of the barber chair and nudged it with his little snub nose. A tinny version of *All I Want for Christmas is You* rose up from the snowman's plush form.

"Fine," Nick said.

It was a formal royal function, not an actual date. Princess Alana was probably even less thrilled about it than he was.

"Shall we begin, sir?" the barber asked, holding up a pair of thin silver scissors.

Nick nodded, and thus began his transformation from a frog into a prince...

If only on the surface.

CHAPTER FIVE

I'd Rather be Stress-Frosting a Yule Log

"I'M NOT GOING." GRACIE DIPPED her frosting spatula into a bowl of chocolate icing, focusing intently on the lump of cake in front of her. "Besides, I thought this was supposed to be a Yule log party. It's starting to feel a little like a royal intervention."

She glanced up. Sure enough, not one other person seated around the kitchen island in her parents' home had started icing their Yule logs. Her mom, dad, and Clara were all just sitting there, staring at her with unfrosted Swiss roll cakes in front of them. Even the family cat was eyeing her with judgment. But maybe that was simply resting feline face. Gracie wasn't sure.

"Of course, it's a party." Jane Clark, Gracie's mother, dropped a dollop of chocolate frosting onto her log. "This is the fifth year we've made Yule logs for the holidays. Can you believe it?"

"*Bûche de Noël*," Gavin Clark, Gracie's dad, said in an

exaggerated Parisian accent. "Mom has wanted to go to Europe and try an authentic French one ever since the Yule log episode of that baking show she loves on television."

"And I fully support that dream," Gracie said.

"Dreams are important." Her mother nodded. "That's all we're saying, sweetheart."

"Really? Because it sounds like you're all saying a lot more than that." Gracie narrowed her gaze at Clara.

If Clara hadn't been an unofficial member of the Clark household for as long as Gracie could remember, she'd be furious at her friend for telling her parents about the contest. As it stood, she wasn't exactly thrilled. If her family hadn't known, she wouldn't be sitting here, stress-frosting a log.

"You never said it was a secret." Clara shrugged. "They were bound to find out when you jetted off to San Glacera."

"Except that I'm *not* jetting off to San Glacera. Or anywhere else, for that matter. Christmas is for family, right Mom?" Gracie said. If anyone would be on her side, her mother would. Christmas was a Very Big Deal in the Clark household.

Every Christmas Eve, Gracie and her parents went to the midnight service at church, and then Gracie spent the night in her childhood bedroom so she could wake up at home on Christmas morning. Mom got up early and made homemade cinnamon rolls from a recipe that had been in the family for more than fifty years. She and her parents stayed in their Christmas pajamas all day and after all the gifts were unwrapped, they watched holiday movies and did a jigsaw puzzle together. After Clara's family celebration was over, she always came over for board games. Hands down, it was Gracie's favorite day of the year.

Always.

"Nonsense." Mom swirled her spatula with a flourish.

Gracie shook her head. "Who are you, and what have you done with my mother?"

"We'll be fine. We can celebrate when you get back," her mother said.

Gavin Clark, Gracie's dad, set down his frosting knife. Clearly, he meant business. "Honey, we love having you around at Christmas. Obviously. But an opportunity like this only comes around once in a lifetime."

"Just think of what you could do with all of that prize money," Mom said.

Gracie plopped another dollop of frosting onto her log. Naturally, she'd thought about the prize money. Since the call from San Glacera a few days ago, she'd thought of little else. Winning the money was the answer to all her prayers. With that kind of cash, she could accomplish every single one of her business goals, from renting a small office to providing Christmas bonuses and benefits for her employees.

If only those things didn't come with some very uncomfortable strings attached.

"Sweetheart, we know it's been a while since you sang in public. But you used to love it so much. Maybe if you give it a try again, it won't be so bad," Dad said.

Just thinking about singing in front of an entire kingdom on Christmas Eve made Gracie's hands shake. Her frosting knife slipped through her fingers and clattered onto the table.

Mom reached over and gave her forearm a comforting squeeze. "Dad's right, honey. We know you can do it. It's time to forget those awful things that Philip said, once and for all."

"Amen," Clara said. Her face scrunched into a grimace the way it always did whenever anyone mentioned Gracie's ex-boyfriend's name.

It had taken them a while to figure out how anyone at the palace even knew that Gracie could sing. She and Clara watched the video three times before they'd realized there was additional footage at the end. Clara couldn't have looked more shocked if Santa himself had popped onscreen and belted out "Grandma Got Run Over By a Reindeer." No one could have faked that degree of surprise, least of all Gracie's best friend. She knew Clara hadn't sent the footage intentionally. After all, Clara had been front row, center, when Gracie froze onstage at her final Juilliard concert while singing a duet with Philip. She'd witnessed Gracie's humiliation firsthand, and she'd helped Gracie pick up the pieces after Philip had broken off their engagement the following morning.

Do you realize what you've done? You've ruined both of our futures. Everyone was there last night—all the big Broadway producers. Everything we've dreamed about is over. We're over.

Philip's hurtful words rang in the back of Gracie's head every time she tried to sing. When she closed her eyes, she could still see the way he'd looked at her onstage: like she'd committed the worst possible betrayal. As if she'd done it on purpose...

As if that one, small moment hadn't completely turned *her* world upside down too.

"I'm perfectly fine playing Princess Snowflake. The business is doing great. There's no reason whatsoever to start singing again." Gracie's Yule log went blurry as her eyes filled with unshed tears. She blinked hard before anyone noticed.

Giving up music had been like losing a part of her soul. She'd *loved* singing ever since joining the church choir as a little girl. She still loved it. She just couldn't do it in front of an audience.

Every now and then, she sang to a special child like the one in the video. It was Gracie's way of expressing herself and trying to give comfort when words failed her. Singing was personal to her now, not something she could do in front of hundreds—or maybe even thousands—of people in San Glacera on Christmas Eve.

"Hon, you've got *thirty thousand* reasons to sing again," Clara said. "Trust me, I would do it myself if I could. But they don't want me—they want you. Because you're amazing. This is your moment, Gracie."

"She's right, sweetheart." Mom picked up Gracie's discarded frosting knife and placed it back in her hand. "When you make a mistake, the thing to do is try again. Just because you froze up once doesn't mean it will happen this time. It's been years. If you don't go to San Glacera, you'll regret it for a long, long time. Dad and I don't want that for you."

Gracie glanced back and forth between her parents. "But it's Christmas..."

It was a last-ditch excuse, and she knew it. But she didn't know what else to say. They were right. If ever there was a time to try and get past her stage fright, it was now. People were depending on her. Clara, her party princesses, the kids she entertained.

Maybe even a faraway kingdom and a real royal family, as crazy as that seemed.

"Oh, sweetheart. Going on this trip and singing again will be the best Christmas gift ever." Mom stood, walked away from her Yule log, and wrapped her arms around Gracie's shoulders. "For us, for your business, but most of all, for yourself."

Gracie squeezed her eyes closed tight. She knew that Clara and her family were right...

Unless things didn't go as planned and she failed spectacularly. She was going to need more than a little Christmas magic to pull this off.

"I still can't believe you talked me into this." Gracie's stomach churned as she gazed up at the Swiss-chalet-style building rising from a mound of freshly fallen snow in front of them.

She still couldn't believe she was here. In San Glacera.

The chauffeur who'd picked them up from the airport had just dropped them off, and Gracie already wanted to climb back into the sleek black car and book a flight home.

What on earth had she been thinking when she'd finally broken down and agreed to get on the plane?

"I didn't talk you into it. It was a group effort," Clara countered. "You know I sent that video by accident, right? I had no idea there was footage of you from one of your hospital visits on that reel. I promise."

Gracie nodded. "I know."

"You promise you're not mad?" Clara's gaze flitted over Gracie's shoulder and lingered a moment on the elegant castle directly opposite the medieval village square. Eyes sparkling, she glanced back at Gracie. "I'm trying my best to look contrite right now, but it's really hard when I feel like we just landed in a winter fairy tale."

It was no exaggeration. The photos on the contest website really didn't do the kingdom justice. The B&B and all the surrounding buildings legitimately looked like they were made of gingerbread, with fanciful white trim and painted gumdrop accents. The windows shimmered like sugar glass, and the gable roofs were covered in deep brown shingles that could have been peppermint bark. Candy cane-striped poles lined the cobblestone walkways. If Gracie hadn't known better, she might have believed she'd been plopped down on a *Candy Land* game board.

Only the world's biggest Grinch would've been able to muster up any real sense of indignation, and Gracie was no Grinch.

"I'm not mad. Everything is going to be fine," she said. A huge understatement.

Once she left San Glacera with a thirty-thousand-dollar check, Perfect Party Princesses would be more than fine. Princess Snowflake and her fairy tale sidekicks would be all set to take over Denver. Maybe even the whole state of Colorado. All Gracie had to do was shake off a years-long case of stage fright sometime in the next seven days.

She could do that, right?

Never be afraid to melt. Gracie had made the adage her tagline way back when she'd slipped into her first snowy white ballgown.

She inhaled a dizzying breath of frosty air.

"Let's go check into our room." Clara rubbed her hands together. "I don't know about you, but I could use a hot toddy and a nap."

Nerves trumped jet lag, but Gracie nodded. Then she reached to grab hold of the handle of her giant suitcase, but it had disappeared. "What happened to our luggage? It was right here a second ago."

"The chauffeur took it inside for us while you were gawking at the castle." Clara winked. "We're getting the royal treatment. You should probably get used to it."

"I wasn't gawking," Gracie countered. On the contrary, she could barely look directly at it. It was like staring straight at the sun, blindingly bright in its magnificence.

You can do this. She had a full day to get acclimated to San Glacera. Tonight, Gracie was scheduled to appear as Princess Snowflake at the official opening of the Ice Village and meet the royal family for the first time. It should be a simple meet-and-greet photo op with children and tourists—the sort of thing Gracie did back home every single day.

With the addition of a king, queen, prince, and princess.

San Glacera's royal family was picture-perfect. At least they'd seemed that way when Gracie and Clara had Googled them and pored over photographs of the royals cutting ribbons, unveiling plaques, and attending state dinners in fancy gowns and tuxedos. The princess was just a teenager but seemed to carry herself with the kind of poise that Gracie was still trying to master with her party princess appearances. Her older brother, the Crown Prince, was so classically handsome that he almost seemed fictional.

Regal square jaw? Check.

Dreamy gray eyes? Double check.

Dark, slightly tousled hair that could only be improved upon by the addition of a crown on his head? Triple check.

Still, they were only people. How hard could it be?

Clara yawned. "Come on, Sleeping Beauty," Gracie said. She tucked her arm through Clara's and pushed open the door to the B&B.

The inside of the quaint chalet looked even more like a Christmas dream than its exterior did. Spun glass ornaments and fragrant pomander balls hung from every square inch of the ceiling, suspended by red velvet ribbons. A fire blazed in an enormous stone hearth, surrounded by a leather sofa and a mismatched collection of overstuffed wingback chairs in various tartan patterns. Dark wood paneling covered the walls, and a platter of homemade cookies welcomed them at the registration desk: Linzer stars with ruby-colored jam in the center, delicately frosted gingerbread snowflakes, and buttery Scottish shortbread.

"That's it. I'm never leaving this place." Clara slipped off her gloves and bit into a crescent-shaped cookie covered in powdered sugar. "So long, Colorado. I live here now."

"Good morning!" A woman with salt-and-pepper hair fashioned into a neat French twist and wearing a ruffly red apron covered in a cute Christmas print came bustling into the room. "You must be the guests of the royal palace. We've been expecting you."

Gracie and Clara exchanged a glance. *Guests of the royal palace.* Gracie was beginning to feel like Cinderella. Not the party princess version, but the real deal.

"Yes, we are. I'm Gracie, and this is Clara. We're excited to be here," she said.

"I'm Ingrid Krieg. My husband Max and I run this place." She waved a hand, encompassing the cozy lobby. "Welcome to our home. I'm sure you're both exhausted from your trip, so I'll be brief. We serve all our meals in the dining room, which is just around the corner. I've placed a schedule in your room, and we have fresh baked goods in the lobby at all times."

Clara reached for another crescent cookie, and Gracie chose one of the Linzer stars. It was buttery soft and melted in her mouth in an instant.

"We're always around to help, and please call me Ingrid." She pressed a hand to her heart. "We're just so thrilled that we've been chosen to host all the royal guests this week."

"All the royal guests? Are there more?" Gracie asked.

Ingrid nodded. "Oh, yes. The royal family of Vernina are scheduled to arrive later this afternoon. King Hans and Queen Sophia, along with their daughter Princess Alana."

Another king and queen? Did *everyone* in this village have a royal title?

"I guess it's a good thing my curtsy has gotten a lot of practice," Gracie said.

Clara laughed. "No kidding."

Ingrid began leading them toward a staircase on the opposite side of the lobby. "I'm sure you won't need to curtsy. We're all like family in San Glacera, especially here at the Krieg B&B."

Gracie tilted her head. "Really? No curtsying?"

Ingrid paused beneath a stone archway. A sprig of mistletoe hung above her head. Her gaze drifted over Gracie's shoulder for a brief moment, and she pulled a face. "Well, maybe once. In the beginning. Some royals are more formal than others."

Gracie turned to see if she could figure out what had

made the older woman reconsider, and she spotted a folded newspaper resting on the arm of a chair by the fireplace. A single black-and-white photograph covered the entire front page, accompanied by a bold headline in all caps—just like the screamy text messages Gracie's dad sometimes sent by accident.

THE ABOMINABLE SNOW PRINCE GOES INTO HIDING.

"Oh, wow." Gracie took in the image of a grizzly, grumpy face with eyebrows caked with snow and a beard dripping icicles. Whoever it was looked like Santa's evil twin. "Who is that?"

"I'm afraid that's His Royal Highness, Nicolas Luca Montavan." Ingrid sighed. "The Crown Prince of San Glacera."

The pictures of the prince they'd seen online must have been ancient. The man on the front page wasn't even recognizable as the same person.

Clara's eyes went wide. "No. Way."

Her gaze flitted to Gracie, and they exchanged a look of mutual confusion.

"It's true. That picture was taken a few weeks ago at the end of his annual Matterhorn expedition. He's developed a reputation of being rather..." Ingrid's forehead furrowed, and she seemed to choose her next words very carefully. "... frosty. But don't worry. The rest of the family is just lovely."

Gracie glanced at the photo again. A shiver went up and down her spine. Frosty, indeed.

"He's in hiding?" Perhaps that was a good thing. Maybe she'd never meet this strange prince in person.

Ingrid shrugged one shoulder. "He hasn't been seen in public since returning from the expedition. I'm sure he'll attend the Ice Village opening tonight, though. Prince Nicolas would never miss something like that. It's a royal tradition."

"Let's hope he manages to defrost by then," Clara said.

"Shall I show you both to your room?" Ingrid nodded toward the staircase. "Max took your luggage up already, and I've turned down the beds in case you'd like to get some rest. Or if you'd rather explore the kingdom a bit, the Christmas market opened this morning. You must try the hot cocoa. San Glacera is rather famous for it."

"That sounds amazing." Gracie was far too wired to sleep, and she wanted to get a feel for her surroundings before she slipped into her velvet ballgown tonight for her appearance at the Ice Village. She also needed to connect with the local actor who had been hired to be her Prince Charming sidekick. She wasn't sure when they were supposed to start doing joint appearances.

"Nap first. Chocolate later," Clara said, and then she blinked hard. "Wow, I don't think I've ever said that before. The jet lag is messing around with my priorities."

Ingrid laughed as she led them upstairs. Clara followed immediately on her heels, with Gracie not far behind. At the last minute, something made her glance over her shoulder for another peek at the Abominable Snow Prince. The nickname certainly appeared to fit the man with the wild beard and eyelashes white with snow. Even his stare looked hard and icy.

No wonder San Glacera's castle looked like it belonged in a fairy tale. A beast lived there.

CHAPTER SIX

Can You Keep a Secret?

"Come on, Emilie. Mittens doesn't like it when we don't get along." Nick gave the little spaniel the hand signal they'd practiced, and Mittens sat up on his hindquarters and pawed at the air.

Emilie cracked a reluctant smile from her favorite chair in the corner of the palace library. Nick and his sister had spent countless hours in the library when they were children, and it was still one of Emilie's regular haunts. "You taught your dog how to beg?"

"Desperate times call for desperate measures. I told you I was sorry. Everyone loves your idea for the contest," Nick said.

"Everyone besides you." She slammed her book closed.

"But I'm willing to give it a chance."

Today was the day. Rows of candy cane-striped tents had popped up along the village square overnight, along with the massive carved ice sculptures that drew crowds of tourists to San Glacera for the annual Christmas market. Tonight Nick would join the royal family to preside over the official opening of the Ice Village, along with his royal blind date, of course.

And the rent-a-princess.

It was happening. All of it.

"Come take a walk with us," Nick said.

Emilie's book slid out of her lap and fell onto the floor with a thud. At last, he'd gotten her attention. Mittens's, too. The little Cavalier's copper-colored ears pricked forward at the sound of his favorite word.

"Take a walk?" Emilie's gaze darted toward the castle window, where the peaks of the tents that made up the Christmas market were just visible. Snowflakes danced against the windowpane. "*Outside?*"

Mittens let out a gleeful yip. They were hitting all the doggie vocabulary highlights.

Nick shrugged one shoulder. "That was the idea."

He wanted to stroll through the vendor stalls and see for himself what challenges the people of his kingdom were facing. He wanted to walk in the footsteps of his grandfather, who used to take Nick to the opening morning of the market every year for cocoa piled high with marshmallows and a single chocolate kiss at the bottom of his cup. He wanted a chance to see San Glacera at Christmas, the way it had always been....

Before tonight, when it turned into a glorified theme park.

Emilie looked him up and down, and Nick gave a silent prayer of thanks that she couldn't read his mind. "But you haven't left the castle since you've been back. Like, at all."

He arched an eyebrow. "Would you, if you'd been the one on the cover of every newspaper in Central Europe?"

"Point taken." Emilie bit her bottom lip, and any lingering resentment in her expression seemed to soften. "Why now? What's changed your mind?"

His time was up, whether he wanted it to be or not. It would be nice to leave the palace on his own terms first, though. "I thought it might be fun for you and I to take a look around the market before tonight. Dress down and be regular people."

Emilie grinned. "You mean like when we used to sneak out of the castle when we were kids? You really think no one will recognize us?"

"Not if we take Mittens." Nick shot a meaningful glance at his dog. "We'll practically be invisible by comparison."

Mittens, like all Cavalier King Charles spaniels, was aggressively adorable. A "sweet, gentle and melting expression" was written right into the official description of the breed in America. Nick's dog was the canine equivalent of a warm hug.

Better yet, Nick had thus far managed to keep the little squirt out of the press. Sarah Jane hadn't mentioned his furry companion, lest the dog's existence make Nick seem in any way warm and fuzzy. Keeping Mittens a secret was probably Nick's way of keeping a small part of his life to himself. He hadn't really examined his reasoning for keeping the dog under wraps. It had just sort of happened.

In any event, Mittens's presence at the market wouldn't signal that the Crown Prince of San Glacera was nearby, especially if Nick and Emilie were dressed down and on their own, with no royal entourage. Nick's recent shave and haircut might also help. As far as the public knew, he was still sporting a full snow monster-esque beard. He doubted anyone would notice him.

If they did, he'd survive. He couldn't hide forever.

"Let's do it." Emilie leaped out of her chair, and it was so good to see her smiling at him again that Nick didn't much care if anyone spotted them out and about. It would be worth it in the end.

Probably.

Minutes later, Nick pulled a cashmere beanie down low over his eyes and Mittens trotted merrily at the end of his dog leash as they exited the castle grounds. Emilie wore pink furry earmuffs and a ponytail high on her head—not the most stealthy disguise.

Still, Nick's prediction had been spot on. Nearly everyone they encountered on the cobblestone walkways oohed and ahhed over Mittens. Most people stopped in their tracks to give him a pat or a scratch on his head, but not a single passerby made eye contact with Nick or his sister.

"I'm almost insulted," Emilie said under her breath as they slowed to a stop near the first tent of the Christmas market. "I never realized how easy it would be for a dog to steal my thunder."

Nick rolled his eyes. "No one is stealing your thunder. I think this is rather fun."

Of course, it would have been more fun if the village square had been bustling like it usually did during the holidays. It was scarcely recognizable as the same Christmas market where Nick had walked hand in hand with his grandpa when he had been a boy. The change had happened so gradually, year after year, that Nick hadn't noticed.

He should have been paying more attention. He should have been worrying less about the details of his personal life being splashed across the papers and more about the state of his kingdom. Maybe if he had, Jaron's ominous chart wouldn't have come as such a shock.

"It's definitely fun." Emilie's gaze lingered on an ice sculpture made up of three enormous, interlocking snowflakes. Sunlight filtered through the chiseled ice, bathing the surrounding snow in pastel shades of pink and lavender.

Nick's sister gave a wistful sigh. "So pretty." She turned to face him. "You know, if you're serious about trying to get back into my good graces, you should probably buy me a cup of hot cocoa."

"It wouldn't be Christmas in San Glacera without it," Nick said.

He wondered if the hot chocolate stand was still in its usual spot, right at the center of the pop-up market, or if that, too, had changed. Mittens's little nose twitched as they wound their way through stalls selling sugared almonds, colorful marzipan bonbons, and warm, fragrant gingerbread. The booth selling chimney cakes—tall, thin cakes that resembled a stack of cinnamon donuts—was exactly where it had always been. Nick inhaled the sticky sweet scent and remembered his grandfather's laughter and the rough calluses on the palms of his hands, the mark of a people's king. Not someone who sat in the castle and ruled, but the first leader of San Glacera to really spend time with the people.

Nick's grandfather, King Noël, had been the monarch who'd started the Christmas market and the Ice Festival in the first place, so many years ago. He'd been the architect of every last detail of the village Christmas celebration. He'd also been the first king to go on mountaineering expeditions with members of the military who'd served the kingdom. Nick's annual Matterhorn trip was an extension of that very program.

There was a reason Nick's grandfather had been so beloved. To Nick, he'd been a larger-than-life figure—more than a grandfather, more than a king. He'd represented the best and brightest of San Glacera, everything Nick wanted to be when it was time for him to sit on the throne.

And now, in Nick's absence, his family had decided to change the single biggest tradition his grandfather had ever started. Intellectually, he understood why. But he was still having a difficult time wrapping his heart around it.

"Look! There it is." Emilie pointed a mittened hand toward the hot cocoa stall, situated at the spot where the rows of tents all came together. The heart of the Christmas market.

Relief flowed through Nick. It was good to know that some things never changed.

He let Mittens drag them toward a cluster of red picnic tables and benches where small groups of people sat warming their hands on steaming cups of chocolate. The Cavalier swiveled his little head from Nick to the cocoa booth, tail wagging back and forth like a pendulum. Mittens's breath came out in tiny puffs of frosty vapor. Then, just as they approached the booth, Nick heard someone let out a sigh. Not just any sigh, but a soul-deep sigh of pure delight. Utter satisfaction.

"Ahhhhhhhh." The woman's head tipped back and loose, dark curls spilled over her shoulders.

Something stirred deep inside of Nick. How long had it been since he'd sighed like that? All he could see of her was the back of her robin's egg blue swing coat and a glossy curtain of chestnut waves falling from a hat topped with a huge white pompon. He couldn't seem to look anyplace else.

"Nick. You're *staring*," Emilie said under her breath.

He tried to drag his gaze away from the cocoa enthusiast. "I'm simply pleased to see someone enjoying one of San Glacera's long-standing holiday traditions. That's all."

Was the woman a tourist? She had to be if she'd never tasted the kingdom's most well-known delicacy before. So much for Jaron and his bar graphs. *Someone* had managed to find San Glacera without adding fairy tale characters to the mix.

"That's all?" Emilie let out a snort that could only be described as *un*regal. She leaned far to the left in an attempt to catch a glimpse of Miss Cocoa's face and blinked. Hard.

Nick said, "I'm not altogether sure what you're implying, but..."

Emilie held up her hand in a wave before he could finish. "Bye." She darted away, weaving through a group of boys and girls in uniform.

"What? Wait, where are you going?" Nick threw up his hands. He could hardly go barreling after her through a class of schoolchildren, an adorable dog in tow, without calling attention to himself. But he hadn't dragged her to the market so she could abandon him. They were supposed to be partners in crime. They could go back to being royal later tonight.

Already at a short distance, Emilie turned around and winked. Then she inclined her head toward the woman enjoying the hot chocolate.

Here, he'd thought he'd finally convinced her to forgive him and all the while, she'd had her own agenda. She'd wanted to get him out of the castle and now that she'd dragged him out of hiding, she was going to double down and play matchmaker.

Seriously?

And just like that, with a flutter of her mittened fingertips, his sister was gone.

Oh. My. Gosh.

Gracie's eyes drifted closed. She might have even sighed out loud.

Scratch that—she'd definitely sighed, and not in a discreet, princess-y sort of way. She sounded more like Goldilocks probably had after greedily gulping down three bowls of delicious porridge.

What *was* porridge, anyway? It didn't sound all that appetizing, frankly. Definitely not as decadent as the sip of rich cocoa Gracie had just taken. Then again, what was?

Ingrid hadn't been exaggerating. San Glacera's hot cocoa was like nothing Gracie had ever tasted before. Creamy.

Luxurious. Like drinking a melted bar of the purest, richest gourmet chocolate in the world.

"What kind of magic is this?" she whispered into her cup.

"Not magic at all. Just one of our kingdom's finest delicacies," someone behind her said—a male someone, if the deep timbre of his voice was any indication.

Gracie turned around and immediately found herself colliding with a flash of white and chestnut fur barreling toward her shins. It took her a second to realize it was a dog. The pup had huge, perfectly round eyes, a short muzzle, and feathered paws that sort of made him look like a character from a Dr. Seuss book.

"Mittens, no," the man holding the other end of the leash called, just as the little spaniel threw himself, belly-up, at Gracie's feet.

The dog pawed at the air until Gracie stooped to rub his belly with her free hand. "Well, aren't you the sweetest thing I've ever seen?"

"Sorry, he's a little excited." The man cleared his throat. "He doesn't get out much."

"That's a shame. Clearly, he loves the attention." Gracie laughed as the dog bit gently at her mitten. Then she stood to meet the strange man's gaze.

Her stomach fluttered. He had eyes like steel, and a perfectly chiseled jaw to match. His spine was ramrod straight, and he carried himself with an air that seemed—dare she think it—regal. Clearly, Gracie had been spending far too much time playing princess.

The man shifted from one foot to the other as if he, too, didn't get out much.

Gracie tilted her head and bit back a smile. "Mittens? Did you really name your dog after a winter fashion accessory?"

He looked at her for a beat before cracking a reluctant smile. "Yes and no. I let my sister name him, so it was either that or Tiara. She's really into that sort of thing."

"Fashion accessories?" Gracie narrowed her gaze at him. "Or princess paraphernalia?"

He barked out a laugh and then seemed to collect himself. "Both."

"Smart girl. I like her already," Gracie said. Her gaze flitted toward the castle. Snowflakes swirled around its slender turrets, and guards dressed in bright crimson coats and tall hats flanked the entrance. They looked like toy soldiers in a magical Christmas fairy tale.

No wonder men who looked like Prince Charming and dogs named Mittens roamed free in this place.

"You just missed my sister, I'm afraid. We came for the *chocolat chaud*, but then she...ran off," Mittens's dad said.

The dog scrambled to his feet and looked back and forth between them. A clump of snow clung to his petite nose.

Gracie felt herself frown. *"Chocolat chaud?"*

He nodded toward the cup in her hand. "French for hot chocolate. We make it in the Parisian style, but with a secret surprise."

Gracie had never been to Paris, or anyplace else that glamorous—which was half the reason she'd let her family convince her to travel to San Glacera during Christmas. If she'd known about the chocolate, she might have been more eager to get on the plane.

You don't have to sing for five more days. You've got loads of time.

Then why did she feel like Cinderella on the brink of midnight?

"What's the secret surprise?" She took another sip, and the decadent cocoa warmed her from the inside out.

A group of people passed by, chatting and laughing into the wind. Mittens's dad quickly looked the other way as they walked by. Gracie followed his gaze in an attempt to see what had captured his attention, but all she could see were the tents of the Christmas market stretching the length of the square.

When she turned back toward him, he smiled and nodded toward her cup of cocoa. "You'll find out what the secret surprise is when you get to the bottom."

Gracie tilted her head. "That's awfully mysterious."

He regarded her for a moment, and his eyes went from steel to a soft dove gray. "Actually, if you're into Christmas treats, there's something else you simply must try."

"Something better than this?" She took another sip of *chocolat chaud*, suddenly anxious to discover whatever surprise lingered at the bottom of her cup. "If so, I'm in."

He held up a finger. "Not better. But almost as good."

Gracie's stomach growled. The airplane meal she'd eaten hours ago wasn't cutting it anymore. "I'm still in, but can I ask you a question first?"

"Certainly." He nodded.

"Why are you doing this?" Denver was a friendly place, but no one there had ever taken such a vested interest in her holiday snack preferences before. "I don't even know your name."

"My name is Nick," he said quietly as his gaze dropped to her cup of cocoa. "And I'm just happy to see a visitor enjoying Christmas in San Glacera. It's a special place."

Gracie nodded. "I can see that already. Okay, lead the way. I'm ready to try this mystery treat."

"Follow me, then."

A few minutes later, at a booth just three tents down, he offered her a paper plate straining under the weight of a stack of round waffles topped with chocolate sauce and something that looked sort of like peanut butter but smelled like gingerbread. Mittens rose onto his hind legs and did a little dance, nose twitching.

"I present Belgian liege with chocolate and speculoos," Nick said.

"Liege?"

"Just a fancy word for a round waffle." He winked, and

it seemed to float right through Gracie, like a snow flurry.

Wait. She wasn't supposed to be attracted to this nice man. He was a stranger playing tour guide, and she was here for the most important princess appearance of her life. There was zero room for flirting on her agenda. Maybe the fluttery feeling was just the hot cocoa talking.

Right. And maybe I'll wake up tomorrow and not worry the slightest about singing off-key on Christmas Eve.

"Speculoos is a spiced cookie butter spread. Lieges with speculoos were one of my favorite holiday treats when I was a kid." Nick smiled, and Gracie's stomach did a flip-flop.

No hot cocoa is that powerful.

Gracie was definitely charmed, which was kind of a problem. She didn't need this sort of distraction. In fact, she should leave right now, go back to the B&B and think about her song selection. Maybe even practice a little, since her first rehearsal was coming up soon.

But the lure of that waffle was just too much. At least, that's what she told herself as she prepared to take her first bite. "So what was it like growing up in San Glacera?"

Their eyes met just as the mix of scrumptious flavors burst on her tongue, sugary sweet with just the right amount of spice. If Christmas could be defined by a single taste, this would be it.

"Life in San Glacera is..." His brow furrowed as he appeared to consider his answer. "Wonderful. We're a small country, built on tradition. People here care about one another. It's the best place on earth, in my humble opinion. So long as you don't mind the cold..."

"I don't mind the cold at all. It's actually kind of my thing." Gracie laughed.

He tilted his head, studying her with those gray eyes of his. It was like falling into a winter sky.

Gracie cleared her throat. "You hesitated just now, though."

"I did?"

"Yep, right before you told me how much you love it here. You paused, like you were thinking about saying something different." What was she doing? She didn't even know this man. Why would he possibly want to have a meaningful heart-to-heart with her? "Ignore me. I'm sorry. It's really none of my business. And I definitely don't need convincing that this place is magical. I mean, look around."

She waved a hand, encompassing the market's peppermint candy-striped tents and the castle, looking more romantic than ever behind a lacy veil of swirling snow.

Nick followed her gaze to the palace's elegant turrets, and his enchanting smile turned ever-so-slightly sad around the edges. "This is my home, and I love it dearly. But you're right—I suppose I did hesitate. The pause wasn't about San Glacera, though. I've just been a bit out of sorts lately."

Mittens let out a tiny whine, as if agreeing to this statement. More likely, he wanted a bite of waffle, but the timing was uncanny.

Gracie's gaze flitted from the adorable dog to his handsome owner. "Me too."

"Is that so?" Nick said, regarding her with an intensity that made her feel like she'd been spinning circles on ice skates. "Why?"

She took a deep breath, unsure quite how to explain. She certainly didn't want to come off as ungrateful about winning the contest, but something about the conflicted look in his eyes made her think he might understand how overwhelmed she sometimes felt. Or maybe she was just reading too much into this entire encounter. Probably so...

It had been a while since she'd opened up to a man like this, with good reason.

"This probably won't make a bit of sense to you at all, but do you ever feel like you've gotten so accustomed to playing a role that you sometimes forget where that role ends and the real person begins?" The words tumbled out of her mouth before she realized what she'd meant to say, as if they'd been waiting right there on the tip of her tongue for just the right time...just the right person to hear them. "Like, to the outside world you've got everything completely under control, but inside..."

He gave her a lopsided smile and finished the thought for her. "But inside, you feel like you're just one mistake away from causing everything to crumble to the ground?"

Gracie blinked. He'd just perfectly described the way she'd been feeling for weeks, starting with all of those horrid bank interviews and culminating with the realization that she'd have to sing in order to collect her contest prize money. She felt like he'd just handed her a long-lost piece to a jigsaw puzzle—the kind her family always did together on Christmas morning.

"That's it exactly," she said, breathless.

"In that case, we're both a little out of sorts in the same way." His gaze locked with hers until a thick lump formed in her throat. A strange sensation washed over her, almost like homesickness.

He held her gaze just a little longer before he looked away. For a second, she could almost breathe again.

"Sometimes it almost feels like the public role is a sort of hiding place, even though it's the part of you that everyone in the world sees," he said. "As long as everyone is paying attention to that very public face, you don't have to worry about anyone knowing the real you and all the messiness that goes with your true hopes and fears." Nick kept looking toward the castle until his brow furrowed. Then he shook his head and glanced back at Gracie. "I have no idea where that just came from. I'm supposed to be feeding you waffles, not a heaping dose of existential angst."

"More like honesty. And that pairs perfectly with everything, in my humble opinion," Gracie said.

"Mine, too." The corner of his mouth turned up in a smile. "It seems that you and I make a fine pair."

Gracie nodded, thoughts in a whirl. "We do, don't we?"

Her heart thumped hard in her chest. She'd traveled halfway across the world and somehow found a kindred spirit—someone who understood exactly what it felt like to wear a princess gown and a perfect royal smile every day. To do her best to spread joy and hope, while at the same time wondering if she was really up to the task. People relied on her. Not just children, but her employees too. If she messed up this trip, she wouldn't just be letting herself down. Her entire business could fail.

How was it possible that a perfect stranger could articulate what that weight on her heart felt like?

"Honesty." The corners of Nick's lips rose. "I like it. One of my favorite virtues, right up there with kindness and authenticity."

I like him. Gracie smiled into her cocoa. *I like him* a lot.

"You haven't forgotten about the secret surprise, have you?" Nick arched an eyebrow and cast a meaningful look at her paper cup.

"Oh, that's right." Hope fluttered inside her as she took the last few sips. Then she looked down and gasped.

An intricate picture was stamped into the bottom of the cup in gilded ink. It depicted a chocolate kiss surrounded by delicate snowflakes and the words *Chef's Kiss.*

"Every cup has a special artist rendering of a chocolate kiss inside. It represents the kiss that's dropped into the cocoa just after it's poured," Nick said.

"So the secret surprise is a kiss," Gracie said, and when she looked up and met Nick's gaze, her cheeks went warm.

A kiss.

Gracie had the sudden, improper urge to rise up on tiptoe and press her lips to his.

She didn't dare, obviously. Good grief, what had gotten

into her? She felt like she'd taken a royally big bite from an enchanted apple.

"Indeed." His eyes flickered with...something. And Gracie got the feeling that neither one of them was talking about chocolate anymore.

She hadn't been imagining the sparks between them, had she? He felt it too.

All her breath seemed to gather in her throat. *Had* she somehow landed in the middle of a fairy tale?

Mittens's wagging tail beat against Gracie's shin, and the little dog looked up at her with huge, melting eyes. The animal was so cute that he almost didn't look real. Gracie wanted nothing more than to keep wandering the kingdom's cobblestone streets with this captivating pair, but her first official San Glacera appearance was in less than two hours and her ballgown was still crammed into her suitcase, along with everything else she needed to transform into Princess Snowflake. She couldn't just wave a magic wand and turn into a princess. These things took time, and tonight would be the most important appearance she'd ever had.

Until Christmas Eve, anyway.

"Um." Gracie let out a shaky breath. "This has been lovely, but I should probably go. I have kind of a big night ahead of me."

Mittens let out a mournful sigh.

"A big night, hmm? Might you be attending the opening of the Ice Festival?" Nick asked.

"Ice sculptures, royalty, and storybook characters?" Gracie bounced on her toes. "I wouldn't miss it."

He nodded. "It's going to be quite something this year."

"Will you be there?" she asked.

"With bells on," he said in a tone that was strangely flat. For someone who loved San Glacera so much, he didn't seem too enthusiastic about what was supposed to be one of the kingdom's biggest holiday traditions.

He'd been so kind to her, and she wanted to reciprocate in some small way. And if she was being honest with herself, she also wanted to see him again.

Mittens peered up at her and cocked his cute little head. If Gracie didn't know better, she would've thought the spaniel could read her mind.

She glanced up at Nick. "Can you keep a secret?"

He chuckled. "Better than you could possibly imagine."

Never in her life had Gracie disclosed her Princess Snowflake identity to a total stranger. Back when she'd started Perfect Party Princesses, she'd read an article about theme park characters and how the actors portraying them weren't allowed to disclose their real identities. Not in real life and not on social media. It was a way to make visiting the park as magical as possible for the attendees.

Gracie had adopted the same policy for all the party princesses, including herself. And here she was, about to break her own rule.

She leaned close to Nick—close enough to breathe in his crisp evergreen scent. Like he'd been off somewhere chopping down Christmas trees. Then she reached inside her coat and pulled out the VIP badge that hung from the lanyard the palace had left at the B&B in her welcome packet, with strict instructions to wear it every time she left the hotel.

She flashed Nick the purple badge and whispered, "I'm the princess."

Mittens dropped into a play bow and wagged his tail. Nick's eyes glittered.

"What an astonishing coincidence." Nick shook his head. Then he dropped his voice to a murmur that sent a chill up and down Gracie's spine. A chill that had nothing to do with the cold. "I'm the prince."

CHAPTER SEVEN

What Kind of Princess Doesn't Believe in Happily Ever After?

"I MET PRINCE CHARMING," GRACIE BLURTED. She shut the door to their room behind her and leaned against it, still the slightest bit weak in the knees.

Clara sat up in her twin bed and pushed her satin sleep mask onto her forehead. "What did you just say?"

"Oops." Gracie winced. "I'm sorry. Go back to sleep. We can talk about it later."

She still couldn't believe it. Gracie had practically floated all the way back to the B&B. She'd never imagined that Nick might be the actor who'd been hired to play Prince Charming opposite her, but looking back now, it made perfect sense. He'd spoken so sincerely about playing a part and echoed everything she felt about being Princess Snowflake. They really were kindred spirits, fake crowns and all.

"Too late. You've definitely got my attention." Clara yawned, then spotted the small plate in Gracie's hand and perked up considerably. "Are those more of Ingrid's cookies?"

"Yes. She just made a new batch. The entire lobby smells like sugar and cinnamon." Gracie unbuttoned her coat as she crossed the room to hand Clara the plate.

Their room was a double, with dark wood paneling and two twin beds piled high with patchwork quilts and faux fur throws. Directly across from the beds was a sitting area with a pair of tufted, overstuffed chairs facing a stone fireplace strung with woolen knit stockings. A blue spruce Christmas tree sat in the corner, laden with mercury glass ornaments shaped like mushrooms and pinecones.

Clara sat up, scooted over, and patted the empty space beside her. "Come. Sit. Tell me everything. Only you could go out in search of hot cocoa and meet someone who seemed like Prince Charming."

Gracie tossed her hat and coat onto her bed, settled beside Clara, and took a deep, pine-scented inhale. She could smell the Christmas tree clear across the room. Her thoughts immediately went to Nick—his fresh pine scent, his chiseled features, the warmth of his breath fanning her cheek as he'd whispered in her ear.

I'm the prince.

She shook her head. "No, he didn't just seem like Prince Charming. He *is* Prince Charming. He's the actor playing the prince opposite me at the Ice Festival."

"And you just happened to bump into each other? That's crazy." Clara bit into a shortbread star decorated with royal icing and gold sprinkles. "How did you know it was him?"

Gracie hesitated.

"What?" Clara frowned. Cookie crumbs dotted her chin.

"I sort of told him I was the princess." Gracie winced. She couldn't believe she'd outed herself like that. "Once I showed him my VIP badge, he spilled the beans."

"Whoa. That's so unlike you." Clara's eyes danced. "He must have made quite an impression."

Gracie leaned against the headboard and sighed. "You have no idea. He had a dog named Mittens, and he fed me the most divine waffles. He was—for lack of a better word—charming."

A bemused smile spread across Clara's face.

Gracie let out a dreamy sigh. "There was a chocolate kiss at the bottom of my cup."

Clara reached for another cookie. "I don't know what you're talking about, but you sound positively smitten."

Gracie's response was automatic. "I'm not smitten."

"Are you sure? Because you just burst in here and woke me up talking about waffles and dogs and a charming prince. And just look at you." Clara waved a hand in Gracie's general direction.

Gracie brushed a stray tawny curl from her eyes. She probably looked like a mess after the long flight. It was going to take an extra dash or two of glitter to get her into perfect Princess Snowflake form for the event later. "What do you mean?"

"You're *glowing*." Clara reached across Gracie to grab her phone from the nightstand—a brand-new device to replace the one that had fallen victim to Jingle's hoof. "That must have been some waffle."

Heat crept into Gracie's cheeks. Was she really glowing? "I'm sure it's just the cold."

Clara looked up from scrolling. She hadn't posted anything about the contest on the Perfect Party Princesses social media accounts yet because she wanted to wait until tonight when Princess Snowflake made her first appearance in San Glacera. Gracie knew the wait had to be killing her.

"It's okay to be excited, you know." Clara gave Gracie a gentle shoulder bump. She gestured at the chalet's cozy room with her phone. "All of this is definitely something to be excited about."

"I know," Gracie said, swallowing hard.

Every time she let her guard down, the realization that she was going to be singing in front of an audience in just a matter of days seemed to sneak up on her. Back home, her family had managed to convince her it was just one tiny part of the trip. But now that she was here, now that San Glacera was a real place and not just a faraway dream...

The enormity of what she'd signed on for was finally beginning to feel real.

"I'll feel better after I get the singing part out of the way," she said, trying—and failing—to keep the nervous tremor from creeping into her tone.

Clara reached for her hand and gave it a squeeze. "You're singing on Christmas Eve. That's the final night of the trip. Are you planning on holding your breath until then?"

"No." Yes. Maybe. "It's crazy. For a while there, I managed to forget about the performance and enjoy the market. It was..."

Magical.

She didn't dare say it out loud. Gracie had been playing princess long enough to know what was real and what wasn't. Fairy tales fell squarely into the latter category.

"It was nice," she finally said.

"Because of Prince Charming." Clara waggled her eyebrows.

Gracie rolled her eyes. "No."

Not entirely, anyway...

"I didn't come here for romance," she insisted. "I came here for the prize money and so we could go back home to build Perfect Party Princesses into the success that I know it can be."

"Who says you can't have a little romance at the same time?" Clara shrugged one shoulder. "Who says a girl-boss princess can't have it all?"

"History," Gracie said, throat going tight. "History says that."

And she wasn't talking about any of the real-life royals whose lives weren't fairy tale perfect. She was speaking from her own personal experience.

The last time she'd fallen head over heels, it had ended in a spectacular mess. It had also been a major contributing factor in her crippling case of stage fright. Now was definitely not the time to be thinking about romance.

"The only way I'm going to get through this week is to focus." Gracie climbed off the bed in search of her luggage. She only had a few hours to transform herself into an ice princess.

"If you say so," Clara said, clearly unconvinced.

"I mean it." Gracie flung her suitcase onto the settee bench situated at the foot of her bed. "After I told Nick I was the princess, he asked if I wanted to meet him ahead of time. We're going to meet at the castle gate thirty minutes before I'm scheduled to appear so we can arrive together, but it's all going to be strictly business."

When he'd issued the invitation, Gracie's knees had turned to water.

This is bad, she'd thought. She was flirting with disaster. This was the most important Christmas of her life, and singing and romance didn't mix. Not for Gracie. But before she'd been able to stop herself, she'd agreed.

I'd love to. Her answer had come out breathy and sweet. Full Disney princess.

Nick's eyes had blazed, as warm as a crackling fire. *It's a date.* Then, in true princely fashion, he'd kissed her hand.

Was that even a thing these days? Gracie had only seen it happen in an old movie starring Grace Kelly, who'd famously gone on to become a real-life princess. Thing or not, as Nick's lips brushed against the pale pink cashmere of Gracie's mitten, tiny sparks of electricity had skittered over her skin. Her hands shook now, just thinking about it.

She had a date.

At a castle.

With a prince.

Clara bit back a smile. "I'm sure you're right. A castle, a princess, a charming prince...none of that sounds romantic in the slightest."

"I'm *not* falling for him." Gracie grabbed a faux fur throw pillow from her bed and threw it at Clara.

But who was she kidding? Those were the literal ingredients of a whirlwind fairy tale romance, and what kind of princess would Gracie be if she didn't believe in happily ever after?

I'm the princess.

Nick couldn't help but smile every time the words spun through his mind. Just the memory of her soft voice, warm against his cheek, made him feel light on his feet as he strode across the palace to Jaron's office.

She'd caught Nick off guard at first. Even after all the talk about public roles and responsibilities—the secret fears so unique to being royal—he hadn't recognized the beautiful woman he'd spent the afternoon with as Princess Alana of Vernina. Now it made perfect sense. Who else could she have possibly been?

No wonder they seemed to have so much in common. Still, Nick had never met another royal who seemed to wear her heart on her sleeve like she did. She was so...*real*. Nick hadn't stopped thinking about her since she'd bid him farewell at the Christmas market and left him standing by the waffle stand, dumbstruck. He barely remembered her as a little girl. They'd been just children the last time he'd seen her, but she'd completely enchanted him today. He couldn't believe he hadn't remembered her straight away.

The American accent had thrown him. That had to be why it had never crossed his mind that the captivating stranger could be the visiting princess. She'd spent years in American classrooms, though. So in retrospect, the accent made complete and total sense. Nick was almost surprised that he hadn't figured out her identity sooner.

Well, now he knew, and it almost felt like a Christmas miracle.

"Do you have a minute?" Nick said as he paused at the opened doorway to Jaron's office.

Jaron sat facing him behind a broad desk covered in neat stacks of paper. Bookshelves spanned the entire back wall of the office, where hardback volumes stood among various royal orders and honors that Nick's family had bestowed on Jaron in recent years. The top shelf was covered with photographs in polished silver frames, some dating all the way back to their prep school days.

"Sure. What can I help you with?" Jaron looked up from his laptop, gaze lingering on Nick's formal military uniform. "Wow, you're already ready for this evening's activities."

"I am." Nick nodded. Why did this conversation suddenly feel awkward?

Just spit it out. It didn't really matter how he phrased things. He and Jarod had known each other a long time. Jaron would surely guess what he'd come to inquire about. Nick was simply feeling a little...restless.

"I met Princess Alana earlier this afternoon," he said.

Jaron cocked his head, brow furrowing. "You did?"

"I did."

"That's interesting." Jaron leaned back in his chair. Nick had stopped by his office unannounced. It happened sometimes, since the two men were friends. But judging by Jaron's expression, this particular visit had caught him off guard. "The last I heard, her flight was delayed. I haven't gotten an update from the Vernina travel office in hours. I assumed she and the king and queen were still waiting to take off."

"Strange. She's definitely here. I met her just a while ago at the Christmas market," Nick said.

"Good. I was about to re-work the seating arrangements in the royal box. I'm really glad you let me know." The furrow in Jaron's brow deepened. "Why did you, though? You don't typically get involved in logistics of this sort."

Nick paused. "I don't?"

"When was the last time you knew a visiting dignitary had arrived in the kingdom before I did?" Jaron's eyebrows lifted. A challenge.

Point taken. "Never."

"So, what's different about this time?" Jaron studied him, and his attention seemed to linger on Nick's hands, currently fidgeting with the cufflinks at his wrists.

"Nothing's different," Nick said, but his racing pulse told him that wasn't quite true. *She* was different. The princess. "I ran into her, and I thought you'd like to know."

"And this was so important that you needed to come all the way to my office and tell me in person?" Jaron sat up straighter, and his mouth twisted into a smirk.

"Stop looking at me like that." Nick lowered himself into the office chair opposite Jaron. He hadn't planned on this little visit taking more than a few minutes, but getting information out of Jaron was clearly going to take more effort than Nick had anticipated.

Jaron shrugged, but his smirk intensified. "How am I looking at you?"

"Like your imagination has gone wild and you're writing a press release for a royal wedding in your head right now," Nick said.

Jaron laughed. "I'm doing no such thing. It's just been a while since I've seen you interested in a woman. A long while, actually. Not since Sarah Jane."

Nick's jaw tensed. "I didn't say I was interested in anyone."

"Aren't you, though?" Jaron looked him up and down, and Nick realized he'd begun fidgeting with the sash stretched across his chest. "It shows, friend."

"We shared a waffle. She's—" Nick struggled for a word to properly describe the woman he couldn't seem to stop thinking about. *Lovely. Everything about her is undeniably lovely.* "Different."

"How so, exactly?"

The princess's luminous blue eyes flashed in Nick's memory, sparkling like mad when she'd spotted the gold rendering of the chocolate kiss at the bottom of her cup of cocoa.

"There's an earnestness about her that I find very charming. She seems passionate." Warmth flooded Nick's chest when he landed on the most suitable adjective. "Authentic."

She seems honest. He couldn't bring himself to say it. The last time he'd placed his trust in a woman had been a monumental mistake. Alana was a princess and, judging by the things she'd said, she understood the importance of maintaining a good public image. She seemed to have the same ingrained sense of responsibility that Nick did. The same desire to do the right thing for the people who relied on the monarchy to watch out for their best interests. But other than romping around the palace as small children, they'd just met. He couldn't possibly *know* her.

No matter how badly he wanted to.

Jaron stared blankly at him. "You got all that from sharing a waffle?"

"I'm curious about her, that's all. I'm meeting her shortly at the side castle gate." He wanted to take a walk with her before they had to take their seats in the royal box. He thought she might like to see the ice sculptures flanking either side of the palace up close. "What can you tell me?"

Teri Wilson

"Well, I don't know much about her, to be honest. As you know, her country has been one of our closest allies for centuries." Jaron shuffled through some papers on his desk until he found the princess's bio on a sheet of thick, ivory-colored parchment paper with the royal crest of Vernina embossed at the top in gold. "This is her first official royal tour. She's been in America the past few years, studying for her graduate degree in international relations at Georgetown University."

"How long was she in the States?"

Jaron glanced down at the paper again. "Quite some time. It looks like she went to boarding school on the East Coast there, as well."

Again, that certainly explained her accent.

"Anything else?" Nick asked.

"She's an equestrian, specializing in show jumping and eventing. Her horse's name is Thunder." Jaron shot him a penetrating look. "But be honest—this isn't the sort of information you're looking for, is it?"

"I have no intention of invading her privacy. I just..."

"You want to know if she can be trusted," Jaron said.

Nick swallowed. Yes, that's exactly what he wanted to know. He just hadn't realized as much until Jaron put it so bluntly.

"I don't blame you for being cautious, but there are never any guarantees about this sort of thing. Sometimes you just need to take a leap." The corner of Jaron's mouth inched into a smile. Not a smirk this time, but a genuine expression of kindness and concern.

Take a leap.

It was so much easier said than done, and Nick wasn't looking for a relationship...with anyone.

But wasn't he getting ahead of himself? All he was contemplating was a walk. It was Christmas. He had an entire kingdom to worry about, with the added bonus of a cartoon character tossed into the mix.

There would be no leaping.

"When was the last time you took a leap, dating-wise?" Nick asked, cocking an accusatory eyebrow.

"This conversation isn't about me," Jaron countered.

"Right. That's what I thought. I should go," Nick said, rising to his feet.

Jaron stood, mirroring his movements. "So you're good?"

Nick nodded. "Perfectly fine, thanks."

Jaron regarded him for a moment and Nick felt like a specimen under a microscope. He should've kept his feelings about the princess to himself.

Not that he had any actual feelings for her. He didn't even know her.

So why are you in such a rush to get to the castle's side gate?

"Very well. I'll see you later in the royal box," Jaron finally said.

Nick said his goodbyes, left the press office, and nearly plowed into Emilie in the process.

"Watch it, Prince Charming," she said, stumbling backward in a pink sweatshirt and her favorite pair of ripped jeans.

"Sorry. I'm in a hurry," Nick said.

"You're already dressed? Before me? This is a first." She crossed her arms. "Where have you been? I've been looking everywhere for you."

He shifted from one foot to the other as the bells on the cathedral began chiming on the hour. He needed to get outside. Now.

"I've really got to go, Em." He stalked past her, toward the corridor leading to the castle's side gate. The hallway stretched long before him.

Emilie scrambled to keep up with him. "Can't you just tell me how you liked—"

He held up a hand. "Whatever it is, we'll have to talk about it later."

"But..." She chased him for a few more strides until giving up with a huff.

The church bells kept ringing as a pair of grand double doors came into view. The footman standing guard beside them jolted into action when he spotted Nick rushing in his direction.

"Your Royal Highness." The footman nodded as he heaved one of the doors open, holding it wide for Nick.

"Thank you," Nick said, sweeping past him.

Snowflakes swirled against the darkening sky. Nick could just see the arms of the clock on the cathedral's great spire ticking into place. He picked up his pace and made it to the castle gate with half a second to spare.

CHAPTER EIGHT

Once a Beast, Always a Beast

GRACIE FELT LIKE CINDERELLA ON her way to the ball.

It was silly, really. The gown that swished around her legs as she made her way toward the castle in the distance was the same dress she wore every single day back home—the frothy, over-the-top cupcake of a ballgown that had seen more kiddie birthday parties, charity events, and children's hospital visits than Gracie could count.

It wasn't the gown that was giving her serious Cinderella vibes at the moment, though. Nor was it the castle, despite its grand turrets and spires topped with glittering gold leaf. When Gracie had landed in the faraway kingdom of San Glacera and first spotted the palace nestled among the jagged, snowy Alps, it had seemed as if she'd been dropped inside a snow globe that had been given a good, hard shake. Everything was so beautiful...a frosted Christmas dream.

Gracie knew good and well that she wasn't in a dream or a snow globe, though. Her glass-slipper-clad feet were planted firmly on the ground, but she couldn't seem to stop smiling. This bubbly, giddy feeling was so unlike her—not the fantastical Princess Snowflake character she played, but the real person beneath all the fluff. The actual Gracie.

Gracie was polka dot T-shirts and soft blue jeans with ragged hems. She drank coffee from a Keurig out of a ceramic mug she'd bought at the farmer's market on a cool Colorado morning. She had a normal, practical life and spent Christmas every year in a normal, ordinary fashion—in her childhood home, with crumpled wrapping paper and an artificial tree dripping with wispy metallic icicles.

But here in San Glacera, the icicles were real. So were the trees, from the slender evergreens surrounding the castle and dotting the mountains to the colossal blue spruce that stood in the center of the skating rink in the village square. Gracie had only landed in San Glacera a few hours ago, but already, her life had become anything but ordinary.

Here, Gracie drank *chocolat chaud* with a secret surprise nestled in the bottom of her cup. Here, she'd sleep in a whimsical chalet that looked like it belonged in a Christmas card. Here, there were sparkling, chiseled ice sculptures on every street corner and the air smelled like gingerbread and romance.

Romance.

Gracie's heart did a little flip. She reminded herself she didn't believe in love at first sight. She wasn't Snow White, for heaven's sake, wandering through the forest and falling for the first man who sang a duet with her.

That was a hard no.

Been there, done that, got the T-shirt. Never again.

Even so, just this afternoon she'd gone all swoony over a prince with regal bone structure and eyes the color of the sky during a winter snowstorm. She'd felt like a snowflake falling...falling...falling...

He wasn't a real prince, obviously. Nick was an actor

playing a part, just like Gracie. But there'd been nothing fake about the way her heart had skipped a beat, and as much as she wanted to chalk it up to surprise at accidentally running into Prince Charming, she knew better.

Could it be that somewhere deep down, she still believed in fairy tales?

She wouldn't have thought so a month ago, a week ago, or even a day ago. But all of her breath bottled up tight in her chest as she looked out over the village square. The buildings shimmered with twinkling Christmas lights, the boughs of the great blue spruce were blanketed with snow and candy cane-striped poles lined the walkway to the castle gates. Snowflakes swirled against the velvet sky.

Gracie had a cute little magic routine that she performed at children's parties when she was in character. It involved some sleight of hand, a few paper snowflakes tucked up her sleeve, and copious amounts of glitter. But this...this was real magic. The sort of magic that made children believe in Santa Claus and adults long to come home for the holidays. This was *Christmas* magic.

If Gracie couldn't muster up the tiniest bit of hope in this glorious place, then she should probably just pack up her tiara and go home.

A sound like church bells filled the air. She turned toward the Gothic cathedral just to the right of the castle, and sure enough, the arms of the big gold clock on the central steeple ticked perilously close to seven p.m. If she didn't pick up the pace, she was going to be late. She wrapped her velvet cape snug around her shoulders and dashed toward the castle, a shivering Cinderella in reverse.

Passersby stopped to stare and smile as she floated past in a diaphanous cloud of tulle. She waved and gave them the full party princess treatment, even as she rushed toward the meeting spot. After all, that's what she'd come here for. She had a responsibility to the kingdom, which she took very seriously. But once the castle gates came into view, everything around her seemed to slow to a soft, dreamy blur. Even the snowflakes appeared to twirl and dance in slow motion.

Despite the cold, warmth radiated through Grace as she saw Nick waiting for her. He was turned toward the side, and at first glance, she had the ridiculous thought that he had the sort of profile that belonged on a silver coin. Or a dollar bill, like Queen Elizabeth in England.

It was a strange thing to imagine, but there was something timeless about that square jaw of his and those piercing gray eyes. Something refined. Stately, even.

His eyes sparkled as his gaze swept the horizon. Gracie's steps slowed. Nick's costume looked so authentic. From the blue sash stretched across his chest to the gold epaulettes on his shoulders, it was detailed in a way that Gracie never could have achieved with her old Singer sewing machine. The cut of his trousers was impeccable. The medals pinned to his chest were buffed to a perfect shine.

She couldn't help feeling a little cheap by comparison...

Like a grown woman playing dress-up.

Gracie blinked, and all at once, everything went back to feeling sweet and magical. Whatever momentary doubts she had melted away like yesterday's snow. She'd never once been ashamed of her job, and she wasn't about to start now.

Why should she? Playing Princess Snowflake made her happy. It made *others* happy, every single day. She felt like she was actually making a difference and helping change her little corner of the world into a brighter, more joyful place. If not for her job, she would have never traveled to San Glacera at all.

"I'm here," she said, breathless as she came to a stop at Nick's side.

Nick turned, eyes dancing as he met her gaze. Then the church bells rang one last time, as the hands of the clock ticked into place.

Just like in a fairy tale.

Nick gulped a deep breath of air as he took in the princess's beautiful face, luminous beneath the Christmas lights glittering overhead. She smiled, and Nick's head spun, like he'd just taken a generous gulp from a love potion in a fairy tale.

It was an absurd notion, but for once, Nick didn't care. In his mind's eye, he could see the tips of his polished shoes creeping over the edge of some imaginary cliff.

Take a leap.

Jaron's words rang in his ears, echoing in time with the church bells. Sonorous and sweet.

And then his gaze drifted lower, toward the explosion of glitter, lace, and tulle that surrounded the princess's graceful frame. Nick blinked and tried to make sense of what he was seeing.

It looked as if she'd had a run-in with a unicorn on her way to the castle. Many unicorns, actually. A whole, sparkly herd of them. Was that...a *crown* on her head? It certainly looked like one, except it was comically oversized. Like she'd taken the topper off of the San Glacera Christmas tree and placed it directly on top of her lush brown hair.

Nick's chest tightened, and his forehead beaded with sweat, despite the cold. He dabbed at it with his white-gloved fingertips, and then he remembered something the princess had said when he'd mentioned San Glacera's famously chilly winters.

I don't mind the cold at all. It's actually kind of my thing.

And like a magnet, his attention went straight to the garish rhinestone snowflake earring dangling from her ear.

No.

Panic seized him. He hadn't shared waffles with Princess Alana this afternoon, after all, had he? He'd spent the day with none other than Emilie's cartoon character.

How had he not recognized her from the video? But there hadn't been any closeups. And in the market, she'd worn a classic winter coat and hat, without much makeup, her hair loose down her back. She'd looked nothing at all like Princess Snowflake.

Just no...

Even her name was ridiculous.

"Hello," he said stiffly.

She smiled at him, all sweetness and light.

A gust of wind picked up the skirt of her gown and it wrapped around both of their legs, threatening to eat them alive. Nick couldn't have fled, even if he'd tried. He was trapped.

"Wow, your costume is really..." He shook his head, unsure how to complete that sentence. There were truly no words.

"Thank you." She spread her hands over the voluminous skirt, utterly clueless as to his sudden and acute mortification. In the distance, the people gathered in front of the castle were beginning to stare.

He needed to do something. This couldn't happen. It just couldn't. If the press even got a whiff of the fact that he'd mistaken a dress-up character for Princess Alana of Vernina, he'd be the biggest laughingstock in Europe. There'd be no coming back from that sort of humiliation.

Or had this entire thing been a setup all along? He didn't want to believe that, but given his past history, he couldn't rule out the possibility that she'd intentionally misled him.

"You're not a real princess," he said flatly.

She gave him an exaggerated wink. "Father Christmas and his reindeer say otherwise."

The rhinestones on her gown glittered beneath the twinkle lights strung overhead, nearly blinding him. But who was he kidding? Clearly, he hadn't been seeing straight for the entire day.

"I'm serious," he said.

She laughed. "Obviously." She gestured toward the gaudy crown on her head. "Newsflash: this thing isn't real either. Just like your medals."

She tapped one of the gold medallions hanging from the sash strung across Nick's chest with a glitter-tipped fingernail—a royal order, *not* a medal. Of course she didn't know the difference.

Nick arched an accusatory eyebrow.

Then Gracie's cheeks went as pink as cotton candy as the reality of the situation finally hit her, and the magic spell that had wrapped itself around them all day was broken once and for all.

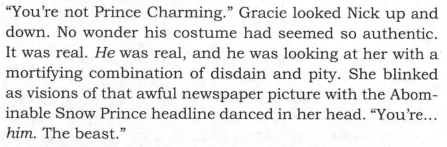

"You're not Prince Charming." Gracie looked Nick up and down. No wonder his costume had seemed so authentic. It was real. *He* was real, and he was looking at her with a mortifying combination of disdain and pity. She blinked as visions of that awful newspaper picture with the Abominable Snow Prince headline danced in her head. "You're... *him*. The beast."

"The beast?" Nick's expression hardened. Every last trace of sympathy in his eyes promptly vanished.

Which was just fine with Gracie. She didn't need this beast to feel sorry for her. She had nothing whatsoever to be ashamed of...

Except that she'd told an actual prince that she was

royal. And now she'd just called him a beast. *To his face.* No biggie.

"Sorry." She swallowed hard. How could this have happened? Forget San Glacera. She wanted to run away and spend the rest of her life in a tower in the middle of nowhere, like Rapunzel. "About the beast thing, I mean."

"You're correct," he said, ignoring her apology. "I regret to inform you that I'm not, in fact, Prince Charming."

Who talked like that?

His gaze went straight to her crown, and his lip curled ever so slightly. "Nice tiara. Princess Snowflake, I presume?"

Seriously? He was judging her?

She lifted her chin and drew herself up to her full height, but he was still a full head taller than she was. If she squinted hard enough, she could imagine him with a beard and eyebrows full of icicles. Someone had clearly introduced him to a razor in recent days.

"That's my character name. My real name is—"

"Gracie Clark." He gave her a frosty look. "I'm aware."

"Then you're also aware that I'm here by royal invitation, so I'm not sure why you seem so appalled by my appearance." She sent up a prayer of thanks that she'd remembered to get the icing out of her crown. "*You* brought me here, Your Majesty."

"Not me, specifically. I assure you. And you don't need to address me as 'Your Majesty,'" he said.

"Thank you." That seemed fair, since a few hours ago he'd told her to call him Nick.

As in, Nicolas Luca Montavan, the Crown Prince of San Glacera. How had she not realized who he was?

"The proper form of address for a prince is 'Your Royal Highness.' No need to call me 'Your Majesty' until I'm king." A muscle in his jaw flexed.

Finally, a joke. Gracie laughed, even though it wasn't technically all that funny.

Nick, however, didn't so much as crack a smile.

She blinked. "Oh, you're serious."

Wow. Just...wow. She was beginning to understand how Nick had gotten his nickname, icicles aside.

Also, he was going to be the *king* someday? Of course he was. That's what happened when a person was a Crown Prince. He moved right up the ladder to king. Gracie couldn't help but think that the last thing Nick needed was a throne.

Perhaps she was being too hard on him. The misunderstanding had definitely thrown her for a loop once she realized what was going on.

"This is awkward, I know. I obviously didn't realize you're a real prince, and you didn't realize that I'm a performer," she said with as much dignity as she could muster.

"A performer," Nick said, and he may as well have made those annoying air quotes as he did so.

Gracie's face went hot, and the shame that coursed through her felt sickeningly familiar. Like she was standing onstage beside Philip all over again.

"Let me guess—you were expecting a genuine princess," she said hotly.

He glowered in response. "Yes, as a matter of fact. Princess Alana of Vernina."

"So suddenly I'm not good enough for your fancy waffles, just because I'm a commoner?" *Commoner.* Gracie had never used that word before in her life, least of all in reference to herself.

"It's not your position. It's your..." His gaze flitted over her costume as his voice drifted off.

"Do you have some sort of problem with party princesses? Do you even really like waffles?" Gracie crossed her arms. She was wearing faux fur-lined opera gloves, part of Princess Snowflake's winter ensemble for outdoor appearances on cold Denver nights. The gloves had always seemed exceptionally regal to her.

Not anymore.

Nick cut his gaze toward a passerby who'd just aimed a camera phone in their direction. The man pocketed the phone immediately and did a little bow.

Everything about this encounter felt surreal.

Nick turned back toward her and lowered his voice. "To answer your question, yes. I love waffles."

Snow was beginning to pile up on the fancy gold epaulettes of his uniform. His dark hair was dusted with a fine layer of white. He probably looked more like her princely counterpart than he realized.

He came closer—as close as her billowing tulle gown would allow. "I particularly enjoyed sharing them with you, if you must know."

Gracie melted. Just a little.

Until she realized he'd completely ignored her question about party princesses.

She stated the obvious. "You're a snob."

"Perhaps." He narrowed his eyes at her. "Tell me the truth. Did you purposefully mislead me?"

She glared at his ridiculously handsome face. It was honestly amazing what a shave and haircut could do, but that was beside the point. Once a beast, always a beast.

Not according to the fairy tale.

Gracie's annoyance flared. She'd had enough of this conversation, enough of feeling like a big royal joke, enough of Prince Not-So-Charming. So she spun on her glass-slippered heel and left him in the dust.

What did Belle know, anyway?

"Wait!" Nick called after Gracie, but she didn't hesitate.

She didn't turn back. She didn't even slow her steps. If anything, she picked up her pace as she stormed away from him in a furious blizzard of fluff and sparkle.

The urge to go after her was overwhelming, as if the compulsion to chase down a fleeing princess was something he'd been born with, along with all the other rights and responsibilities of being a prince. He was almost surprised when she didn't leave one of her glass shoes behind. Nick scanned the surrounding cobblestones for one, just in case.

What are you doing?

He shook his head, as if doing so could jolt some sense back into him. As Gracie had so succinctly put it, he was no Prince Charming. He most definitely didn't need to be chasing after a woman wearing a pseudo-Cinderella costume.

No matter how badly he wanted to.

He didn't *truly* want to, though, did he? That would be crazy. He simply felt bad for upsetting her. Plus, he was being unduly influenced by a fairy tale that had been around for centuries.

The doors to the castle swung open with a groan behind Nick as he peered into the distance for a final glimpse of that ridiculous dress. But snow flurries clouded his vision, and he couldn't see a thing beyond the crowds of people heading toward the village square for the big event.

"Oh, good. I caught you," Jaron said just over his shoulder. "It seems there's been a mistake..."

Nick turned around. "You think?"

"So you've figured out that whoever you met earlier today isn't really Princess Alana?" Jaron looked around, as if searching for a royal imposter.

"It was rather obvious when she showed up in costume," Nick said.

"In costume?" Jaron's face went blank. Then his eyes went wide. "No!"

"Yes," Nick said with a sigh.

"It was *Princess Snowflake*?" Jaron's body shook with silent laughter.

"I'm glad someone thinks it's funny." Gracie sure hadn't, but that was undoubtedly Nick's fault. "And can you please call her by her proper name instead of that silly stage name?"

"Absolutely." Jaron nodded, and a quiet laugh escaped him. He cleared his throat and seemed to do his best to regain his composure. "May I ask where Miss Clark is now?"

"She left. It seems she wasn't any happier about the misunderstanding than I was." Nick tugged at the collar of his uniform. The regalia felt stifling all of a sudden.

Jaron studied him for a beat. "That's certainly an interesting development. Are you...disappointed?"

"Not in the slightest," Nick lied. "It's for the best."

Jaron's eyebrows lifted. "If you say so."

Nick narrowed his gaze at his friend. "I do say so. Everything is fine. We just need to move on and forget this unfortunate mistake ever happened."

"How did it happen, exactly? If you don't mind my asking."

"We spent the afternoon together at the Christmas market. I took her to all the best food booths." Nick's heart seemed to turn over in his chest as he remembered the delighted sparkle in her eyes as she'd spotted the kiss at the bottom of her cup of cocoa.

For a moment, he'd imagined what it might be like to give her a real kiss, right there on the snowy sidewalk. But princes didn't go around kissing strangers, unless it was to wake them up from an enchanted nap in a fairy tale forest. Even then it was borderline creepy.

Since when do you have so many opinions about fairy tales?

Nick's head hurt. He should have never come back from the trip to the Matterhorn. "Anyway, just as we were about to part, she asked me if I could keep a secret. Then she told me she was the princess."

"And you told her you were the prince. She must have thought you were the actor we hired to play Prince Charming. He's only scheduled to appear with her on Christmas Eve when we unveil the ice ballroom. We wanted to keep the focus on her this week, since she's the contest winner." Jaron drew in a long breath. "This *is* a rather strange turn of events."

"One I'd like to forget." Nick looked up at the snowflakes floating overhead. He'd always loved a good Christmas snowfall. Snow made everything so peaceful and pure. He wondered why Gracie had chosen to be a snow princess, of all things.

Then he reminded himself he didn't care.

"After you left my office, I got an update from the royal staff in Vernina. Due to inclement weather, the plane carrying the king, queen, and princess still hasn't been able to take off. They're going to have to postpone their trip for a day or two. You'll be escorting Princess Alana to another Christmas event later in the week. I pressed to make certain that she couldn't have arrived on her own, and they assured me she hadn't left the country, so I knew there had to be some sort of mistake. I got here as soon as I could," Jaron said.

"I appreciate it," Nick said, even if Jaron had arrived too late to prevent him from making a fool out of himself.

"Where did you say Miss Clark has gone?"

Good question.

Nick was as clueless as the befuddled prince in Cinderella. At least that poor guy had a glass slipper to go on. "Your guess is as good as mine."

CHAPTER NINE

Snowflake Made of Steel

"**W**HAT ARE YOU DOING HERE?**" Clara's eyes went wide when Gracie burst through the door of their room. "I thought you were meeting—"

"Don't say it." Gracie held up her hand. "Do *not* say Prince Charming. I never want to hear that name again."

Clara blinked. "Hon, Prince Charming isn't a real person. He's a storybook character."

"You said it," Gracie groaned and collapsed face-down onto her bed. A cloud of tulle puffed up around her.

Clara sat down gingerly on the edge of the mattress. "Gracie, what's going on? And what are you doing? You have an appearance in less than half an hour and your dress is getting wrinkled."

"He wasn't Prince Charming. He was the *real* prince of San Glacera." Gracie still couldn't believe it. She felt like the girl who'd kissed the frog, only instead of kissing a lowly amphibian and turning him into a prince, she'd kissed a prince and he'd turned into a horrible, warty toad.

Also, there'd been no kissing, much to Gracie's disappointment.

Her heart clenched. Her stupid, stupid heart.

"The real prince?" Clara shoved her, and she nearly fell off the bed. "Get. Out. Are you kidding me?"

"You don't understand." Gracie sat up to meet her friend's gaze. "He's awful. Way worse than Ingrid made him sound."

"How on earth could you mistake him for Prince Charming? I don't understand how this happened."

"He shaved." Gracie could barely wrap her head around it herself. "And got a haircut."

Clara nodded knowingly. "The classic royal makeover."

"He loathes my costume."

"He's a monster. Clearly," Clara deadpanned.

"You seriously don't understand how awful it was just now. Do yourself a favor and the next time a prince asks you out on a date, run in the opposite direction as fast as you can."

"Weirdly, that opportunity doesn't present itself to me all that often. As in, never." Clara hopped off the bed and clapped her hands. "Come on, get up. We can trash-talk Prince Nicolas—or *Nick,* as you so affectionately call him— all night long, but first, you have to get out there and help the royal family officially open the Ice Festival."

"You're hilarious." Gracie snorted and began the long process of unpinning her tiara from her hair.

Clara looked on in horror as she removed the first bobby pin. "I'm dead serious, Gracie. Come on. This is why we came here."

"I'm a joke to them, Clara." She blinked furiously as her eyes filled with tears.

She couldn't do this. *Wouldn't.* First, the stupid banks and now this. Hadn't she already been humiliated enough? Did she really need to travel thousands of miles, only to be disrespected yet again? And, bonus! This time, the people who were mocking her lived in a castle.

"Not them. *Him.* Don't you remember what Ingrid said?" Clara picked up the discarded bobby pins and began jamming them back in Gracie's hair.

"Ouch!"

Clara stuck another pin into Gracie's braided updo. "She said the prince was rather frosty but the rest of the family was just lovely. In fact, they're *so* lovely that they want to give you thirty thousand dollars."

Right. That.

"You can't let Prince Nicolas intimidate you. Princess Snowflake is better than that." Clara paused from her bobby pin assault long enough to smile. "*You're* better than that."

She was right. His Royal Rudeness wasn't the only person in San Glacera. There were children waiting to see Gracie. Ordinary people, just like the ones she met every day back home—people who needed to believe in kindness and bravery.

And magic, especially this time of year.

Gracie needed to believe in those things too. She hadn't realized quite how much until she'd been on the receiving end of a princely scowl.

She scrambled off the bed as quickly as she could. "You're right. I'm going to perform. Sorry, I don't know what I was thinking."

"You were thinking with your heart and not your head. Ordinarily, it's one of your better qualities. It's the reason you're such a great party princess." Clara aimed an appreciative glance at Gracie's ballgown. "The dress doesn't hurt, though."

Gracie hugged her friend. "You're the best, you know that? I'm so glad you're here with me."

"Me too. Now let's get out there and show your prince how it's done." Clara took Gracie by the shoulders and pointed her toward the door.

She gathered her skirts in her hands and charged forward but stuttered to a halt to make an important correction to Clara's little pep talk.

"Just so we're clear, he's not *my* prince."

He never was, and he never would be. San Glacera could keep him.

Nick stood beside his father as the royal family prepared to take their seats in the royal box, unable—or possibly unwilling—to believe what he was seeing.

The crowd at the Ice Festival was on its feet, cheering for Princess Snowflake as she stood at the foot of the majestic Christmas tree in the kingdom's square, waving with an exaggerated royal flourish. They were *besotted* with her. All she'd done so far was toss a little glitter around and talk to the children near the front of the audience, and they were reacting as if she'd invented Christmas.

Also, did Gracie really think that was how royals waved? Because it definitely wasn't. Nick had never once held his pinky finger that extended. Had *any* real-life human being? Ever?

"She's quite something, isn't she?" the king said as Gracie twirled her hands in sweeping, graceful movements and produced a glittery paper snowflake out of thin air.

She bent to offer it to a little girl on crutches wearing a plastic tiara. The child was one of hundreds who'd turned out to see the magical ice princess on opening night of San Glacera's Ice Festival. When Gracie had been introduced, the squeals had been so loud that for a minute, Nick had thought his ears were bleeding.

Ah, but now it was his turn. Tradition dictated that the members of the royal family took their seats in the royal box just as the event got under way. They were announced in reverse order of succession, which meant Emilie was already sitting in the enclosed area in a plush velvet chair, waiting for Nick to join her. She gave him a quick wave—no extended pinkie finger, Nick noted—as the announcer called out Nick's name and title.

"Presenting His Royal Highness, Crown Prince Nicolas Luca Montavan of San Glacera."

Nick walked from the shadows into the luxury box, waving at the people gathered below. Their reaction was substantially less enthusiastic than it had been when Princess Snowflake arrived on the scene. He was met with scattered applause and a half-hearted standing ovation that only managed to make its way through about a third of the crowd.

Ouch.

Nick tried to breathe, but it felt like a tight band had been placed around his ribs, squeezing out all the air in his lungs. So this was what being instantly and acutely humbled felt like.

Nick didn't much care for it. Would the audience be more impressed if he pulled a snowflake from his sleeve?

Somehow, he doubted it.

He sat ramrod straight as the king and queen took their seats, doing his best not to pay attention to whatever adorableness Princess Snowflake was up to. But his gaze kept finding her, no matter how hard he tried to ignore her overly bedazzled presence.

"Thoughts?" His father cast a pointed look at Gracie.

"She's got quite a way with children," Nick said, an understatement if there ever was one. The royal box was situated high above the square, where Gracie mingled with the crowd in front of the village Christmas tree. Even from this distance, he'd been able to spot tears in a young girl's eyes as Gracie had spoken to her.

"She does, indeed. The adults appear to be charmed by her, too." The king slid a glance at Nick. "Are you ready to admit your sister was right about all of this?"

On a personal level, yes. Obviously. Nick had certainly been charmed.

But as part of the kingdom's leadership? He still wasn't convinced. This was one night in December. They still had no real idea if her snow queen act would have any impact whatsoever on holiday tourism.

"We'll see, won't we?" Nick said under his breath.

He glanced over his shoulder at Emilie, seated in the second row. As heir, Nick always sat beside the reigning monarch. When he'd been a little boy and his grandfather was king, Nick's father sat in this very chair. Nick could remember begging to sit in his father's place in order to be closer to his beloved grandpa. The answer had always been no because tradition reigned supreme.

Tradition was important. It's what gave everyone who lived in San Glacera a sense of comfort and belonging. And now here they were, breaking with tradition in the most flashy, sentimental way possible. What would Christmas look like next year? And the year after that?

He tried to catch Emilie's gaze. They needed to talk, but Nick may as well have been invisible. She had stars in her eyes as she watched Gracie down below.

He faced forward again, eyes trained on Gracie's megawatt smile. As role models went, he had to admit she wasn't the worst. No one had ever spoken to Nick like she had earlier. She was determined, he'd give her that. And she certainly wasn't afraid to stand up for herself. Beneath all that sparkle and cheer was a snowflake made of steel.

She glanced up at him, and time stood still for a moment as their eyes met. Nick became acutely aware of his own heartbeat, pounding in his ears like a drum. He tried to avert his gaze and couldn't. When she turned away, a cold breeze washed over him, and his gaze remained fixed on the delicate rhinestone snowflake barrettes that glittered in her upswept hair.

He swallowed and swiveled to face his father. "Have we gotten any concrete numbers from Jaron yet about the Christmas market?"

The king shook his head and answered without taking his eyes off the action below. "It's too early, son. We'll know something soon enough."

"And do you have plans to talk to the visiting royals from Vernina about extending the peace treaty between our two kingdoms?" They still had another year remaining on the fifty-year agreement, but while the king and queen were in San Glacera, it seemed like the perfect time to discuss an extension.

His father didn't respond for a full minute, leaving Nick to wonder if he'd heard the question.

"Father?" he prompted.

"Son." The king turned kind eyes on him. "It's Christmas. Perhaps just take a minute and let things go."

This was the way things had always been with his dad. His father never hesitated when it came to things like teaching him to ride a bicycle or attending his school functions. But the minute Nick wanted to talk about anything involving the kingdom, Dad shut down. For all of Nick's life, his father had let King Noël take the reins when it came to preparing Nick to be king someday.

Now his grandpa was gone, and Nick had been trying to elbow his way into matters of state for the better part of a year. Thus far, it wasn't working.

He stiffened beside his father.

Nick didn't feel like letting things go. He couldn't. The last time he'd let his guard down, he'd ended up on the news and he was still paying for it a year later. Letting go wasn't all it was cracked up to be. Just tonight, he'd come dangerously close to doing so again, and look what had happened—he'd accidentally made a date with a dress-up character.

It was so preposterous that it was almost funny.

Gracie blew into the palm of her hand and tiny iridescent snowflakes filled the air. From where Nick sat, it was hard to tell the fake snow flurries from the real deal. The Ice Festival had officially begun, and San Glacera sparkled with frost, both real and imaginary.

Nick's frozen heart beat hard in his chest.

If accidentally making a date with Princess Snowflake was so funny, then why aren't you laughing?

CHAPTER TEN

Believe

THE FOLLOWING MORNING, GRACIE TORE a piece from the gloriously braided loaf of bread in the center of the table she shared with Clara during breakfast at the Kriegs's and nibbled half-heartedly at it.

"What are you doing? You didn't dunk." Clara waved a hand at the crock of warm cheese situated next to the braided loaf.

"Oh, right. I guess I forgot," Gracie said.

"You forgot there's a bowl of melted Gruyere within arm's reach?" Clara's gaze flitted to the fondu crock and then back at Gracie. She frowned. "I'm starting to worry about you. You love cheese."

Who didn't? Especially the gooey melted variety. By some miracle, fondue was a common breakfast treat in San Glacera, as it was in the surrounding Swiss region. As a chips-and-queso connoisseur, Gracie should have been beside herself.

"The crowd last night was amazing. They *adored* you." Clara gestured with a chunk of bread. "It was like Bobbi Bell's sixth birthday party on steroids."

Bobbi Bell's mother sat on the board of directors for the Denver Children's Museum. The museum had also been the site of little Bobbi's sixth birthday celebration, complete with a petting zoo, a bouncy castle, and a red carpet stretching the entire length of the walkway that led up to the museum's curved entrance. Bobbi's mother had even hired pretend paparazzi, which had seemed like a bit much in Gracie's opinion. Most of the fifty-plus children in attendance just stared blankly when the photographer shouted, *Who are you wearing?* But to those kids, Gracie had been a bona fide rock star.

"You're right. The crowd was nice. Prince Nicolas, on the other hand..." Gracie rolled her eyes. She'd been painfully aware of Nick's presence in the royal box while she'd been talking to the children and posing for pictures. "Every time I glanced in his direction, I saw him watching me. He didn't smile at all—not even once. What is his problem, anyway?"

Gracie had never misjudged a person so severely in her life. It was amazing what you learned about someone when you tossed a princess costume into the mix.

"They were more than nice. Nice is an understatement. You were a massive hit." Clara wrinkled her nose. "Who cares what the abominable prince thinks?"

I do.

Gracie didn't want to care, but no matter how hard she tried to brush it off, she did care. Very much.

"Are you sure he wasn't simply surprised?" Clara's eyebrows crept up closer to her hairline. "Not to play devil's advocate or anything, but it was a pretty major misunderstanding. He couldn't have been the only one caught off guard."

Gracie pushed her plate away. She was too upset for

cheese—a concept that would have seemed utterly impossible before she'd started cavorting with actual royalty.

"Of course I was caught off guard. How was I supposed to know he was the *real* prince and not an actor? He looked nothing at all like those pictures in the papers," she said.

Clara bit back a smile. "I saw him last night in the royal box. He didn't look abominable in the slightest. He's hot, Gracie. Like, I'm pretty sure I saw some of the ice sculptures melt."

"That doesn't make him a good person."

"Obviously, it doesn't. I'm just saying..." Clara sighed. "I can see why you were smitten at first glance."

Gracie glared at her. She didn't care to revisit the teensy crush she might have developed on Nick before she learned his true identity. Ever.

Clara held up her hands. "Got it. You don't want to talk about it. We don't have to. You probably don't even need to see him again—at least not up close. Clearly, he doesn't have much to do with the contest. I seriously doubt he'll be joining you on any of the Christmas activities this week."

"Maybe you're right," Gracie said, trying her best to feel relieved.

But Nick—she absolutely refused to think of him as His Royal Highness Prince Nicolas, when he'd lied and let her believe he was a normal person for an entire afternoon— would surely be in attendance at the opening of the ice ballroom on Christmas Eve. Which meant she was going to have to *sing* in front of him.

She pressed a hand to her stomach. "I think I might be sick."

"Oh no, dear. Is something wrong with the fondue?" Ingrid paused at their table, wiping her hands on another frilly holiday-themed apron. This one was covered with rows of gingerbread men doing cartwheels.

Gracie shook her head. "Not at all. It's delicious."

"I second that," Clara said as she dunked another chunk of bread into the melted Gruyere.

"Perhaps it's a bit rich? It's tradition here, but we'll be happy to make you an American breakfast if you prefer. Bacon and eggs, maybe?" Ingrid waved a hand toward a big buffet table at the back of the wood-paneled dining room. "We also have a selection of breakfast pastries every morning. Today my husband made a lovely cinnamon roll wreath."

"Did you hear that, Gracie? Homemade cinnamon rolls," Clara said.

Cinnamon rolls were Gracie's favorite. Although, save for Christmas morning, the ones she typically ate came from a tube with the Pillsbury Doughboy's picture on it.

"Please don't go to any trouble, Ingrid. Everything is lovely." Even Prince Abominable couldn't get between her and a cinnamon roll wreath. Could he? "I'm just not feeling like myself this morning."

"Yourself, as in Gracie, the American tourist? Or yourself, as in Princess Snowflake?" Ingrid flashed her a wink. "You were wonderful last night. Just what the Ice Festival needs, if you ask me."

"Thank you. That means a lot." Gracie felt herself smile. "Truly."

"You're probably just feeling a little overwhelmed. Maybe the two of you need to get out and do something fun today." Ingrid's gaze swiveled from Clara to Gracie and back again.

Clara picked up her phone and scrolled through her calendar app. "Actually, we don't have anything going on until tomorrow when Gracie has her first rehearsal for the performance on Christmas Eve. It's only supposed to last an hour or so. The next major thing on Princess Snowflake's agenda is a ride around the kingdom in a horse-drawn carriage with Princess Emilie tomorrow evening."

A ride in a horse-drawn carriage? Like the one Prince

Harry and Meghan Markle rode around in after their wedding? That sounded excessively royal. Thank goodness Princess Emilie was scheduled to accompany Gracie, and Nick wouldn't be there. Gracie would rather ride a horse bareback over the Swiss Alps than share a carriage with him.

Ingrid clapped her hands. "Perfect. I know just the thing. Have you heard about the Christmas tree maze?"

Clara shook her head. "Like a huge maze made from evergreen trees?"

"Exactly! It's another San Glacera tradition. Just lovely, especially when it's snowy out." Ingrid nodded toward the window. The entire village square was covered in a pristine blanket of white. "Make sure and bundle up. The maze is quite large, with lots of twists and turns. When you find your way to the middle, there's a surprise."

Gracie's thoughts went straight to the kiss stamped onto the bottom of her cup of cocoa yesterday and the way it had seemed so dreamy and romantic at the same. So *fated*, as if she and Nick had been characters in a fairy tale.

She'd had enough surprises lately, thank you very much. But getting lost in a maze of Christmas trees sounded like just what Gracie needed. With any luck, no one would find her ever again—especially San Glacera's not-so-charming prince.

* * *

Two hours later, Gracie and Clara stumbled their way down a snowy path that looked awfully familiar.

"We've been this way before." Clara pointed at a cluster of Scotch pines. "I definitely recognize that tree."

"How can you tell? They all look the same," Gracie said.

They were surrounded by evergreens on every side—live

ones, sparkling with snow. It was like being lost in the world's most chaotic Christmas tree farm. On the plus side, thus far it had proven to be the perfect distraction. Gracie hadn't given a single thought to her recent humiliation or Prince Nick since they'd embarked on this impromptu adventure.

Okay, maybe Nick's lopsided smile had popped into her head once or twice. Three times, tops. It was too bad he didn't seem to know how to smile when he was on official prince business.

"I know that pinecone." Clara pointed at a pinecone nestled in the lower branches of the tree directly in front of them. Then she made a quarter turn and pointed at one on a different tree. "Or maybe it was this one."

"I'm pretty all the trees have pinecones." Gracie laughed.

Clara's shoulders sagged. "I'm starting to wonder if we're ever going to find our way out of here. No wonder we've hardly run into anyone else. The locals must know this is a trap."

"I doubt it's a trap. I, for one, am having a great time," Gracie said.

She would have been perfectly happy spending the rest of the week right there, stuck in a twisty Christmas forest—so long as she could still leave San Glacera with thirty thousand dollars in her pocket.

Clara's gaze narrowed. "You're hiding in here, aren't you? Have you been sabotaging us this entire time?"

"I've been doing no such thing." As appealing as the thought of hiding might be, doing so in an outdoor tree maze was less than practical. Gracie's hands were already getting numb, despite her mittens.

"I think we should split up," Clara said.

"What?" Gracie tucked her hands in her pockets and wished she'd thought to pack some of those hand warmer heat packs that she sometimes used for outdoor princess appearances in Denver. "No. That's a terrible idea."

"Think about it. I'll make right turns, you make left."

Clara pulled her cell phone from the pocket of her puffer coat. "Whoever gets to the center first calls the other and tells them what to do."

"I'm not sure that's how mazes work," Gracie said.

Clara shrugged. "It's how we found the center of the corn maze at the Botanical Gardens when you and the other princesses appeared at their annual HarvestFest. Left turns all the way."

"That's right." Gracie had forgotten all about the corn maze. She did so many events that sometimes they started to run together.

"I'll head left." Clara pointed to the fork in the path where they'd just come from.

Gracie nodded. "Okay, I'll go right. But if neither of us gets to the middle within an hour, I say we call each other and come up with another plan."

"Like what?" Clara arched a brow.

"I have no idea." Gracie laughed again. It felt so good to do something normal. Something Christmas-y. Maybe the rest of the week wouldn't be so bad.

"I'm glad you're having fun, but we have to get back to the B&B eventually. My phone is blowing up." Clara looked down at her device's screen again, then held it out for Gracie to see. "The palace posted a picture from your meet and greet last night on the monarchy's main account."

"Seriously?" Gracie squinted. There she was, on the House of Montavan's Instagram grid, in all her party princess glory.

"Of course. You won their contest. They're probably going to be posting your picture all week. It's getting loads of likes, by the way. They even tagged the Perfect Party Princess account." Clara pocketed her phone again. "I'm telling you—this trip is going to be the best thing that ever happened to you."

Gracie wanted to believe her. She really did, but so far,

the journey hadn't been anything like Gracie had imagined. And she was even less convinced that she could get through a song on Christmas Eve than she'd been before she'd ever set foot in San Glacera.

"Don't argue," Clara said, as if she could see straight inside Gracie's head. "Just believe."

Then Clara promptly spun around and disappeared among the evergreens.

Believe.

It was the kind of thing that grown-ups said to kids while they waited in line at the shopping mall to see Santa. Department stores printed the word on shiny red shopping bags in whimsical calligraphy. If ever there was a time to believe, Christmas was it.

Maybe it wasn't too late to salvage a modicum of her dignity. Maybe if she tried hard enough, she could forget everything that had led up to the Ice Festival last night, including ever setting eyes on the Abominable Snow Prince in the flesh. Maybe Clara was right, and this Christmas would be her best one yet.

Gracie lifted her gaze to the snowy sky and whispered, "I believe."

Then she took a deep breath and let herself get lost.

"What are we doing here?" Nick frowned in the direction of the cluster of trees that seemed to appear out of nowhere as he and Emilie turned down the cobblestone avenue that ran behind San Glacera Cathedral. He stopped dead in his tracks.

"It's the Christmas tree maze." Emilie shot him her brightest, most hopeful grin.

She still had a lot of explaining to do. Nick knew without a doubt that his sister had recognized Gracie Clark at first glance, and instead of doing the right thing—the *grown-up* thing—and telling him who she was, Emilie had fled with a wink and a nudge. She'd just left him there, primed to make a complete and total fool of himself.

And now Emilie had tugged him outside by the elbow, promising to make it up to him.

Nick wasn't sure what he'd expected, but it wasn't this.

"You loved this place when we were kids," Emilie added.

He'd loved everything about Christmas in San Glacera. But at the moment, he was in no mood to get lost in a maze of evergreens. Every time his thoughts strayed to anything Christmas-related, he saw Gracie dressed as an ice princess last night, expression open and trusting. Breathless with anticipation. It was like a movie playing over and over in his mind, and no matter how many times he tried to press pause and rewind the scene back to the very beginning, it just kept on going...

All the way to the frame where he'd accused her of orchestrating their meeting or working with the press to intentionally embarrass him.

He'd gone too far. Gracie didn't seem like the type of person to be involved with something so underhanded. Nick had made the mistake of trusting the wrong person before, though. He was as lost out there in the real world as he'd probably be in this festive maze his sister was trying to force on him.

He shoved his hands in his pockets and didn't budge. "You knew it was Gracie at the market. Don't even try and deny it."

Emilie dropped her gaze to the snow-covered walkway. "I recognized her from her contest submission video."

"Then why didn't you say anything?"

She shrugged in that maddening way that teenagers had

been doing since the dawn of time. "You were in such a good mood, and she clearly loved the hot cocoa. I figured if I left, you'd talk to her about San Glacera's great Christmas cocoa tradition, the two of you might get along and you'd realize how wrong you were about the contest. She seemed utterly charming."

Nick glanced at the clouds overhead, swollen with snow. What was he supposed to say to that? Emilie hadn't been wrong. He and Gracie had indeed gotten along. Nick had been more charmed than he wanted to admit...even if he still thought the contest was an awful idea.

"It never occurred to me that you wouldn't recognize her. And for the record, I *tried* to talk to you about her before you went running off to meet her. My plan was for you to get to know her, so you'd soften to the idea of incorporating her princess character into our Christmas celebration, not for you to ask her out." The corners of Emilie's lips crept upward.

Nick narrowed his gaze at her. "I didn't ask her out."

"Are you sure? Because I definitely noticed some Cinderella vibes when Gracie ran up to the castle gate. If she'd lost a shoe, you looked like you would have moved heaven and earth to find it."

"When I'm king, I'm banning romcoms and Disney films from the castle. Mark my words," Nick muttered.

Emilie snorted.

"I thought she was Princess Alana, and I merely suggested that we take a walk together before the opening of the Ice Festival since we were supposed to be seated next to one another in the royal box," Nick said quietly.

Really? Was that all there was to it?

There had been more to the invitation than simple convenience, and Nick knew it. Things were just so complicated now that he knew who Gracie really was...

Not to mention the fact that she'd clearly decided she

despised him.

"It's kind of a funny misunderstanding when you think about it." Emilie pressed her lips together, as if trying not to laugh.

"Pardon me if I fail to find the humor in the situation," he said stiffly. He'd hurt Gracie's feelings, which was the last thing he wanted, no matter how he felt about inserting Princess Snowflake into San Glacera's holiday festivities.

He needed to find her and apologize. And he would... just as soon as he managed to forget that she'd called him a beast, right to his face.

"Oh, come on. Can you just let it go and have a little fun with your kid sister while you have the chance? This week is going to be nuts. Let's go get lost in the Christmas trees." She nodded toward the entrance to the maze.

Nick sighed. "Fine, but we're following the same rules from when we were younger."

"We go our separate ways and the first one to get to the center wins. Loser sneaks to the kitchen to make midnight ice cream sundaes later tonight." Emilie nodded.

"Let's do it," Nick said.

The moment the words left his mouth, Emilie took off running toward the maze, ponytail swinging and boots kicking up puffs of snow as she went. Nick paused for a beat, then chased after her.

He'd let himself get talked into doing this. He may as well do it right.

CHAPTER ELEVEN

Were All Princes This Annoying?

G RACIE LET HER FINGERTIPS GRAZE the stiff needles of the Christmas trees as she wound her way through the maze. Just about every variety imaginable was represented—bushy noble firs, moody blue spruce trees, and bright green Scotch pines. Gracie's favorites were the white spruce trees. Tall and elegant, with softly needled branches sloping gently downward, heavy with snow.

She took a deep breath, grateful for the respite. She could breathe out here, surrounded by the peaks and valleys of the Alps. It reminded her of home. If she tried hard enough, she could almost convince herself that she was out for a hike in the foothills of the Rocky Mountains.

She wasn't, of course. Every so often, a group of locals would pass her on the footpath, chattering in French or German. Gracie would immediately remember where she was, and a knot would form in her stomach.

Clara was right, though. Professionally, things were

going great. Far better than Gracie had anticipated. She just needed to hold it together until Christmas Eve and get through the vocal performance, so she could accept her prize money and go back to Colorado.

Maybe if she practiced a tiny bit more, she'd be able to relax. It couldn't hurt. She'd have to give it a go in San Glacera eventually, and now, out here all by herself, seemed like the perfect time. Definitely better than waiting until her rehearsal tomorrow morning. So she wrapped her arms around her middle, closed her eyes, and with the evergreen trees as her only audience, she began to sing a Christmas carol. "Winter Wonderland," the obvious choice, given the setting.

She started out quietly at first, her voice little more than a whisper floating gently among the trees. With each line of the song, she grew more confident, and her voice became louder. And louder still, until it echoed back to her. Lyrical and delicate, almost like a wind chime.

Joy welled in Gracie's heart, and for a brief, shining moment, singing felt like it used to. Natural, free…glorious. Without anyone listening, she could almost let loose.

She spread her arms out wide and let the echo wash over her, an angelic chorus. When she got to the part of the song about the parson asking if the couple in the lyrics was married, her eyes drifted open.

And Gracie realized she wasn't alone, after all.

She blinked. It was *him*—Nick. Or technically, His Royal Highness, Prince Nicolas. He stood just a few feet away with his royal hands in the pockets of his jeans, watching her intently. Like she was giving him his own private concert.

Gracie abruptly closed her mouth. Her face went so hot that she fully expected the snow flurries swirling around her to sizzle when they landed on her cheeks.

"Please don't stop." Nick smiled, and his eyes crinkled in a way that seriously tugged at Gracie's heart. "That was beautiful."

Gracie shook her head. She couldn't manage to form words, much less sing. "I...I..."

Nick continued the verse. He tried, anyway. But his voice was comically off-key.

So he's human, after all.

Gracie cleared her throat to keep from laughing. Then she remembered that she wasn't supposed to be amused by someone she disliked so much, so she crossed her arms and glowered at him. "What are you doing here?"

"The same thing you are, I imagine." He glanced at the maze of trees. "Engaging in a little Christmas cheer."

"I didn't think *cheer* was your specialty," she retorted.

The happy crinkles near the corners of his eyes promptly vanished. "Right. Because I'm a beast."

"Sorry. That was mean. I'm sure you love Christmas cheer." Gracie squirmed. She was never this rude.

On the other hand, why on earth was she apologizing when he'd looked at her last night like she was a seven-year-old trick-or-treater who'd crashed a royal ball?

"And, for the record, I apologized for the beast comment last night right after I said it." As opposed to Nick, who hadn't said he was sorry for a single thing. Sure, he'd complimented her singing, but was she supposed to simply forget everything that had happened last night? "Anyway, I've got to get going. I'm not going to find the center of this maze so long as I'm standing still. Goodbye."

Gracie spun around and nearly plowed straight into the snowy arms of a spruce tree.

"It's the echo trail," Nick said, as if she hadn't just said goodbye and announced her intention to leave.

Couldn't he just say goodbye in return, like a normal person? More importantly, were all princes this annoying?

Gracie glanced over her shoulder at him. "Excuse me?"

He twirled his pointer finger, indicating their surroundings.

"This maze is located in an area of the kingdom known as the echo trail. It's got the best conditions in the entire region for reflecting sound."

"Oh. Wow." Gracie blinked. He suddenly seemed more like the Nick she'd met at the Christmas market, sharing his love for San Glacera, instead of the stuffy and abominable Prince Nicolas. "That's why my singing sounded so special just now."

He flashed a meaningful smile. "Not the only reason."

Gracie didn't quite know what to do with the compliment. "I don't really sing. I know that sounds weird, since I'm scheduled to perform at your big event. But trust me, I usually don't do that sort of thing."

Nick's brow furrowed. "But I just heard you, and you also sang in the video you sent for the contest. You have a lovely voice."

He'd seen her video? Gracie's stomach fluttered. She'd assumed that a palace aid or some other high-placed commoner had chosen the contest winner. Not the royal family.

"That song just now...it was a private moment." She blew out a breath. "I thought I was alone. And that part of the video was also private. It was included in my contest submission by accident. No one was supposed to see it."

"It was a large part of why you won." Nick frowned. "You do know you're expected to sing on Christmas Eve?"

As if she could forget.

"I do." Gracie crossed her arms, uncrossed them, and then crossed them again. Why did he make her so nervous? Things had been so natural between them at the Christmas market. "Can we talk about something else now?"

"Shall we talk about last night?" he asked, tilting his head in a way that reminded Gracie of his adorable dog.

"Let's not. Once was enough." She told her feet to start walking in the other direction, but they flagrantly disobeyed. Ugh, why was she still standing here talking to him? "Where's your dog? I'll bet Mittens would love running around in circles in a place like this."

"He's back at the palace," Nick said.

At the palace. Where Nick lived. "That's right. You mentioned he doesn't get out much," she said. Poor Mittens.

"Let me guess—you think that makes me abominable. Like I'm locking my dog away in a tower."

"I didn't say that." But she'd been thinking it, and they both knew it.

"No one outside the palace knows about Mittens," Nick said. He looked away for a second and then back at Gracie. "Except you."

"Oh." Before last night, knowing that she was the only non-royal who knew about Mittens's existence probably would have made her feel special. Now, she knew better. Still, her heart de-thawed an infinitesimal amount.

"I don't understand, though. He's so sweet. Why keep him a secret?" Gracie stopped short of pointing out the obvious—the presence of a marshmallow of a dog in his life might help his "abominable" reputation.

"I'm not going to use my dog to rehabilitate my image, if that's what you're implying." A knot in Nick's jaw ticked to life. Had she accidentally awakened the beast? "It's also nice to have a bit of privacy when most of your life is spent in the public eye."

Well, that certainly explained a lot.

Gracie nodded. "So that's why you lied."

Nick's eyes flashed. Beast mode definitely activated. All that was missing was the beard full of icicles. "When have I lied to you?"

"Are you serious?" An incredulous laugh escaped Gracie. "'My name is Nick.' Sound familiar?"

"My name *is* Nick." The knot in his jaw flexed again. Gracie couldn't seem to take her eyes off of it.

She blinked and looked away. "You left out some crucial

information, and you know it. If you'd told me you were a prince right off the bat, we both could have avoided last night's awkwardness."

Her face went warm. *Awkwardness* was putting it mildly. Much to her mortification, Gracie's feelings had ventured dangerously close to heartbreak territory. Which was preposterous. She didn't even know this man.

The way he'd looked at her, though...

His entire countenance had changed the moment he'd spotted her costume. She felt like she'd been sitting across the desk from a bank manager all over again. Or worse...as if she'd been singing a duet with Philip back at Juilliard.

Nick took a step closer, so close that she could see tiny flecks of gold in his gray irises. Out here among the evergreens, his eyes appeared more blue than gray. It was a striking contrast to his dark hair. Pure Disney hero. "I did tell you I was a prince, remember?"

He had, hadn't he?

"Not until after..." Gracie's voice drifted off.

Not until after I'd developed a giant crush on you.

Nick stared at her for a beat, waiting for her to finish. When she didn't, the corner of his princely lips quirked into a knowing grin.

"You know what? Never mind. I have more important things to do right now than talk about your royal status." Gracie huffed. "Like get out of this stupid maze."

He held up his hands. "It was an honest mistake. I realize that now. I'm sorry I accused you of manipulating the situation."

Were her ears deceiving her? Had he just offered her an actual apology? Gracie softened ever so slightly.

And then he went and ruined things again.

"It was just a shock when I realized you weren't Princess Alana and instead just someone who plays dress-up for a living. A big one," he said.

Gracie crossed her arms and stared daggers at him. "What did you just say to me?"

He held up a finger. "That might have come out the wrong way."

"Is there a *right* way to mock what I do? I'm a small business owner. I empower women to earn a living, pay their college tuition, and take care of their families." Why did this keep happening? Why did everyone who crossed her path seem to underestimate her? "I spread *joy* and *happiness* to *children.*"

Granted, she wasn't spreading much happiness at the moment. She was borderline yelling. At a freaking royal prince.

She marched past him. Crown or not, he had to be the most smug person she'd ever shared a waffle with. Not that that was a particularly long list of individuals, but still.

"You're going the wrong direction," he said to her back as she trudged through the snow.

And that was it. That was the moment that Gracie lost her head and showed Prince Nick how she really felt about the little prince-in-disguise game he'd been playing at the Christmas market. If she got thrown into a dungeon somewhere, so be it.

The snowball hit Nick smack between his eyes with a wet thud. He hadn't seen it coming at all, and for a stunned moment, he wasn't sure if it was shock that kept him frozen in place or if the tightly packed snowball had done actual damage.

He scrubbed a hand over his face, brushing the snow from his eyes. A bit of feeling returned to his numb skin.

When he cracked an eye open, he found Gracie watching him, wide-eyed.

"Oh my gosh." She swallowed, and he traced the movement up and down the slender column of her throat. "I... I'm sorry."

"I highly doubt that," he said with exaggerated calm as he crouched to scoop a handful of snow into his palms.

"No, really. It was a dumb impulse, and I..." Gracie's gaze dropped to the snowball he was busy forming. "What are you doing?"

"You wanted a snowball fight? You've got one." He drew back his throwing arm.

Gracie squealed and dashed down the nearest tree-lined path. Nick followed, and once she was within perfect striking distance, he let loose with the snowball.

Thwack.

It exploded in the center of her back.

"You did *not* just do that," she wailed. But when she turned around, a smile danced on her lips, even as her eyes widened in surprise.

"You started it," Nick said.

"You sound like a five-year-old."

Nick felt himself smile. At least he could fully feel his face again. "Says the woman who just threw a snowball at me."

Her mouth twitched, as if she was doing her best not to grin even wider at him, and then her expression turned back to astonishment as he crouched to gather another handful of snow.

"What are you doing?" She held out her hands and backed away. "This is crazy."

"Is it?" Nick rotated the snowball in his hands, forming it into a perfect round shape.

"I'm not having a snowball fight with you. I don't even like you."

"You sure about that?" Nick asked with a wink.

He threw the snowball at her, narrowly missing her beautiful head.

"You're a dead man." She kicked at a snowbank, spraying him with fresh powder, and then took off running.

Nick chased after her, and the pursuit quickly gave way to a messy snow battle of epic proportions. They alternated hiding behind trees and ambushing each other. Each direct hit was punctuated with squeals and vows to decimate the other person. Until somewhere along the way, they dropped the comical threats. The trail echoed with laughter. It rang in Nick's chest like church bells.

She hit him again in the face, and he laughed so hard he could barely catch his breath. He wiped his eyes, choking on a mouthful of snow.

"Well, well, well. What do we have here?"

Nick froze.

He forced his eyes open, blinking against the ice crystals that had gathered in his eyelashes during Gracie's most recent assault.

"Hi, there." Emilie waved at him with one of her gloved hands. She held a steaming cup of cocoa in the other one.

A woman stood beside her, thumb paused over her iPhone, mid-scroll. Her jaw dropped open as she glanced from Nick to Gracie, both covered head to foot in snow. During the melee, they'd apparently stumbled upon the center of the Christmas tree maze.

Nick straightened and snuck a glance at Gracie, who appeared to be ignoring his existence altogether.

Should he feel insulted? Probably. He wasn't, though. People had been overly solicitous to Nick his entire life—to his face, anyway. Whether it was because of his cold reputation or the fact that he would one day sit on the throne, Nick wasn't entirely sure. But no one had ever told him point-blank that they didn't like him before, and he'd certainly never been on the receiving end of a snowball to the face. Not even Emilie had dared to go that far before.

"Thank goodness that's over with," Gracie said, brushing her mittens together. Snow flew every which way.

"You're Princess Snowflake." Emilie's face split into a huge grin.

The woman beside her looked Nick up and down before switching her attention to Gracie. "Have you two been lost together in the maze this entire time...while having a *snowball fight*?"

"No," Gracie said, while Nick simultaneously nodded and said yes.

She glared at him as a chunk of snow fell from the pompon on her hat and landed on her cheek. Nick's fingertips tingled, and he had to stop himself from reaching to brush it away.

He cleared his throat. "Miss Clark and I ran into one another in the maze, and I gallantly led us to freedom."

She rolled her eyes. "Oh, please."

"I'm loving this." Emilie clapped her hands and turned to the woman beside her. "Aren't you?"

"There's nothing to love, I assure you," Gracie said. She glanced at the table in the center of the maze with a big silver cistern in its center. A sign strung over the table read *Congratulations! You've Reached the Heart of Christmas in San Glacera.*

She could *definitely* go for some cocoa right about now.

Gracie stomped past Nick as he made his way to the cistern and began filling a paper cup.

"We ran into each other by accident. End of story." She took a gulp of her hot chocolate.

"I'm not thirsty, but thanks, though. You go right ahead." Nick winked at her again.

Gracie's cheeks blazed pink.

"Ignore him," Nick's sister said with a dismissive wave of her hand. She scurried toward Gracie. "I'm Emilie. It's so nice to meet you. You have no idea."

"Thank you," Gracie said, looking genuinely pleased.

"The contest was my idea, and I knew as soon I saw your video that you *had* to come here." Emilie beamed.

"You're the one responsible for the whole thing? That's amazing and thank you so much. Winning the contest is really going to change things for me." Gracie's voice halted a bit, as if she couldn't believe what Emilie was saying. She studiously avoided Nick's gaze. "You're officially my favorite royal. Am I allowed to say that?"

"Absolutely," Emilie said.

Brilliant. Nick sighed. He was back to being the Abominable Snow Prince again.

"Hello, I'm Nick," he said, extending a hand toward the woman Emilie had befriended while he'd been otherwise occupied.

"Oh, I know who you are." Her eyes narrowed, and for a second, it seemed like she was going to refuse to shake his hand, but she finally relented. "I'm Clara from Perfect Party Princesses."

Nick was beginning to feel woefully outnumbered.

"It's a pleasure to make your acquaintance, but I should probably be getting back to work," he said.

Nick had a meeting scheduled with Jaron this afternoon to go over the numbers from last night. His dad might be eager to give things time, but Nick intended to monitor the situation daily. He also needed to look into the whereabouts of the royals from Vernina. As Jaron had mentioned last night, Nick would be expected to escort Princess Alana to another event upon their arrival since she hadn't made it in time for the Ice Festival the night before. He kept forgetting about his royal blind date for some reason.

"We need to get going too." Gracie shot a beseeching glance at her business partner. "Right, Clara?"

Emilie sighed. "Bummer. At least let me take your picture

first. You two look adorable, all covered in snow." She pulled her cell phone out of the pocket of her parka.

Nick and Gracie looked at each other, but neither one of them moved.

"Nick, go put your arm around her," Emilie said.

He raised a brow at Gracie. He wasn't about to force her into posing with him if she truly didn't want to.

She waved him over, smile frozen in place. "Come on. One photo won't kill us."

"I'm fairly certain that's what the photographer said when he took my photo at the Matterhorn," Nick murmured once they were snuggled up close to one another.

"Just smile and pretend we like each other," Gracie said through gritted teeth.

"Yes, Princess," he whispered.

Gracie dug her elbow into his ribs, and Nick flashed his most princely of princely grins.

No pretending necessary.

CHAPTER TWELVE

A Royal Mess

W HEN GRACIE WAS A LITTLE girl, she never slept as soundly as she did after a snow day.

Once a year or so, a blizzard would blanket Denver beneath a thick layer of glittering white, prompting city-wide school closures. For Gracie—and most other children—those precious snow days were like Christmas.

She and her friends would spend the entire day outside. Sometimes they went sledding on the big hill behind the neighborhood church and, if the roads were clear, her dad might take them up into the mountains to go snowshoeing. They'd clomp their way through the thin, silvery Aspen trees, looking for animal footprints on the snowy path. Gracie's dad would point out deer and elk tracks. Gracie always looked for signs of the little white bunnies that hopped through the forest during winter—snowshoe hare, her father called them. On the very best snow days, she'd spot one, darting from tree to tree. Then they'd go home and build a huge snowman in the front yard.

The only thing that could have made those days better was an appearance by Santa himself. Gracie sometimes dreamed of his magic sleigh, flying over her sparkling white street. Other times, she fell into a deep, dreamless sleep. But those precious winter nights were always calm. Always bright. And Gracie would awake the following morning and stretch like a cat who'd gotten the cream.

Which was exactly what she did the morning after her snowball fight with Nick.

"I slept great last night," she said, reaching her arms overhead and wiggling her toes in her bed at the B&B. "I must be getting over the jet lag."

"Oh, good. You're awake." Clara sat up straight in the other bed and flicked on the lamp on the nightstand. "I've been waiting forever for you to get up. Look at this."

She shoved her phone toward Gracie.

Gracie threw an arm over her face. "It's too early for screens."

"It's nine in the morning, sleepyhead," Clara countered.

Gracie's eyes flew open. "I never sleep that late. Are you sure?"

"Positive." Clara tossed her covers off and hopped out of bed. "If we don't hurry and get ready, we're going to miss breakfast downstairs. But first, you really need to see this."

She thrust the phone toward Gracie again. The last time she'd been this anxious to turn her device over to Gracie, it had been a phone call from the palace, so Gracie relented, took hold of the phone, and squinted at the screen.

Notifications pinged, one right after the other, scrolling across the top of the screen faster than Gracie could read them.

"What's going on?" she said.

Clara leaned over and tapped the screen a few times. "You and your prince. That's what's going on."

"Me and my what?" Gracie said, and then spots started swimming before her eyes, like she might faint.

You and your prince.

She blinked, doing her best to focus. And then, to her horror, she realized she was looking at an Instagram photo of her and Prince Nicolas. Snow coated their clothing, their boots, their hair. Nick's arm was wrapped around her shoulders and she was tucked against his side, as if she'd been made to fit snugly in his arms. Gracie looked directly at the camera, smiling her best and brightest party princess smile, but Nick wasn't looking at the camera at all. He gazed directly at her instead, with a smile on his face that made it look as though they'd just been frolicking in the snow together.

Which they had, technically speaking.

"You posted this?" Gracie's gaze flew to Clara. This could *not* be happening. "You didn't ask me first! And for the record—again—he's not *my* prince."

"The camera doesn't lie. Also, I was there. You two definitely seemed cozy." Clara jammed a hand on her pajama-clad hip. "And no, I didn't post it. If you'll recall, I wasn't the one who took the photo."

Gracie scrolled to the top of the page to check the profile picture of the account. The little circle contained an official looking crest with a crown emblazoned across its center. Immediately to the right of the crest was a tiny blue checkmark and the name of the account—*sanglaceraroyal.*

"The palace posted it from their official account. Can you believe it?" Clara said.

No, she couldn't. "Are you sure? This has to be some sort of mistake."

"Read the caption. Princess Emilie posted it herself." Clara flicked the pad of her thumb over the screen and pointed at the fine print below the image.

Princess Snowflake melts the Abominable Snow Prince's

Heart...Gracie Clark, winner of the Royal Winter Wonderland Contest enjoyed a romp through the Christmas tree maze today with Crown Prince Nicolas. ~E

Gracie groaned. "This. Is. Mortifying."

"Are you kidding? We couldn't buy this sort of publicity if we'd tried. This is way better than the princess photo Jaron posted after the Ice Festival the other night. This post came from Princess Emilie herself. She signed it with her initial and everything." Clara plucked the phone from her hand. "Our follower count is going through the roof. I shared the post to the Perfect Party Princess page an hour ago, and it's already got thousands of likes."

Gracie pulled a face. "So deleting it is out of the question?"

"I'm going to pretend you didn't just ask that." Clara held the phone protectively to her chest. "What's the big deal? It's just a picture."

Did Gracie really need to spell things out? "It's a picture of me and the royally big thorn in my side."

Gracie didn't want to be photographed alongside Nick—especially while he gazed at her as if she'd hung the moon. As if he didn't think her job was a joke. As if he really and truly enjoyed her company.

She'd mistaken him for an actor, but perhaps that assumption hadn't been too far off the mark.

Just smile and pretend we like each other.

Those were the words Gracie whispered to him just as Emilie snapped the picture. She'd expected a big cheesy grin, not a soulful expression that put a pang in her chest the moment she'd seen it.

It was too much. Too cozy. Too romantic.

And if Gracie wasn't careful, she might accidentally let herself believe it was a bit too real.

"There's been a change of plans." Jaron brushed past Nick, straight into his quarters without so much as an invitation.

"Do come in," Nick said drolly. He really needed to stop answering unexpected knocks on his door.

Mittens disagreed. Vehemently. The moment Jaron crossed the threshold, the little Cavalier King Charles spaniel hopped down from Nick's bed and scrambled toward their surprise guest. He wiggled his entire backside and danced around Jaron's feet as if Gracie's implication had been true and Nick did, in fact, keep the dog locked away in a tower, starved for attention.

"Hey, Mittens. How are you, bud?" Jaron scooped the dog into his arms and let the Cavalier lick the side of his face. The greeting lasted a full minute—maybe two—until Jaron put him back down.

Mittens sat with his little rump situated on the toe of Nick's Armani loafer.

Nick gave Jaron a pointed look. "You were saying?"

"What?" Jaron gave him a blank stare, as if he'd forgotten why he'd stopped by. "Oh, right. Sorry. It's been a crazy morning. Completely crazy. You have no idea."

"Enlighten me, then," Nick said.

He'd rarely seen Jaron this discombobulated. Jaron was the consummate palace professional. Nick sometimes thought he knew more about royal protocol than the royals themselves.

"Yesterday's photograph is causing quite the stir. The Christmas market is packed."

Nick still didn't follow. "What photograph?"

"The picture of you and Princess Snowflake."

"I didn't pose for a picture with Princess Snowflake,"

Nick said.

"Then who is this?" Jaron slid his phone from his pocket, tapped the screen a few times, and handed it to Nick.

His image filled the screen, arm wrapped around Gracie and gazing at her like she was the queen of his heart. The Christmas tree maze was a blur in the background, and they look like they'd just climbed out of a snow cave together.

"But..." Nick shook his head. *But we look like a couple.* "But this wasn't an official appearance. Why is there a picture of it on social media?"

Jaron lifted his chin. "Emilie posted it, and you should be grateful that she did. You look accessible here. Human."

Nick's jaw clenched. "Human? As opposed to what, exactly?"

Jaron pocketed his phone and winced. "Sorry. Poor choice of words. The point is that this is just the sort of publicity the press office had in mind when Emilie suggested the contest. And it's working."

Jaron nodded toward the window.

Nick sighed and walked toward it with Mittens trotting obediently on his heels. He peeled back the heavy damask drapery and glanced down at the village square, teeming with people. Lines snaked down each row of the Christmas market. Groups of tourists posed for selfies at the palace gate. Some of them looked as though they were wearing plastic snowflake tiaras over their knit winter hats.

On one hand, it was great to see the holiday crowds back to their normal levels. On the other...

"This can't possibly have anything to do with the picture." He stepped away from the window and jammed a hand through his hair.

Mittens cocked his head and whined.

The dog gets it. Why doesn't Jaron?

The photograph had been taken in an unguarded moment, one that hadn't been intended for public consumption. Seeing it making the rounds online almost felt like seeing Sarah Jane's interview for the very first time.

"Oh, good. You're both here," Nick's mother said as she bustled into the room, along with Nick's father.

Mittens immediately forgot about Nick's angst and romped toward the king and queen, tail wagging like mad.

"This is where we have meetings now?" Nick said, but no one seemed to hear him.

"Good morning, son." His dad smiled broadly. "Has Jaron filled you in on the latest developments?"

"Not yet, sir," Jaron said.

Nick angled his head at him. "Didn't you?"

"Not entirely." Jaron adjusted his tie while the king and queen exchanged a loaded glance.

It was then that Nick remembered Jaron's words as he'd bustled inside Nick's quarters.

There's been a change of plans.

Everyone in the room focused intently on Nick. The king and queen. Jaron. Even Mittens. Nick's gut churned. He had a feeling he wasn't going to like whatever came next.

"They want me to do *what*?" Gracie's fork slipped out of her hand and landed on the table with a clatter.

The other B&B patrons looked up from their breakfasts, heads swiveling in Gracie's direction. One by one, they each appeared to identify her as the source of the commotion and nodded in recognition. Princess Snowflake had become an unofficial San Glacera celebrity, literally overnight.

"Sorry." Gracie flashed a smile and waved at the room at large before turning her attention back to Clara. She dropped her voice to a whisper. "What did you just say?"

"I just got an email from Jaron Lutz. The palace press office is delighted at the response to the picture of you and Nick. Apparently, there are record crowds at the Christmas market today." Clara waggled her eyebrows. "I told you this trip was going to be a huge success."

"Not that part." Gracie shook her head. "There was something else." Something far more troubling.

"Oh, you mean the part about the prince?" Clara said, feigning obliviousness.

Gracie grimaced.

"Relax. It's no big deal. You're still going to be doing the Christmas tour, as planned. But they're adding a few more things to your agenda. They've scheduled a stand-in for your rehearsal today because the carriage ride is going to take longer than originally anticipated. They can figure out the lighting and everything without you. I've already given them your song selection."

"Oh." Relief coursed through her. She'd been dreading rehearsal. At least now she could postpone singing for a bit longer. "But there's still more. I know I heard it. Go ahead and say it again."

"It's really no big deal," Clara said. "They've also decided that Prince Nick is going to be your escort for all the holiday activities."

No big deal? Was she serious?

Gracie shook her head. "No. Absolutely not. That's not what was supposed to happen."

"Newsflash: there are worse things than having to sit beside a handsome prince in a horse-drawn carriage," Clara said.

Gracie wanted to crawl under the table. She'd completely forgotten about the carriage ride. And wasn't that happening *today*? "I can't. This is just too awkward. I'm starting to feel like I won some weird royal version of *The Bachelor* instead of a holiday contest."

Clara's head tilted. "Huh. I hadn't thought of it that way. I guess it *is* sort of like an episode of *Fairy Tale I Do*."

"No, it most definitely isn't." Except for the part about the carriage. And the castle. And the poufy princess gown.

Nick couldn't possibly be on board with this idea. He'd probably rather abdicate and flee the kingdom than ride around in a horse-drawn carriage with her while she was dressed as Princess Snowflake.

"I thought Nick was supposed to be spending time with a *real* princess this week?" Gracie picked at the flaky pastry of the croissant on her plate.

It wasn't as if she truly despised him. Things would be a lot easier if she did. But no matter how hard she tried, she couldn't seem to forget how much she'd liked him on her very first day in San Glacera. How butterflies had floated through her like snow flurries while they'd walked through the Christmas market together. How her head had spun when he'd asked her to meet him at the castle gate later that evening. Or how she'd gone warm all over when he'd told her that her singing was beautiful. She'd wanted to throw her arms around him right here in the Christmas tree maze.

The croissant lodged in her throat. She needed to forget all about that. Nick had certainly had no trouble pretending they'd never had any sort of chemistry once he'd found out who she really was.

"Speak of the devil." Clara aimed a pointed glance toward a group of people who stepped inside the lobby of the B&B, just visible through the dining room's stone archway, where another sprig of mistletoe hung from a velvet ribbon. "That's got to be her, right? Princess Alana? She looks every inch a princess."

Gracie followed Clara's gaze and immediately knew who her friend was referring to. A woman who looked to be about their age stood beside a middle-aged couple busy chatting with Ingrid's husband Max at the registration desk. She had smooth blonde hair twisted into an artfully arranged low bun, wide green eyes, and a peaches-and-cream complexion. A hat was jauntily perched on the young woman's head, but it wasn't a knit beanie topped with a fluffy pompon like the one Gracie always wore. This one was a red cloche, decorated with an elaborately folded cluster of felt flowers and paired with a matching scarf tucked neatly into the collar of a coat that had a swingy cape attached to the shoulders. It looked like something the Duchess of Cambridge would wear to church on Christmas morning.

Gracie swallowed hard. "I think you're right."

Visions of her Princess Snowflake costume danced in her head, along with her gaudy, over-the-top crown, dotted with pink cupcake frosting. Somehow she doubted Princess Alana had anything remotely resembling the get-up packed in her posh Louis Vuitton suitcases.

"Oh, look! Our royal guests have arrived." Ingrid smoothed down her apron—yet another ruffled holiday creation, this time in a print covered with Christmas Bundt cakes. She darted past the table and headed toward the lobby, where she greeted the royals with a deep curtsey.

Clara's eyes went wide. "Did you see that?"

"I sure did." Gracie couldn't have missed it. She'd almost forgotten that real curtseys were a thing anymore, outside of theme parks and children's princess parties. Ingrid had made it sound like they weren't that important.

Clara's forehead scrunched. "Do you think we're supposed to be curtseying to Nick and Emilie?"

"I would rather die," Gracie said.

Seriously, though? Were they? If so, why hadn't Nick said anything?

Gracie didn't have much time to dwell on the matter because the Kriegs were escorting Princess Alana and her parents into the dining room.

"Everyone, can we have your attention, please?" Max

said as he stood next to the buffet table, which was flanked on either side by a Christmas tree decorated with shiny ribbon that looked like it had been chosen to match Princess Alana's Kate Middleton ensemble.

Maybe it had.

"We're pleased to welcome some very special guests this week—Their Majesties King Hans and Queen Sophia of Vernina, and their daughter, Her Royal Highness, Princess Alana." Max beamed.

Gracie half expected a liveried footman to pop up out of nowhere and blow a trumpet like in an animated princess movie.

This is all so surreal.

There were more kings, queens, princes, and princesses running around this place than there were at the children's parties that Gracie organized back home.

The royals moved from table to table, greeting the Kriegs's guests and making a few minutes of small talk. It seemed to be an unofficial icebreaker, and Gracie supposed the Kriegs had arranged it so the king, queen, and princess would feel comfortable moving about the B&B all week. Just part of the holiday family.

Except Princess Alana seemed anything but regular. Gracie couldn't take her eyes off her as she floated through the room. Her posture was so elegant and so impeccable that she could've been walking around with a book on her head. She spoke English, but with a European lilt to her tone that made her sound like Audrey Hepburn. She oozed royalty from every perfectly poised pore. If this was the woman Nick had mistaken Gracie for, no wonder he'd been so visibly distressed when she'd shown up in character.

"It's a pleasure to make your acquaintance," the princess said as she stood beside Gracie and Clara's table. She was wearing stilettos, despite the weather. And they didn't have a speck of snow or salt clinging to the luxe red suede.

"Nice to meet you, Your Royal Highness," Gracie stood and immediately dropped into her party princess curtsey, as if by rote. Her gaze dropped ever so slightly and she realized the front of her ugly Christmas sweater was covered in croissant crumbs.

"Call me Alana." The princess winked. Even her eyelashes seemed regal, nothing at all like the exaggerated extensions that were part of Gracie's Princess Snowflake costume. "Please."

"Of course." Gracie swallowed. "Merry Christmas, Alana."

"Happy Christmas. My parents and I are so pleased to be here this week for the holidays." Call-me-Alana smiled, and somehow it seemed to be a true princess smile instead of the bubbly grin that Gracie had practiced in the mirror over and over again when she'd first created her party princess persona.

Then, with a dainty flutter of fingertips, Alana waved goodbye and moved on to the next table.

Gracie sat back down, stumbling a little as she collapsed into her chair.

"She's really lovely, isn't she?" Clara whispered.

"She sure is," Gracie said, and as much as she didn't want to admit it, the deer-in-the-headlights expression on Nick's face when his gaze had landed on her Princess Snowflake ballgown suddenly made a lot more sense.

If Alana was the sort of woman Nick was accustomed to spending time with, what must he think of her?

His opinion doesn't matter, Gracie told herself...

Except for the wholly inconvenient fact that the palace had decided he should escort her on a Christmas tour of the entire kingdom, starting with a cozy, fairy tale-esque carriage ride.

She blew out a breath. If she'd had a fairy godmother, Gracie would've been tempted to make a wish and go back to a time when crippling stage fright was her most pressing problem.

"Gracie?" Clara said.

She looked up. "Hmm?"

Clara gestured toward the front of Gracie's ugly Christmas sweater, which was beginning to feel uglier by the second. Crumbs still dotted the red and green yarn. "You've got a little bit of a mess going on."

Truer words had never been spoken.

CHAPTER THIRTEEN

Forget Protocol

NICK DID HIS BEST TO keep his expression neutral as he held the door of the carriage open for Gracie, but it was nearly impossible.

Honestly, he deserved a medal for the effort. Per the palace's official request, Gracie had arrived at the castle dressed in full Princess Snowflake mode—from the heavily embellished crown on her head to the glitter-strewn glass slippers on her feet. Nick had only gotten a brief glance of one of the shoe's pointed toes as she'd swished toward him across the palace courtyard. It was a miracle he'd caught so much as a glimpse because her ballgown pretty much swallowed anything and everything in its path.

Hence the struggle not to smile.

"Hello, Your Royal Highness," Gracie said without meeting his gaze. She seemed to be focusing intently on his forehead.

Nick felt himself frown, and before he could ask why on earth she'd suddenly decided to start calling him by his

HRH, she dropped into a deep curtsey.

His chest tightened, right in the vicinity of his heart.

What was she doing? And more importantly, why? Sure, they'd gotten off to a rocky start, but he'd thought they'd moved past mere formalities.

"Gracie, don't." He let out a ragged exhale and pinched the bridge of his nose. "Please."

She lifted herself to a full standing position and at long last, looked him in the eye. "Why not? Curtseying is the proper protocol when greeting the Crown Prince, isn't it?"

Nick narrowed his gaze at her. Same lovely blue eyes. Same bow-shaped lips. Same billowing gown, decorated with a profusion of shimmering rhinestones and lace. This time, she'd added a faux fur-trimmed velvet cape and a white fur muff for her hands, as though she'd prepared for a stylish trip to the Arctic tundra. But the overall effect was the same—snow queen meets glitter bomb.

So why the sudden change in demeanor?

"And how are you so well-acquainted with royal protocol all of a sudden?" he asked. There was a telltale ache in his voice that he hoped she didn't notice.

She blinked up at him. "Google."

He felt the corner of his mouth hitch into a grin.

She jabbed her pointer finger at his chest. "Do *not* laugh at me."

Ahh, there was the fiery American girl he knew and loved. Not *loved* loved. Loved, as in *liked*. A lot. Far more than he should, if he was really being honest.

He held up his hands. "I'm not laughing. I promise. I just find it interesting that you Googled me."

She studied him for a moment with those icy blue eyes of hers. "What about you? Have you done any Googling lately?"

"Maybe," he said, choosing not to mention the embarrassing amount of time he'd spent poring over the photographs on the slideshow page of the Perfect Party Princess website late last night. Mittens had finally given up and gone to bed without him.

Gracie's lips twitched as if she was trying her best not to smile. But the sparkle in her eyes gave her away.

Right answer.

"Please don't curtsey to me," he said, just as a gust of wind blew a lock of hair free from her elaborately braided chignon. He reached a tentative hand toward her face, and when she smiled at him, he took it as permission to brush the stray curl from her eyes.

"Why not?" she asked with an inflection that Nick knew all too well. It was the same vulnerability he'd heard in her tone in the contest video when she'd been singing to the child in the hospital bed.

Nick drew his hand back, and then paused with his fingertips just a whisper away from her porcelain skin.

He wanted to kiss her. Was that crazy? It was, but Nick didn't care. He longed to cup her face, lower his lips to hers, and kiss her until she forgot he'd one day sit on San Glacera's throne.

Or maybe he was the one who needed to forget...

Even if just for a moment.

"Why don't you want me to curtsey to you, Nick?" Gracie asked in a soft voice—so soft that he had to lean in to make sure he heard her correctly.

Her breath fanned over his face, warm and sweet in the winter wind. Nick had never wanted to kiss a woman so badly in his life.

He rested his forehead gently against hers instead and brushed a tremulous finger down the soft curve of her cheek. "You don't need to defer to me, Gracie. I want to be your friend, not your prince."

"Your friend," she repeated. Her breath hitched, and before either one of them could say another word, a throat cleared nearby.

Gracie sprang away from him as if he were the last person on earth she'd want to be seen with.

"Sorry to interrupt," Jaron said.

"You're not." Gracie shook her head. A lovely flush flooded her cheeks, as pink as the lush carnations that grew wild outside the castle gates in springtime. "We were just talking."

"About carriages," Nick added. If she was so desperate to pretend they hadn't just shared a moment of tenderness, he'd go along with it.

For now.

Jaron glanced back and forth between them.

"I was just wondering how I'm supposed to get inside this thing," Gracie said, eyeing the coach.

Good question. It *might* be a challenge for both of them to fit inside of it along with approximately ten miles of glitter chiffon and lace.

"Not to worry. The coachman is right behind me, and he's got a step stool," Jaron said, and then he turned to Nick. "I'm glad I caught you. I need to let you know that the visiting royals have arrived, but your presence is no longer required at dinner later this evening. Princess Alana won't be in attendance."

Nick blinked. He'd forgotten all about Princess Alana. *Again.* Why did she keep slipping his mind? And why wasn't she planning on attending dinner? Had his abominable reputation scared her off?

He didn't want to think about that right now. For once, he was going to listen to his father, try to let things go, and enjoy himself.

"Very well. Thank you for letting me know," he said.

Jaron regarded him through narrowed eyes. "So, you're fine with it?"

"Yes, that's what I just said."

"Great." Jaron glanced over his shoulder. "Here comes

the coachman now. He'll get you all settled, Gracie."

"Good evening, sir." The coachman nodded at Nick and Gracie in turn. "Miss."

"Good evening, Charles," Nick said. Charles had been part of the palace staff for as long as he could remember. He'd driven the carriage on Nick's first Christmas ride around the kingdom, back when he'd been just a small boy sitting alongside his grandfather.

"Hello." Gracie removed one of her hands from her muff to wave at the coachman.

Charles glanced at her ballgown in alarm. Even the four white horses connected to the carriage with harnesses strewn with silver sleigh bells had to be wondering how this was going to work.

"Shall we?" Nick took the step stool from Charles's hand and placed it at the foot of the carriage door. He'd already made Gracie feel self-conscious enough about her costume. The best thing to do was just plow forward.

He offered Gracie his hand.

She took it, stepped gingerly onto the stool and into the carriage. The dress took up every square inch of the small space. She patted it down around her. It was like watching someone trying to cram one of those exploding snakes back into a fake can of nuts.

Once she was situated, Nick joined her and the dress spilled over...everywhere. He could barely see over the profusion of airy fabric in his lap.

"Charles is going to take you for the usual ride around all four sides of the village square," Jaron said, focusing on Gracie. "Afterward, if you're enjoying yourself, he'll exit the square and take you on a spin through the countryside. It's surprisingly peaceful away from the hustle and bustle of the kingdom proper. Any questions?"

Gracie nodded. "What do you mean by 'the usual ride'?"

Nick batted a swathe of tulle from his face. "This is the

annual candy cane toss. Every year, a few members of the royal family take a ride through the kingdom and toss candy canes to the children gathered in the square."

"We thought this would be a perfect tradition for you to take part in." Jaron's gaze flitted to Gracie's snowflake crown. "Considering your affinity for kids."

"It sounds wonderful. Hopefully, Prince Nicolas here won't scare them all away."

Charles didn't flinch. He just sat staring straight ahead on the driver's seat. Jaron, on the other hand, laughed a little too hard for Nick's liking.

"Oh, come on." Gracie nudged Nick with her elbow. "What's a little joke between friends, right?"

Maybe this exercise in indignity wouldn't be so bad. The iciness between them was beginning to thaw. They were friends now, just as Nick had proposed.

The horses clip-clopped along the cobblestones in the palace courtyard, propelling the carriage forward with a sudden jolt. Gracie let out a delighted squeal, and Nick's chest filled with warmth. Despite the occasional mouthful of ballgown, Nick realized he was actually enjoying himself. It was like being lost in the Christmas maze all over again. Rituals that he'd known for his entire life had a tendency to feel brand-new as seen through her eyes.

Friends.

Nick glanced at Gracie, and the warmth in his chest felt weighted down all of a sudden, tinged with a bittersweetness he didn't recognize. He didn't really know this woman. He wasn't even sure what had prompted her to enter the Royal Winter Wonderland contest in the first place, other than the prize money. He should have been more than satisfied by the simple fact that she no longer found him abominable.

Why, oh why, didn't it seem like enough?

The closest Gracie had ever come to a ride in a horse-drawn carriage had been the Cinderella sheet cake at her sixth birthday party. The cake's topper had been a fanciful replica of Cinderella riding in her pumpkin-turned-carriage on the way to the royal ball, dragged through a two-inch layer of vanilla frosting by a pair of Barbie-sized plastic horses. Gracie had adored that cake. The topper had held a place of honor on the bookshelf in her bedroom well into high school. If she closed her eyes, she could still see those grand white horses prancing their way through buttercream, flanked on either side by a path of piped roses.

Now she sat in an actual royal carriage, and she couldn't deny that the real deal was decidedly superior to the cake-topper variety. The snowy white horses trotted with their heads held high as the carriage bounced along the village square. Jingle bells on their harnesses chimed with each step, and children gathered along the route, anxious to receive one of the large candy canes with special silver foil gift tags embossed with San Glacera's royal seal.

"It's the princess!" A little girl in a bright red coat jumped up and down as the carriage approached a yarn shop with balls of colorful wool and angora in the window.

The child was surrounded by about half a dozen other girls who squealed Gracie's name. "Princess Snowflake!"

"Your adoring public awaits," Nick said.

Gracie stared straight ahead, bracing herself for a sarcastic comment, and when none was forthcoming, she slid her gaze toward him. "This seriously doesn't bother you?"

He arched a brow. "What? The fact that I need a party princess to help me look good?"

"I'm sure that's not true." Sympathy closed up her throat.

Since when did she feel sorry for Prince Abominable?

"Gracie." He gave her a penetrating look as the carriage slowed in front of the crowd. "It's okay. That's why you're here. I'm a big boy. I can handle it."

"Of course you can." She swallowed hard. For a minute there, she'd forgotten why they were sitting next to each other in a royal carriage.

What was *happening?*

She pasted on a smile and greeted the children, aware of every move Nick made beside her.

"Hello, snowflakes," Gracie sang out as she tossed candy canes to the girls.

"On behalf of her royal highness, Princess Snowflake," Nick said as he leaned over the side of the carriage and passed out candy.

They gazed up at him like he was a Prince Charming action figure come to life. Gracie caught herself doing the same a few seconds later as they resumed their ride around the square.

She marveled at the care Nick took to make sure each child received a treat. Gracie was accustomed to dealing with throngs of excitable children. She did it every day, but even she could barely keep up. As the carriage sped up after a pause in front of a flower shop with lush pine wreaths frosted with snow decorating the windows, Nick called out to the coachman.

"I think we missed one, Charles," he said.

"Yes, sir." Charles pulled lightly on the reins and the horses slowed to a stop.

Gracie swiveled on the tiny bench seat and spotted a small boy with a sweet round face standing in front of the florist, empty-handed.

She pressed a hand to her heart. "Oh, no. Shall we turn around?"

Before she'd finished uttering the question, Nick leaped

over the side of the carriage. He just jumped right out of it and ran toward the child, as if the girls at the yarn shop had been correct and he was, indeed, a Prince Charming action figure.

Gracie's mouth dropped open as she watched him kneel so that he was on eye-level with the child. They exchanged a few words, and Gracie strained to hear what they were saying.

"I came back because it looks like you didn't get a treat," Nick said.

The boy pulled a candy cane out of the inside pocket of his coat. "I did, sir. I'm saving it for my sister. Mommy said she couldn't come because she has an ear 'fection."

"That's too bad. I had ear infections when I was a kid." Nick pulled a face. "They're the worst."

The child' nodded and tucked the candy back inside his jacket for safekeeping.

"It's nice of you to save your candy cane for your sister, though. You're a very thoughtful boy." Nick held out his hand. Two new candy canes rested in his palm. "So thoughtful that I want to make sure you have a candy cane of your own. And one for your mommy, too."

The boy's face lit up like a Christmas tree. "Thank you, sir."

Nick ruffled his hair. "You're very welcome. Merry Christmas to you and your family."

"Merry Christmas," the boy said as he threw his arms around Nick's neck with the pair of candy canes gripped tightly in his small fist.

Gracie melted like a snowflake on a summer day.

Nick bid the child goodbye, ran back to the carriage, and hopped over the side like he did these sorts of things every day—vaulting in and out of coaches, charming small children. Who knew? Maybe he did. Gracie was beginning to think she didn't have the first clue what Prince Nicolas was really like.

"You've been holding out on me," Gracie said as the carriage trundled forward again.

The wind rippled Nick's hair and his breath came out in a puff of vapor that lingered in the cold air after running to leap back into the coach. "What do you mean?"

"You're not all that abominable." Gracie narrowed her gaze at his chiseled face. Dare she say it? "In fact, you can be downright charming at times."

A dimple she'd never noticed before flashed in his cheek. "Ah, so I've managed to trick you into thinking I'm actually a *good* prince in disguise. My devious plan is working."

"Kid all you want, but I see you." Gracie let her gaze sweep over the surrounding gingerbread-style houses and rambling cobblestone alleys with a chocolate shop on every corner. Nick's kingdom, his home, his heart. "You care deeply about this place and everyone who lives here."

That earnestness was what had first attracted her to him in the very beginning. She'd simply lost sight of it in light of recent embarrassing events.

"I do." Nick nodded, and his smile turned a bit sad around the edges. "Even if the press doesn't always realize it, I really do."

His eyes went tender, and if Gracie hadn't been holding onto an armful of candy canes, she would have been tempted to reach for his hand and give it a squeeze. Maybe it was a good thing she couldn't, because she wasn't sure she would have been all too eager to let go.

This isn't supposed to be happening. Gracie swiveled to face forward on the plush seat of the carriage. She wasn't supposed to be softening toward Nick, and she definitely wasn't supposed to be holding hands with him. For a crazy moment back in the palace courtyard, she'd actually wanted to *kiss* him.

She lifted her gaze to the heavens. It was clear today,

as blue as the bluest of Christmases as twilight began to fall over the kingdom. Snow covered the ground, but there wasn't a flake in the sky—perfect winter weather for taking a ride in an open-air royal carriage.

Gracie let her eyes drift shut, face tipped upward toward the stars.

Things were so much easier when he was abominable.

And then, as if on cue, a cheer rose up from a small crowd gathered near a tiny, out-of-the-way building on the edge of the village square.

"We love you, Prince Nicolas!"

"Happy Christmas!"

"Three cheers for Prince Nicolas!"

She peered around the front of the carriage for a closer glimpse of the group as they let loose with a string of hurrahs and gasped at what she saw. Half a dozen or so adults stood along the walkway cheering, but that wasn't the surprising part. Each one of them held a puppy with a bright red bow around its neck. A few even juggled a tiny dog in each arm.

"What is this?" Gracie turned wide eyes on Nick. "*Puppies* are cheering for you now?"

"No, not really." He waved at the group and grinned wider than Gracie had ever seen before. One of the people held up a shaggy black and white dog's tiny paw so it could wave back.

Gracie couldn't believe what she was seeing. "That dog literally just waved at you. What's going on?"

Clearly Nick was a massive hit with San Glacera's canine population for some unknown reason.

Charles pulled the carriage to a stop without Nick having to ask. Then Nick leaned out of the side of the coach to personally greet each individual and hand them candy canes while Gracie petted the dogs. They were adorable, all decked out for the holidays. She sort of wished they could ditch the rest of the carriage ride and cuddle puppies all night.

"Let's go, fellows," Charles said to the horses. They tossed their thick white manes and trotted toward the horizon where the buildings and shops gave way to a wide valley covered by a sparkling blanket of untouched snow.

"Are we in the lyrics of a Christmas carol right now?" Gracie's heart squeezed and she slid her gaze toward Nick. "I can't believe this is your life."

His eyes crinkled. "It has its moments."

"Seriously, what was that back there? With the dogs."

"It's a local pet rescue organization—San Glacera Animal Friends. I'm their royal patron," Nick said.

Gracie had heard of royal patronages but wasn't sure what all they entailed. "What does that mean, exactly?"

"I lend them my name and support. The idea behind a patronage is to get more visibility for the charity and hopefully increase donations. In this case, we obviously also hope to facilitate more pet adoptions." Nick's fondness for the cause showed in the way his eyes sparkled as he spoke.

Gracie regarded him closely. "That's where you got Mittens, isn't it?"

"It seems you really do see me." He tilted his head and let out a low laugh. "Sometimes, anyway."

Happiness sparkled inside her.

Why only sometimes, though?

Gracie didn't need to ask. She knew. Nick didn't show his true self to just anyone. If he did, the whole world would know about Mittens. Something—or someone—had made him approach his public life with caution. Gracie knew that particular brand of self-preservation all too well.

"The shelter has always struggled. We're a small kingdom with limited public resources for pet rescue. Most shelters rely heavily on things like foster families and donations for the care and feeding of the animals. Tourism is such a vital part of San Glacera's economy. I'm worried the downward trend of our biggest industry could affect San

Glacera Animal Friends." Nick's smile hardened in place. "My grizzly face in the news probably isn't doing them any favors. It's the exact opposite sort of attention I should be bringing to their cause."

That hardly seemed fair. They were only pictures, and from what Gracie had read, they'd been taken after he'd been on an extended climbing trip with wounded veterans.

Okay, so maybe she'd spent more time on Google than she was ready to admit. She'd also learned that an ex-girlfriend had given a tell-all interview to San Glacera's biggest tabloid, painting Nick as cold and unable to say the words *I love you*. Frankly, Gracie felt like betraying Nick's trust in such a way said a lot more about the girlfriend than it did about Nick.

"I wish there was something I could do to help," she said.

Everything had gone so quiet all of a sudden. So still. The only things Gracie could hear besides the jingle bells on the carriage were the swish of the wheels through snow and the calm, contemplative breath of the man sitting beside her.

The *prince* sitting beside her.

"You're already helping, just by being here. That's what this whole week is about." Nick shrugged one shoulder. "And apparently, it's working, because here we are."

"Here we are," Gracie said, and her smile wobbled ever so slightly.

For a minute, she'd forgotten that neither one of them wanted to be sitting in this carriage together. This wasn't a date. It was duty.

"My turn to ask a question now." Nick slid his gaze toward her. The jagged peaks of the Alps rose up behind him, silvery-blue in the moonlight. "What did you mean the other day when you said that winning this contest would change things for you? I know what we're getting out of it, but what about you?"

"The prize money, of course." Gracie swallowed. She felt

a little bit strange about taking money from Nick's family all of sudden, even though the cash prize had always been part of the terms of the contest, and she was earning it fair and square. "I've been wanting to expand the party princess business—make the other princesses employees with full benefits. Maybe get a real office instead of running our operations out of the house that Clara and I rent together. The prize money from the contest will allow me to accomplish some of those goals."

"I see." He nodded.

She searched his gaze for signs of judgment, like the disapproval that had been rolling off of him the other night when he'd been expecting a real princess and ended up with a knockoff royal instead. Try as she might, she couldn't find any.

"Winning the contest was kind of a lifesaver. I've been trying to get a business loan for a while, but no one seems to want to lend money to a woman playing dress-up." She glanced down at her gown, filling every square inch of the space around them in the carriage. Then she looked back up at Nick, expecting a laugh. Or at the very least, a smile.

Instead, his expression turned serious. Gentle. "I shouldn't have said what I did in the Christmas tree maze, Princess. You do a lot more than simply playing dress-up."

The cool winter air felt different somehow. Enchanted, almost.

"There you go, turning on the charm again," Gracie said, trying her best to hide the giddy smile on her lips.

He winked. "Just part of the job description."

Maybe, just maybe, she'd met a Prince Charming, after all.

CHAPTER FOURTEEN

Like Being in a Snow Globe

IT WAS LATE WHEN GRACIE returned to the Kriegs's after the carriage ride. A fire glowed in the hearth, but the lights in the lobby were dim and the overstuffed chairs facing the fireplace stood empty. The handmade quilts the guests used as throws in the comfy sitting area had been neatly folded and stacked on an antique chest near the Christmas tree.

Gracie took a deep inhale, hoping to breathe in some of the serenity in the peaceful room. Today had been...unexpected. If she went straight up to her room, she knew she'd immediately spill every detail of the carriage ride to Clara. And she just wasn't ready to share the experience yet—not when she was still trying to wrap her head around it herself. If she wasn't careful, Clara was going to think she was starting to fall for Nick, which was silly. Of course she wasn't.

Was she?

"Get your head out of the clouds. This is business," she whispered to herself, tearing her gaze away from the gold lights twinkling among the branches of the Christmas tree.

But Nick wanted to be her friend, and there'd been nothing businesslike about the shiver that had gone up and down her spine when he'd called her *Princess* again. Gracie smiled to herself as she gathered her fluffy skirt and began climbing the stairs. She couldn't quite help it, and she was still all starry-eyed and distracted when, halfway up the steps, she nearly crashed into Princess Alana.

Even at this late hour, she didn't have a hair out of place. In fact, the princess looked like she'd just stepped out of a blow-out bar, dressed in a luxe, ivory-colored cashmere sweater and skinny jeans. An oversized Louis Vuitton tote was slung over her shoulder.

"Oh, my goodness." The princess stepped to the right and then to the left in a fruitless attempt to pass Gracie.

It was no use. Gracie's dress took up the entire width of the staircase and then some.

"Hi there. I'm sorry I almost plowed into you." Gracie winced. "I wasn't paying attention, and this dress sort of has a mind of its own."

Gracie let out a little laugh, fully expecting Alana to join in and laugh too. She'd seemed so kind when they'd met in the dining room. So down to earth.

Not this time, though. She didn't even crack a smile. She just stood there, tightening her grip on her designer bag as her cheeks went pink.

"Um, is everything okay?" Gracie asked.

"Fine," Alana said, and without another word, she turned around and sprinted back up the stairs toward her room.

Her door opened and slammed shut behind her before Gracie could move a muscle.

That was weird. Gracie's mouth went dry.

Was it, though?

She'd nearly taken out an actual princess with her over-the-top Cinderella ballgown. Alana was probably as horrified by Gracie's appearance as Nick had been the first time he'd set eyes on her. No wonder she'd wanted to get away from her as fast as possible.

And that's all it took for Gracie's swoony post-carriage-ride bubble to burst. She was just a regular girl, as far away from being real royalty as she could possibly get. Nick could call her *Princess* all he wanted...

But that didn't make it real.

The following morning, Nick once again contemplated the feat of engineering required to cram Gracie's snowflake ballgown into a confined space. This time, instead of a carriage, he and Princess Snowflake would be riding one of San Glacera's famed gondolas across the snow-covered peaks of the surrounding Alps.

"The ride is approximately five minutes each way. The gondola will take you from here to the summit of Mount Vit and back again." Jaron consulted the notes on his tablet and continued briefing Gracie as they stood in the tiny log cabin that served as the headquarters for the gondola operation. "You'll be traveling over three thousand miles above sea level, with views of glacial crevasses, mountains, and snow."

Nick glanced at Gracie. "*A lot* of snow." *If* they could see over her dress once they were situated in the tiny glass box that would carry them over the mountain range.

Gracie grinned. "It sounds really fun. This is one of San Glacera's Christmas traditions?"

"The gondolas run year-round, but during the holidays, they're decorated for Christmas and local schools bring the kids up here for a special holiday ride," Nick said.

"Which is taking place today." Jaron nodded toward the cabin window, which overlooked a line of children near the platform where the gondolas stopped for disembarking. "You and Nick will help the kids get on and off the cable cars for an hour or so, and then you'll take the ride yourselves. Does that sound good?"

"It sounds great." Gracie went to work fastening the glittery silver buttons on her velvet cape.

"I'm going to go make sure the kids and teachers are ready. I'll be right back to fetch you two." Jaron glanced up from his iPad and gave them one last smile before striding toward the door.

Was Nick imagining things, or had there been a hint of innuendo in his eyes? *You two.* He'd looked at them like they were a couple. Then again, it seemed like a lot of people were doing that lately.

Nick slid his gaze toward Gracie, still fastening her cape. "Here, let me help. That can't be easy with those long satin gloves you're wearing."

She shrugged. "Princess problems."

Her eyes locked with his as he went to work on the buttons. A pink flush made its way to her cheeks, and Nick could have sworn he saw her pulse beating in the graceful hollow of her throat.

"All done," he said, fingertips lingering on the top button.

"Thank you," she said. Her voice was soft and breathy. For a second, Nick felt like they were back on the echo trail. All alone.

Then the door swung open, and Jaron walked back inside the cabin.

Gracie cleared her throat. A practiced smile came to her lips, but at least she didn't bolt away from him like the last time Jaron had stumbled upon them in a cozy moment.

Why did that keep happening, anyway?

"The kids are ready for you," Jaron said.

"Shall we?" Nick waved for Gracie to go in front of him.

The moment they stepped out into the snow, the children squealed so loud that Nick legitimately worried about the risk of an avalanche. The orderly line descended into chaos as the kids rushed forward to crowd around them.

Not *them*, actually. Gracie was the one they all wanted to see. Children ran straight past him; he might as well have been invisible. A little girl in red snow boots plowed into his knees in her haste to get near Princess Snowflake.

"This way, sweetheart," Nick said as he took her by her narrow shoulders and steered her toward Gracie.

Then he braced himself for the inevitable coldness that had come over him in the royal box the other night after his half-hearted welcoming ovation—that sinking feeling of irritation laced with just enough humiliation to make him feel like an extra on the set of a Disney princess movie instead of the Crown Prince of a very real kingdom.

Oddly enough, it didn't come. He was okay with being invisible, it seemed.

"Good morning, snowflakes! Are you all ready to go for a ride in a snow globe this morning?" Gracie said, clasping her hands to her heart.

A ride in a snow globe?

Her gaze flitted toward him, and he winked at her. *Cute, Princess.* The gondolas were glass on all sides, and each one spun a full three hundred sixty degrees as it made its way across the Alps, affording a breathtaking view of the snowy landscape. It was very much like being inside a snow globe, although Nick had never quite thought of it in that way before.

His mouth quirked into a smile. She had a tendency to do that, didn't she—make him see the everyday things around him in new and different ways? It had been the same yesterday on the carriage ride when she'd told him she felt like they'd been in the lyrics of a Christmas carol.

"Prince Nicolas, Evan here wants to know why no two snowflakes are alike. Does anyone know the answer?" Gracie touched a graceful fingertip to her chin and looked directly at him, drawing him into her snowy princess act. She fluttered her eyelashes. "Do *you* know the answer, Prince Nicolas?"

Dozens of pairs of little eyes turned toward Nick, as if noticing him for the very first time.

"Tell us, Prince Nicolas," the girl in the red boots said in an adorable singsong voice.

He stepped forward, and the children parted for him to make his way to Princess Snowflake's side.

"Let's see." He pretended to ponder the question. "Could it be because snowflakes are made up of molecules and there are an endless number of ways molecules can stack together?"

Gracie let out a gasp of delight, as if he'd just solved the mystery of how Santa could visit every house in the world, all on the same frosty Christmas Eve. Nick knew all of this was part of her sugary-sweet party princess persona.

Pride swelled inside him, all the same. What was *wrong* with him?

"Prince Nicolas is right. Snowflakes are made of molecules stacked together in thousands of different ways. But also, every snowflake that falls to the ground has its own special journey. That journey eventually determines what they look like. Every snowflake follows its own path, just like people do." Gracie turned her princess smile on Nick, and darned if his breath didn't catch in his chest. "Princes and princesses, too."

He nodded. "Princes and princesses, too."

Their conversation from the Christmas market replayed in his head, like a favorite song.

This probably won't make a bit of sense to you at all, but do you ever feel like you've gotten so accustomed to playing a role that you sometimes forget where that role ends and the real person begins?

His journey through life was nothing whatsoever like Gracie's. If they'd been snowflakes, they'd look nothing alike at all. But in some small way, they understood each other—despite all their differences. Maybe even because of them.

And now here they were, worlds apart, but right beside each other. Doing the same work. Serving the people of San Glacera...

Together.

"Thank you for that," Nick said later when it was just the two of them inside a glass gondola suspended high above a snow-capped glacier. Ice glistened like blue diamonds among the snowy crags. "It meant a lot."

Gracie tore her gaze from the view below to give him a quizzical look. "Why are you thanking me, exactly?"

"For pulling me into your interaction with the kids," he said. Snow flurries whirled against the glass behind her. If they'd been inside a real snow globe, it would have been one that had just been given a shake. Nick felt the loss of equilibrium down to his center, and he knew it didn't have anything to do with the ride itself.

It was her.

"Don't be silly. You don't need to thank me. Of course I included you—this is your home." Her baffled expression morphed into a generous smile. "Anyway, we're in this together, right?"

"Together." Nick nodded. "You and me."

And as the gondola floated higher, he went weightless. Just a snowflake against the vast December sky...

Twirling into a freefall.

CHAPTER FIFTEEN

Christmas Casual

THE FOLLOWING MORNING WHEN GRACIE picked up her phone, she found three texts from Nick.

The attire for today's activity is Christmas casual.

That means no puffy ballgown, in case you were wondering.

And just to be clear, you can also skip that monstrosity you call a crown.

When she texted back, demanding to know what exactly this activity was, he just said, *It's a surprise.*

Really?

Jaron would tell her, she figured. He understood how important advance planning was. But when she texted him and asked for more information, even he wouldn't spill the beans. Now she was trying to get ready while Clara sat propped up on her bed working on the Perfect Party Princesses schedule on her laptop. Their bookings were getting a little bit out of control. Clara's phone had been pinging all night long.

"Look at this." Gracie held her phone toward Clara. "Nick just told me not to wear my costume."

Clara read the text messages with an unmistakable smirk on her face and then handed the phone back to Gracie. "Your prince is flirting with you. You do realize that, don't you?"

"No," Gracie said automatically, even as her cheeks went hot. She chalked it up to the old-fashioned radiator in their room at the B&B. That was her story, and she was sticking to it. "He's not flirting. He's insulting me. Did you actually read the texts?"

Clara crossed her arms. "I certainly did read the texts, which begs the question—since when does Nick have your phone number?"

"Since yesterday. We exchanged numbers after the gondola ride. It only makes sense, since we're being forced to spend so much time together this week," Gracie said.

There was a royal prince in her iPhone contacts now. An annoying one, but still—an actual prince. One who texted with full punctuation.

He's not that annoying, and you know it.

The more Gracie got to know Nick, the more she began to realize that he wasn't annoying in the slightest. He was actually pretty wonderful.

"You're being 'forced' to spend time together." Clara snorted. "If it's such a hardship, then why are you trying on every single thing in your suitcase like you're getting ready to go on a date?"

Gracie surveyed the pile of Christmas sweaters, jeans, and other items of clothing in assorted varieties of red and green tartan on her bed. What did "Christmas casual" even mean?

"It's not a date. It's an obligation," she said.

"Maybe a few days ago spending time with him was an obligation, but not anymore. Face it, girl." Clara pointed directly at her. "You like him."

Gracie's stomach did a rebellious little flip. She *did* like him. Too much.

She shook her head, as if she could rattle all flattering thoughts about Nick right out of her brain. "I can't like him, Clara. Not even if I wanted to. He's a prince."

"So?" Clara shrugged, as if things were really that simple. As if something as major as a *throne* couldn't get in the way.

"He's supposed to be with a real princess. Someone like Alana—who seems to be avoiding me, by the way. I think it's obvious that I'm not royal material." Gracie couldn't believe they were even talking about this. It was absurd. "And have you forgotten that I'm only here for a week?"

"Maybe none of those things matter nearly as much as you think they do. Maybe what you're really afraid of is being hurt again, and *maybe* your prince is nothing at all like Philip," Clara said.

"And what if he is?" Gracie countered. "You know what? It doesn't matter, because this isn't a date. It's an Instagram moment, nothing more."

She grabbed a random sweater off the top of the pile and marched to the bathroom to shower and put it on, just to prove her point.

Gracie closed the door behind her, then opened it to stick her head out for another important clarification. "And he's not *my* prince. Why do I have to keep saying that?"

An hour later, she descended the stairs of the B&B, ready for Nick to pick her up for their mystery Christmas activity. Just as she reached the bottom of the steps, Princess Alana dashed past her.

"Excuse me," the princess said without making eye contact.

"No problem," Gracie said, but Alana was already way out of earshot.

Again?

Gracie wished Clara had been there to witness the strange interaction. This was exactly what she'd been talking about earlier—and she couldn't deny that it stung.

She took a deep breath and marched outside to sit on one of the pretty benches in the front of the B&B. She couldn't worry about Alana right now.

One royal at a time.

Nick arrived at the B&B to pick her up in a sleek sports car that looked like something James Bond would drive. She didn't realize it was him until he climbed out of the driver's seat to open the passenger door for her.

Gracie rose from the bench where she'd been waiting and strolled toward the vehicle. "This is what you drive?"

He tilted his head. His hair was a little rumpled today, as if he'd just raked his hand through it, and he wore faded jeans paired with a charcoal cashmere sweater. This was his idea of Christmas casual? He was basically dressed as a lump of coal.

The sweater really brought out the gray in his eyes, though. Not that Gracie particularly noticed.

"You were expecting another horse-drawn carriage?" he asked.

"Ha ha." She'd actually thought he'd arrive in something sleek and black driven by a uniformed chauffeur. She'd envisioned those little flags flapping above the headlights like diplomats always had. But she wasn't about to tell him that.

"Your chariot awaits, m'lady," he said, waving her inside the passenger seat. "That's prince-speak for 'let's go.'"

"Let's go where, exactly?"

He let out one of his low, rumbly laughs. "Nice try, Princess. You'll find out soon enough."

Gracie rolled her eyes. "Have I mentioned that you're impossible?"

"Many, many times," he said drolly, but Gracie could have sworn she saw the corner of his mouth inch up into a smile.

Was Clara right? Was Nick flirting with her? And—oh, goodness—was *she* flirting with him?

Gracie vowed to stop as she slid into the passenger seat. The supple leather interior was buttery soft, and she immediately recognized the scent that lingered in the air—warm flannel meets Christmas tree farm. As much as she wished it could be attributed to an air freshener or a special limited edition of Febreze, she knew that wasn't the case. It was just how royals smelled, apparently.

This particular royal, anyway.

"Where are we going?" she asked as he maneuvered the car through San Glacera's narrow alleyways. "And why didn't you want me to wear my costume? Are you embarrassed by it?"

He ignored her first question and went straight to the second.

"Absolutely not. In fact, the ballgown is growing on me," he said, and she had no idea if he was being serious or if he was teasing her. "It's just not quite appropriate for today."

They rode the rest of the way in silence. Snowflakes pattered against the windshield with a muffled hush. Gracie's gaze kept straying to Nick's hands on the steering wheel. He had nice hands—big and strong. Not at all what she'd expect of a man who lived in a palace. Maybe they were a result of his ice-climbing hobby.

Oh, no. Were they going *ice climbing*? Or mountaineering, or whatever the abominable snowman version of Nick liked to do?

A flare of panic sparked in Gracie's chest. She wasn't dressed for that. Then again, neither was Nick in his understated lump-of-coal sweater.

"Here we are." Nick slowed the car to a stop in front of a modest brick building with wide windows facing the Alps.

Gracie still had no idea where they were, but she didn't

want to give him the satisfaction of asking about it again when she knew that was what he expected from her. So she unclicked her seatbelt and reached for the door handle but in a flash, Nick was already on her side of the car, opening the door for her.

She wasn't at all accustomed to being around men with such impeccable manners, and as much as she loathed to admit it, being treated with such courtesy made her go a little fluttery inside.

He placed his hand in the small of her back and ushered her toward the entrance of the building. When they grew closer, she noticed a small silver plaque next to the door with a quote engraved on it in understated script.

She read it out loud. "'For I was hungry and you gave me something to eat... Matthew 25:35.'"

She broke down and asked the question. "Nick, where are we?"

"This is the San Glacera Soup Kitchen. Today is their Christmas party, and we're volunteering. The members of the royal family always serve the patrons and the staff every year." He tilted his head. "Is that okay with you?"

Of all the possibilities that had been racing through Gracie's mind, she never would have guessed that they'd be volunteering at a soup kitchen. Or anywhere, for that matter.

"It's more than okay," was all she could manage to say.

Nick nodded. "Good."

The other members of his family were already inside, donning festive aprons that looked like they'd come straight from Ingrid's pantry over their dressed-down "Christmas casual" attire. Unlike Nick, though, their sweaters were actually holiday-themed. King Felix's was decorated with broad red and green stripes, and as he moved through the dining room delivering plates of warm food to the guests, Gracie caught a glimpse of his socks—a perfect match.

Queen Livia's earrings were shiny round Christmas ornaments, and Emilie wore a headband topped with oversized, light-up Christmas bulbs in the shape of a halo.

"Thanks for making sure I didn't wear my costume," Gracie said as Nick slipped an apron over her head.

"Of course. Thank you for being here. This is probably one of my favorite holiday events. The soup kitchen is named after my grandfather." The dimple in Nick's cheek gave another surprise appearance. "He would have hated that, though, so we never put a sign out front."

Gracie was so mesmerized by this secret side of Nick that she couldn't seem to figure out what to do with her hands. Her apron strings hung loosely as she kept standing there, quietly regarding him with a goofy-feeling smile on her face.

"Cat got your tongue, Princess?" He took a step closer, reached for the ties of her apron, and gently fashioned them into a bow at her waist.

"Um..." Her mouth went dry. "Were you close to your grandfather?"

Nick nodded. "Very. What about you? Do you come from a big family?"

"No, I'm an only child. It's just me and my parents." Gracie swallowed.

This would be the first year they wouldn't be together for the holidays. She didn't like the idea of her parents spending it alone, back in Denver. But when she'd said as much before leaving for San Glacera, they'd waved off her concerns and insisted it was fine.

An opportunity like this only comes around once in a lifetime. Her father's words had sounded like just something to say at the time—a way to encourage her to forget about her stage fright and get on the plane. Weirdly, though, they were beginning to feel true. This trip was nothing like Gracie had thought it would be.

"They're probably missing you this time of year, if it's

just the three of you," Nick said with a slight frown.

Gracie nodded. "I'll miss some things this year—like my mom making her grandmother's cinnamon rolls on Christmas morning. But it's okay. We're going to exchange gifts and celebrate when I get home."

"Where you'll get each and every present all to yourself because you're an only child," Nick said, deftly moving the conversation to less personal territory.

"I knew you'd go there," she said, biting back a smile.

"Excuse me." A young man who was wearing an apron and carrying a pitcher of water came to a stop beside them. "I'm sorry to interrupt, but someone is asking if they can get a photo of you, Prince Nick. Maybe as you're serving some of the patrons?"

"I'm afraid not," Nick said. "It would be an invasion of privacy for our guests. Also, not quite in the spirit of what we do here. Right?"

The man nodded. "Understood. I thought so, but I didn't want to answer on your behalf without asking you first."

Nick rested a hand on the young man's shoulder. "No worries. You're doing a great job, Sven."

"Thank you, sir." He beamed at Nick, and a flush crawled up his neck as he turned to go back to filling glasses at the long tables in the dining room.

"Sven's new here. He's been at the soup kitchen just a couple of weeks. Great kid, though," Nick said as swiveled to face Gracie again.

Her head spun. Nick was clearly more involved with this place than she'd realized and seeing him turn down what would clearly be a flattering photo opportunity made her go a little weak in the knees.

"Ready?" Nick gave her a lopsided grin.

Gracie swallowed. Did he have any idea how absolutely smitten she felt right now? Goodness, she hoped not.

She nodded. "Ready."

King Felix put Gracie on bread duty, and she spent the day passing out warm sourdough, homemade pretzels, and soft yeast rolls. Nick was in charge of ladling out soup, so they didn't talk much for the rest of the party. Guests came in shifts, so once each meal was over, they regrouped and did it all over again.

"I'm so glad you joined us today." Emilie smiled at Gracie as they wiped down tables together at the end of the day.

"I wouldn't have missed it," Gracie said. Her feet ached like they sometimes did after a full day in glass slippers, but it was a good ache. The very best kind. "Nick told me this is one of his favorite holiday events. He must look forward to coming here every year."

Emilie ran her dishrag in the circles over the table. "Oh, Nick volunteers here at least a couple of times a week. This party is actually his thing. He's been organizing it for years. He didn't tell you?"

Gracie's gaze flitted to Nick across the room. He stood with a small group of the soup kitchen patrons, talking and laughing like they were all old friends. "No. He definitely failed to mention that."

Emilie nodded toward the Christmas tree in the center of the dining room. "He even strung that popcorn garland, all on his own. Although, I'm pretty sure Mittens helped, if you know what I mean."

She laughed, and Gracie did the same. But a lump formed in her throat at the thought of Nick putting all of this together in secret. No publicity, no press. Just him and his lovable dog.

Who are you, Nick? She could no longer reconcile the thoughtful man in the lump-of-coal sweater with the prince who was supposed to be cold and distant.

And for some reason, that frightened her even more than when she'd thought he was a beast.

Mittens was in full sulk mode when Nick returned to the palace after the party at the soup kitchen. With the entire family out for the day and Jaron busy juggling all the work that came with the kingdom's sudden popularity, the Cavalier had been doomed to spending several hours alone.

The dog retaliated by refusing to get off of Nick's bed. Nick also spied some minor retaliatory evidence in the form of a sock with a hole chewed in it, but he decided to overlook it. He'd had a good day—the best in recent memory. He wasn't going to let a destroyed sock toss a wrench in it.

He also knew exactly how to garner his dog's forgiveness. It only required a single word.

"Walk?" Nick said as he stood near the foot of the bed with his arms crossed.

Mittens sprang off the bed and turned a series of manic circles as soon as his paws hit the floor. In a fit of optimism, he also ran to grab a favorite tennis ball from his toy basket and dropped it at Nick's feet.

"Your wish is my command," Nick said.

He grabbed the tennis ball, slid his arms into a coat, and crisscrossed the castle's long hallways with Mittens prancing alongside him. When he opened the door that led to the courtyard, Mittens took off like a rocket. He ran a wide loop around the open space, kicking up snow in his wake, until he came back and plopped into a sit position in front of Nick, eyes trained on the ball.

Nick gave it a good throw. Mittens chased after it, ran back, and dropped it at Nick's feet. This went on for exactly half a dozen repetitions until Mittens grew bored of structured playtime and commenced with romping aimlessly through the snow. He'd just taken off after an alpine marmot—San

Glacera's answer to the squirrels that American dogs on television seemed to enjoy tormenting—when Nick spotted his father walking toward him across the courtyard.

"Here you are." The king tucked his hands in the pockets of his wool overcoat. "Jaron has been trying to call you."

Nick turned a variety of possibilities over in his mind. "Is something wrong? Did the two of you want to meet about the tourism numbers?"

"Relax, son. Everything is fine."

Nick really wished his father would stop telling him to relax. Didn't he realize it usually had the exact opposite effect than he'd intended?

"He just wanted you to know that the princess won't be attending dinner tonight. Since you were to be her escort, you're free to bow out too if you like," the king said.

An unexpected surge of disappointment sagged through Nick. "I didn't realize Gracie was expected to join us this evening."

His father's head drew back. "Miss Clark? I wasn't talking about Gracie, son. I meant Princess Alana. She was to be your companion this evening at dinner. But like I said, something has apparently come up, and she's been forced to cancel."

"Right." Nick nodded. The winter scarf he'd wound around his neck felt too stifling all of a sudden. "Princess Alana, of course."

"You've been enjoying your time with Gracie, then?" the king asked, eyes sparkling with amusement.

Nick really didn't see what was so funny about the mix-up. Except that he kept making it over and over again.

"I'm happy to spend time with Gracie if it helps the kingdom," he said.

"Keep telling yourself that, son." His father gave him a slap on the back. "I watched the two of you together at the soup kitchen, and I've seen the photographs of your joint appearances this week. She brings something out in you. I've seen you smile more this week than I have in quite a long time. Something tells me there's more than just business going on."

Nick paused. He couldn't really protest, could he?

The king smiled. "Miss Clark has managed to do something that I've been trying to accomplish all your life."

Nick's pulse kicked up a notch. This might be the most serious conversation he'd had with his father in, well, *ever*. "What's that, Dad?"

"She's showing you how to live in the moment. You've got the rest of your life to be king. Your grandfather prepared you well. When the time comes, there's no doubt in my mind that you'll be ready. But you have an entire life to live until then, son. Don't waste it. If I've been hesitant to include you in matters of state, it's only because I want you to enjoy your life as a prince. You don't need to carry the weight of the kingdom entirely on your shoulders. Not yet—that's what I'm here for."

Nick reeled. "I had no idea, Dad. I thought you were disappointed in me. I thought—"

"I know what you thought. But surely you realize that I know my son better than the press does. I could never be disappointed in you. And neither could your grandpa." The king's smile went tender around the edges. "Miss Clark is helping the world see who you really are. I get the feeling the two of you are more alike than you realize."

How so?

Nick almost asked the question, but by the time he trusted himself to speak without a telltale hitch in his voice, his father was gone.

Gracie returned from the party at the soup kitchen to find Ingrid, her husband Max, and Clara wrapping the front door of the B&B in bright red wrapping paper to look like a Christmas gift.

"Hello, you three," she said, cocking her head to admire their handiwork.

"It looks great, doesn't it?" Clara stepped back to give the door a once-over, then darted forward again to tuck a piece of tape back in place.

"Did you have a nice time with Prince Nicolas?" Ingrid asked.

Max nudged her with his elbow. "Don't be nosy, dear."

"I'm not being a busybody. I'm simply making polite conversation with our guest." Ingrid turned back toward Gracie and lowered her voice. "I do hope he wasn't too frosty."

If only she knew. "He wasn't frosty in the slightest. He's actually a really nice person."

Nice? Was that really the word she was looking for?

"They *text* each other now." Clara waggled her eyebrows. "I'm pretty sure I saw a string of emojis in their chat earlier."

"There were no emojis," Gracie said firmly. This seemed like an important detail to get out in the open. There had been lots of formal punctuation, but no cute little smiley faces whatsoever.

Clara, Ingrid, and Max exchanged amused glances.

"Stop it. The three of you realize that Nick and I are not a couple, right? It might look that way on Instagram, but we're not." Gracie couldn't believe she even needed to say it.

Sure, a new crop of pictures had been posted from their carriage ride the other day, and they'd looked awfully cozy snuggled together in that fairy-tale coach. Who wouldn't, though? It was a *coach*. With white horses and tinkly jingle bells. Yesterday, a batch of pictures from the gondola had popped up. In them, Nick and Gracie had drawn a heart with their fingertips in the frost that clung to the glass window of their gondola. Gracie hadn't even realized the moment had been captured on film.

She almost dreaded seeing the pictures they'd just posed for. On the way back from the soup kitchen, they'd visited a chocolate shop—San Glacera's oldest chocolatier, to be precise—where they'd sipped more of that yummy hot cocoa made from creamy milk chocolate, drinking it out of little cups. Jaron had met them there, and he'd gone crazy with his camera phone when Nick offered her a chocolate kiss. She could see the Instagram captions and headlines already.

Prince Nicolas gives Princess Snowflake a kiss!

A hot flush crawled up her neck.

Clara's phone was going to implode. They'd already gotten so many calls about princess parties that Gracie could promote every one of her employees to full-time hours and still need to hire more help. The value of the publicity that those Instagram posts were generating was priceless...even if they did manage to leave her just a little confused over what was real and what wasn't.

"We're coworkers," she said with a nod.

It was the best way she knew how to describe their unusual relationship, but it didn't feel altogether accurate. Gracie had never gone all breathless while working alongside one of her party princesses—or anyone, for that matter. It wasn't what romance novels made it all cracked up to be. The fluttery sensation she had whenever she was around Nick was beginning to feel unnerving.

"Anyway." Why were they talking about this, again? A change of subject was definitely in order. "The door looks awesome. I saw a few other doors decorated the same way in the shops along the square just now. Is there a special meaning behind the red wrapping?"

"Yes!" Ingrid clapped her hands. "It's the Living Advent Calendar, another of San Glacera's Christmas traditions."

"Every year, for the five nights leading up to Christmas,

the palace chooses a different local business to open its doors for a special holiday open house," Max said.

"The red doors mark the businesses that have been chosen as hosts." Clara gestured to the Kriegs's newly wrapped door. Clearly, she'd already gotten the scoop on this particular tradition.

"Our open house is scheduled for the twenty-third. We hope you'll be able to attend." Ingrid glanced back and forth between Gracie and Clara.

Gracie grinned. The Kriegs had already shown them so much hospitality. There was no way she'd risk disappointing Ingrid. "Of course we'll be there. And we'd love to help. Is there anything we can do?"

"Actually, there is." Ingrid bit her bottom lip.

"Get that idea right out of your head, dear." Max shook his head.

Ingrid waved a dismissive hand at him before turning a solicitous smile on Gracie. "Do you think Prince Nicolas might come?"

"Um." Gracie honestly didn't know. He certainly seemed devoted to doing whatever he could to support the people of San Glacera, but so far, everything they'd done together had been arranged by the palace.

Not everything, a little voice in the back of her head whispered.

There'd been the Christmas market. And the snowball fight. And the ill-fated meeting on the first night of the Ice Festival...but none of those things counted.

Did they?

"I'll see what I can do," she heard herself say.

"Oh, thank you so much." Ingrid threw her arms around Gracie.

She closed her eyes. The comforting scents of fresh-baked cookies and cake right of the oven clung to the older woman, and it gave Gracie a sharp pang of homesickness.

She wondered if her mom would still bake cinnamon rolls on Christmas morning without Gracie there to eat them.

Ingrid released Gracie as someone else paused to admire the red-wrapped door. When Gracie's eyes opened, she found herself looking at Alana, dressed in another Kate Middleton ensemble with her large designer tote slung over her shoulder.

"You've done such a wonderful job on the door," the princess said.

Ingrid beamed. "It's for the Living Advent Calendar. We'd be so happy if—"

"So sorry." Alana held up a hand and shifted her bag from one arm to the other. "I wish I could stay and chat, but I need to get back to my room."

She dashed inside the B&B before anyone could respond.

Clara frowned as she shut the door behind her. "That seemed weird, right?"

Gracie shrugged. "I don't know. Every time I run into her, she makes an excuse to leave."

"If she seems a little standoffish, I'm sure she has a good reason." Ingrid pasted on a smile. "From everything I've heard, that behavior is very out of character for her."

"Well, you can't believe everything you hear," Gracie pointed out. "Just because someone in the media says it doesn't make it true."

As in the case of a certain prince who wasn't nearly as frosty as he seemed to let people believe.

CHAPTER SIXTEEN

Where's a Dungeon When You Need One?

"**Y**OU WANT ME TO SING?" Gracie blinked up at Nick as he handed her a small book of sheet music. "In public?"

She'd gone pale the moment he'd arrived at the B&B and mentioned that tonight they'd be singing Christmas carols in the village square. Nick wasn't sure what to make of the strange reaction.

"I've heard you sing before. You have a beautiful voice." He hesitated before adding, "And you'll soon be singing for a lot more people than a handful of locals."

"I'm trying not to think about that," she said, as though Christmas Eve weren't the day after tomorrow.

"It's just Christmas caroling," he said.

"With the *entire kingdom*," Gracie countered. "Everyone will be watching us."

Nick nodded. People were always watching—that was the entire point of their pretend royal romance.

185

Gracie let out a shaky breath. "I don't understand. I thought tonight was supposed to be another meet-and-greet. Caroling wasn't on the schedule. Believe me, I would've noticed."

"It's one of the activities Jaron added to the revised agenda. I'm sorry if it caught you off guard," Nick said.

He had to do something. He didn't like seeing her frightened like this. She already looked so tiny in that voluminous white gown of hers. And now her eyes had gone so huge in her face that she looked lost among all the glitz.

Nick took the sheet music from her and steered her toward the fireplace. "Why don't you sit down for a moment. I'll be right back."

She nodded with her gaze semi-focused on the fire in the hearth as he went to speak to the woman at the small registration desk.

"Prince Nicolas!" She untied her apron, yanked it over her head, and stuffed it somewhere behind the dark wood desk, and curtseyed. "Welcome to the Krieg B&B."

"Thank you, and please call me Nick. No need for formalities." He lowered his voice. "Or curtseys."

She giggled like a schoolgirl before composing herself. "Is there anything I can get for you?"

"A cup of herbal tea, perhaps?" He glanced at Gracie, still watching the flames dance in the fireplace. "It's for Gracie."

"Coming right up. I've got a new one called Nutcracker Spice. I'll put the kettle on," she said, nodding at him as she dashed toward the kitchen.

Nick returned to Gracie's side and lowered himself into the chair next to hers. He pulled it closer so they could have a little privacy and said a silent prayer of thanks that the lobby was empty. Most of the guests must have already headed out to stop at one of the hot cocoa or roasted chestnut stalls at the Christmas market on the way to the tree for caroling.

"Hey there, Princess. Can I ask you something?" Nick bumped the mass of Gracie's skirt with his knee. Her leg had to be somewhere under there, didn't it?

She blinked and then turned to face him. "Sure. What is it?"

"Why a snow princess?" He let his gaze drop to the snowflake earrings that dangled from her earlobes. "Why not Cinderella or Snow White?"

The question had been nagging at him for days, even though he couldn't quite imagine Gracie without her snow-flake crown and silver glitter. As much as he was curious about her origin story, he also wanted to get her talking so she'd stop worrying about singing.

"Oh." She smiled. Clearly, he'd landed on a favorite topic of conversation. "I created Princess Snowflake based on a fairy tale that my grandmother read to me a lot when I was a kid—*The Snow Maiden*. Have you heard of it?"

Nick shook his head. "I can't say that I have. Tell me about it."

"It's the story of a girl made of snow. In the book from my grandmother's bookshelf, she was the daughter of Spring and Frost. She's also traditionally known as the granddaughter of Father Christmas. In some European countries she's just as popular as Santa."

"I can believe it," Nick said, flashing her a smile. He couldn't imagine a world where children wouldn't be de-lighted to meet a princess like Gracie.

"You haven't heard the best part yet." Her eyes glittered. Tiny flames from the fire reflected back at him from the depths of her irises.

Anticipation skittered through his veins, but he'd have to wait a bit longer to find out the snow maiden's secret because Ingrid had returned with Gracie's tea.

"Here you go, dear," she said quietly as she handed the steaming mug to Gracie.

"Thank you." Gracie warmed her hands on the tea and blew softly across the top of the steaming liquid.

Nick's gaze went immediately to her bow-shaped lips. And lingered.

"Just let me know if you two need anything else," Ingrid said.

Nick blinked hard and refocused his attention on the kind older woman. "Thank you, Ingrid."

She must have sensed they were talking about something personal, because instead of returning to the registration desk, she slipped into the kitchen and closed the door behind her.

Nick swiveled his head back toward Gracie. "Please go on. The suspense is killing me."

"Well, in my grandmother's book, the snow maiden lived deep in the forest. Her friends were reindeer and woodland creatures, but she longed for real, human love. She dreamed of romance and falling in love. She wanted it more than anything in the world." Gracie's eyes blazed.

Something about the way she looked at him made Nick's chest go tight. *Real, human love.* He couldn't seem to breathe.

"So the snow maiden's mother, Spring, granted her daughter's one true wish. And as love blossomed inside of her, the girl's snowy heart warmed..." Gracie sighed. "And she melted."

Nick felt his face go slack. "She *melted?*"

"Yep." Gracie sipped her tea.

"Princess, that's the saddest story I've ever heard."

"It is, I suppose. But I find it so inspiring." She peered at him through the thick fringe of her party princess eyelashes. "Can you imagine wanting something so much, so fiercely that you'd risk melting to have it? Even for a moment?"

Nick let his gaze sweep over her—her kind eyes, her generous smile—and he didn't even hesitate. "Absolutely."

Gracie's lips parted...just a little...just enough to let

Nick know they were both thinking about the same thing. He could kiss her. He could do it, right now. He'd been wanting to for days.

But it didn't feel right, given that she'd just been a nervous wreck about singing. He didn't want to take advantage of her vulnerability. If and when Nick kissed Gracie Clark, he wanted it to be at the right moment—the *perfect* moment. She deserved that much. She deserved the best that Christmas had to offer.

He cleared his throat and leaned back in his chair. "That's a great story. Terrible ending, but still great. I'll certainly never look at this costume the same way again."

She nodded, and for a small, heartbreaking second, Nick caught a hint of disappointment in her gaze. She'd wanted that kiss just as badly as he had. "I'll admit that when I created Princess Snowflake, I was also fresh from a bad breakup. So maybe there's a hint of that heartbreak lurking beneath the surface." She held her finger and thumb a fraction of an inch apart. "Just a tiny bit."

Nick's jaw tensed. He liked the direction this story was going even less than the one with the melting snow maiden. "What happened?"

"It was nothing." She put on a brave face, but Nick could see the pain behind it. "It happened while I was away at school—Juilliard. I was a vocal performance major."

Nick couldn't help the smile that came to his lips. "I knew it."

He'd known her voice was special the instant he'd seen that video of her in the hospital room and again when he'd heard her singing on the echo trail. She was one of a kind.

Gracie's cheeks went pink. "Stop. I used to be pretty good, but not anymore. Not really."

She was dead wrong, and Nick just knew that something terrible must have happened to make her think that. Whatever—or *who*ever—it was had stolen the joy she found in music.

"Gracie, you're immensely talented. What happened to make you think otherwise?" It had something to do with the breakup, didn't it?

Even though he was asking, Nick wasn't sure he wanted to hear the rest of this story. Was he going to need to scour America, find her ex-boyfriend, and toss him into a dungeon?

Not that the San Glacera castle had one. And not that kings and princes did that sort of thing anymore. Still, the urge was very real.

"My boyfriend Philip and I sang duets together, and our senior year, we got selected to perform at a recital in Madison Square Garden. It was big deal, obviously. My parents came all the way from Denver to watch us perform. Clara was there, too. We've known each other a really long time," Gracie said.

Nick wasn't surprised. Gracie seemed like the type of person who cherished her friends. She lived with her heart open wide. It was one of the things he liked best about her.

"Anyway, the music started and when it was time for my cue, I just sort of froze. I panicked. I looked at Philip, hoping he'd take the hint and jump in until I could gather my thoughts and sing. But..." Her voice drifted off, and for a second, Nick lost her. She seemed trapped in a memory.

"But he didn't, did he?" Nick said.

She gave him a watery smile. "No, he didn't. He just stood there, letting me crash and burn. The music kept playing, and everyone just kept looking at me, Philip included. I finally ran offstage. The next day, Philip broke off our engagement. He said he couldn't trust me anymore. We'd had so many plans, and he said I'd ripped all of them right out from under him...that I'd embarrassed him. I haven't been able to sing in public since. I've tried, and every time, I hear his voice in the back of my head telling me that I'd ruined both of our futures."

Nick shook his head. *No. Just...no.*

"Gracie, that's not true. Look at you. Look at all the joy you bring to people. You have a special gift. This moment right here, right now, is the future he was talking about. And from where I'm sitting, it doesn't look ruined at all." He fixed his gaze with hers. He needed her to understand how serious this was. "It couldn't be more beautiful. *You* couldn't be more beautiful, and I don't only mean what's on the outside. I'm also talking about your snowy princess heart."

A tear slipped down her cheek—a single, glittering tear-drop that looked like ice in the flickering light from the fire.

"The ballgown really is growing on you, isn't it?" she said. Her voice broke, and something inside Nick broke along with it.

He stood, took her by the hand, and lifted her out of her chair. "Come on, Princess. I want to sing a Christmas carol with you. If you don't want to join in, you can mouth the words. It's going to be all right. Either way, I'm right there with you. Okay?"

She nodded. "Okay."

He squeezed her hand tight and started heading for the door, and in the moment before they stepped outside, Gracie lifted her face to press a gentle kiss to his cheek.

"Thank you," she whispered.

Nick swallowed hard, and deep down, something in his soul began to thaw.

Gracie returned to the B&B later that night with a song in her heart and a certain royal prince right at the forefront of her mind.

Nick had totally come through for her earlier. His speech about how her life had turned out had really helped...more than she could really express. She'd been able to sing, right out in the open with everyone else—Christmas carol after Christmas carol. And Nick had never let go of her hand. Not even once.

It hadn't been the same as performing, obviously. Her Christmas Eve solo loomed large, but for the first time, the thought of it didn't fill Gracie with dread. Maybe she could really do this.

Something had shifted between her and Nick tonight, too. At least Gracie thought it had. She couldn't be entirely sure. She knew without a doubt they were friends, but was there really something more developing between them?

Gracie certainly thought so. But was that just wishful thinking on her part? What had Nick called the starry-eyed dreamer that still lurked deep down inside her?

Your snowy princess heart.

She shut her eyes, sighed, and leaned against the closed door of the B&B.

"That's certainly the look of one happy princess," someone said.

Gracie's eyes flew open. Princess Alana stood at the foot of the stairs, watching Gracie with a smile on her face. She held a small empty bowl in her hand and was dressed in a pair of red plaid Christmas pajamas instead of her usual regal coat dress or fine cashmere.

For a minute Gracie thought she might be dreaming. "Are you really talking to me right now?"

Alana's eyebrows drew together. "I think so, yes."

"Sorry, it's just that I sort of got the feeling that you didn't like me. I thought maybe you didn't approve of"—Gracie waved a hand at her costume—"this."

Alana scurried toward her. "Oh, no. That's not true at all. I think it's rather marvelous. You're giving princesses everywhere a good name, I assure you."

Gracie sagged in relief. "I'm so glad to hear that."

"It's my fault. I know I've been acting strange lately, but I've got a good reason. I promise." Alana looked Gracie up and down for a minute, from the top of her crown to the hem of her ballgown. "You seem really trustworthy. I can't imagine someone who'd wear a dress this fabulous betraying someone's secret. Would you like to see it?"

Gracie wasn't following. The conversation seemed to be going in circles. "See what?"

Alana flashed a smile. "The reason."

"Yes?" Gracie answered, without any idea what she was getting herself into.

"Come on." Alana grabbed Gracie's hand and dragged her up the stairs, her princess poise forgotten.

It was a relief to know she was human, even if Gracie stumbled over her glass slippers once or twice on the way up.

When they reached the second floor, Alana paused to help Gracie smooth down her ballgown. During the journey up the steps, the tulle had puffed out of control.

"I told you this gown has a mind of its own," Gracie said.

"I see that." Alana laughed. "Sorry about the rush, but we need to hurry. She tends to get into trouble when left alone."

"Who?"

Alana pressed a fingertip to her lips—the universal sign to speak in a hushed tone. "Gumdrop," she whispered.

Then she opened the door to her room to reveal a tiny black and white ball of fluff with a red bow tied to its collar.

Gracie gasped. "Hey, I know that puppy."

"You do?" Alana scooped the dog into her arms just as it tried to scramble out the door. She clicked it shut behind her.

"I saw this little sweetie at the animal shelter the other day." Gracie ran a hand over the dog's soft head. "She waved at Nick."

Alana gave her a funny look.

Gracie shrugged. "She had some help. Can I hold her?"

"Of course. The poor thing has been trapped inside this room for days. I'm sure she'd love to make new friends. I adopted her the other day as a gift for my father for Christmas."

Her father... King of Vernina.

"That's so sweet," Gracie said.

"He lost his beloved dog a while back, and I want to surprise him. It's not easy hiding a puppy, though. I've been cancelling events all week so I can keep an eye on her. Sometimes I've even resorted to carrying her around in a puppy purse."

All the run-ins Gracie had been having with Alana suddenly made a lot more sense. "You were hiding her in your bag yesterday when Ingrid and Max were outside wrapping the front door, weren't you?"

"I was." She nodded. "I'm so sorry if I've seemed rude this week. I just really want my dad to be surprised. I'm thinking of giving Gumdrop to him at the Advent Night Party. I already confessed and told Ingrid about the dog, and she thinks it's a good idea. I just have to figure out how to keep her hidden until then."

"Oh, don't you worry about that." Gracie rocked the puppy in her arms. She had a round little belly, puppy breath, and the tiniest ears Gracie had ever seen on a dog. The whole puppy package. She couldn't believe the shelter was having trouble finding funding to support dogs like this.

She also never would have guessed Alana was hiding a puppy...though given the way Nick had kept Mittens from the press, maybe she shouldn't have been surprised. Appearances could be so tricky. Everyone had their own private story—their own struggles. Even royalty.

"Clara and I would love to help take care of Gumdrop,"

Gracie said.

Alana's eyes lit up. "Are you sure?"

"Definitely. We princesses have to stick together."

Clara tore her gaze away from her phone and gaped at the puppy when Gracie snuck into their room. "Did you and Nick adopt a dog together?"

"What? No. We're not a couple, remember?"

"Right. You keep saying that, but there are pictures of you all over Instagram holding hands with him at the caroling tonight." She thrust the phone at Gracie. "Wanna see?"

"No, I actually don't." Seeing their pretend romance play out on social media was getting more confusing by the day. Gracie couldn't quite tell where the pretending ended and the truth began. "I'm a party princess from America. Nick is going to be an actual king someday. Why would we be adopting a dog together?"

"For the same reason you were holding hands." Clara twirled a lock of her hair. "I knew you liked him."

"I'm just visiting, remember? My real life couldn't be further from this fantasy world."

"Maybe you should forget about your real life for now. It's Christmas...the perfect time to have a little fun while it lasts," Clara said.

The puppy craned its neck to lick Gracie's cheek as she turned Clara's words over in her mind.

"I know you're in the middle of a romantic crisis right now, but please tell me what that dog in your arms has to do with any of this. I'm dying over here."

Gracie couldn't help but laugh. "This is Gumdrop. Alana adopted her from the animal shelter I told you about. She's a surprise for King Hans for Christmas. I sort of told Alana we'd help her keep the puppy under wraps."

Clara tossed her phone onto her bed and held her arms out toward the dog. "Come here, you little monster. Come to Auntie Clara."

Gracie laughed as she transferred the dog into Clara's embrace. "So you're okay with it?"

"Yes. Duh. I told you I want to get a dog when we get home."

"Good, because there's something else I need to talk to you about. Something important." Gracie took a deep breath.

She couldn't believe what she was about to propose. Clara might think she'd lost her mind—or at least lost sight of the entire reason they'd come to San Glacera to begin with. But the thought had been nagging at her for days, and after tonight, she knew she wouldn't be able to shake it.

"What's up?" Clara said, climbing onto her bed with the puppy tucked under her arm.

Gracie held up a finger. "Just one second."

If she didn't ask Nick now, while his words about her princess heart were still floating through her mind like snowflakes, she knew she'd lose her nerve. Maybe Clara was onto something.

It's Christmas, the perfect time to have a little fun while it lasts.

Gracie grabbed her phone from the dresser and scrolled through her contacts until she landed on Nick's name and sent the text.

I know we're not scheduled for any events tomorrow evening, but would you like to attend Advent Night with me at the Kriegs's?

Nick answered right away.

I'd love to. Just tell me when.

Whenever you're free, Gracie texted back. *I promised to help Ingrid with logistics.*

In that case, why don't we do something special?
Like?

After a few moments, his next text appeared. *Do you think we can make that family cinnamon roll recipe you told me about?*

Gracie's heart turned over in her chest.

I do.

Sounds like we have a date.

Gracie stared at the text for a moment before replying.

It's a date.

Three little dots flashed again, indicating Nick was sending another message. This one took longer to come through than the others. She held her breath, and then it finally appeared. A trio of emojis—a blue heart, flanked on either side by snowflakes.

My snowy princess heart.

Despite all her doubts, despite all the craziness of the reality of their situation, and despite all the ways she'd tried to tell herself that a romance between a party princess and a real-life prince would never work, Gracie smiled. She held the phone close to her chest and beneath the layers of lace and glittering rhinestone snowflakes, her real snowy princess heart ran wild.

CHAPTER SEVENTEEN

After the Ice Melts

THE FOLLOWING MORNING, GRACIE AND Clara took Gumdrop for a walk while Princess Alana had breakfast with her parents in the dining room. The puppy smelled everything in sight, leaving tiny pawprints in the snow. A bit of frost clung to her black button nose, and when they got back to the B&B after a stroll around the square, she could barely keep her little eyes open.

"I think we've successfully exhausted her." Clara lifted the puppy from the cobblestone path and tucked the little ball of fluff inside her puffer jacket. "My guess is we can sneak her upstairs without anyone noticing. What do you think?"

Gracie snuck a peek inside one of the B&B's frosty windows. A few guests sat in the lobby, facing the fire, but the King and Queen were nowhere to be seen. "I think we're good. They must still be eating."

Clara nodded. "Let's do it."

Gracie pushed the door open and held it for Clara.

Gumdrop was a barely visible lump beneath her coat, and they managed to make it upstairs without anyone noticing anything amiss.

"Whew." Gracie let out an exhale when they reached the second floor.

"That wasn't hard at all. Hiding this little sweetie is going to be easy as pie." Clara unzipped her jacket. Gumdrop burst from its confines, but she caught the squirming pup and nestled her close to her chest.

Gracie eyed the dog. "Don't jinx us. Alana just needs to keep her under wraps until the party tonight."

"Like I said, easy peasy." Clara shrugged. "What are we supposed to do with her now? I promised Ingrid I'd help with party prep."

Gracie nodded. "I know. Nick is coming over later, and she told us we could use the kitchen. I told her she could put me to work until he gets here. Alana gave me a copy of her key and said we could put Gumdrop in her puppy crate so long as she's quiet."

"Perfect." Clara headed toward Alana's room, situated directly across the hall from theirs.

"Just a sec. I left the key on our dresser," Gracie said.

She unlocked the door to their room but only made it halfway to the dresser when she heard voices coming from the staircase. Her head whipped back around, and her gaze crashed into Clara's.

"It's them," Clara mouthed.

"Get in here," Gracie whispered, waving her inside.

But it was too late. Just over Clara's shoulder, Gracie spotted King Hans and Queen Sophia. Alana stood between them with her perfectly groomed eyebrows raised in alarm.

"Good morning, Clara," the king said.

Great. She couldn't even turn tail and run—not without looking terribly rude.

Eyes wide, Clara let go of the puppy and nudged Gumdrop

toward their room. Then she turned around to greet the king.

"Good morning," she gushed. "How was breakfast? Gracie and I are getting ready to head down there right now."

"Breakfast was lovely," Queen Sophia said as her gaze flitted past Clara toward their room, where Gumdrop was currently scampering toward one of Gracie's glass slippers.

"Yes, it was. But er, what was that?" The king followed his wife's gaze and peered inside the room.

"I'm sure it was nothing, Dad." Alana grabbed her father by the elbow and tried to drag him down the hall. But he didn't budge. He just kept standing there like an immovable, overly curious rock.

Gracie didn't know what to do, short of slamming the door closed. That wasn't a viable option, though. She was too far away. There was no way she could make it to the doorway before the king or the queen spied the dog.

Then Gumdrop dragged the glass slipper toward the wardrobe, where Gracie's Princess Snowflake gown hung on the outside of the door, because even a fairy godmother wouldn't have been able to cram twenty yards of tulle inside the antique bureau. But maybe that glittering cupcake of a dress could do a little magic all by itself.

Gracie gave the king and queen an exaggerated wave. "Good morning, Your Royal Highnesses!"

She moved toward the hallway and pretended to stumble into the wardrobe in the process. The bureau wobbled, and the gown's hanger teetered from its precarious position and slipped off the edge. An avalanche of organza and rhinestones tumbled to the ground, successfully burying a startled Gumdrop in a mound of fluff.

"Oh, dear. Your dress." Queen Sophia's hand flew to her chest.

"Clumsy me." Gracie shrugged and glanced down at the pile of diaphanous fabric. The lump that was Gumdrop shifted ever so slightly.

"Am I seeing things, or did that gown just move all by itself?" the king asked.

"You're not seeing things," Gracie said.

Alana bit her lip, eyes wide with panic.

Gracie winked at her. "As I keep telling Alana, sometimes this gown just seems to have a mind of its own."

"Have you ever made homemade cinnamon rolls before?" Gracie looked up to Nick from the recipe her mom had emailed her late last night. After the close call with Gumdrop earlier this morning, she'd spent the day helping Ingrid prepare for the open house, and now Ingrid had graciously turned her kitchen over to Gracie and "her prince."

No matter how many times Gracie protested, people kept calling him that. She was starting to get used to it.

"I can't say that I have. But I've eaten my fair share of cinnamon rolls, so I'm betting I'll be pretty good at this." Nick grinned.

Gracie's great-grandmother's cinnamon rolls had been a Christmas morning tradition for as long as she could remember. After her great-grandmother had passed away, her grandma had taken over, rolling out the dough late every Christmas Eve so it could rise overnight.

A few years ago, after her grandmother died, her mom had taken up the tradition and it had become a family affair, with everyone chipping in on the process. Helping form the dough into soft spirals and inhaling the familiar, comforting scents of cardamom, vanilla, and warm brown butter was Gracie's favorite part of Christmas morning. A cherished holiday ritual.

And now she was sharing that tradition with Nick.

"I can ladle soup with the best of them, but baking is new to me," he said as he tied one of Ingrid's frilly Christmas aprons around his waist.

Gracie bit back a smile. He looked ridiculous, albeit in an adorable sort of way. "I suppose you haven't had much of an occasion to bake. You really don't know what you're missing."

His forehead creased. "I don't?"

Gracie shook her head as she began getting the ingredients together and lining them up on the kitchen island. "Nothing beats making a pan of brownies when you're home alone on a Friday night."

"Does that happen often?" Nick asked.

"Making brownies?" Gracie glanced at him and paused when she realized his expression had gone soulful—just like the way he'd looked at her in the photograph from the Christmas tree maze.

"Finding yourself home alone on a Friday night."

Their eyes met, and Gracie forgot how to breathe for a second.

This was new. They'd spent so much time together this week, but they'd never had a direct conversation about either one of their dating lives. It felt like they'd been dancing around the topic for days. Sure, they'd talked about Philip and Sarah Jane, but those discussions had been in the past tense. Gracie had no idea if Nick dated or if he had plans to marry someday.

Surely he would, eventually. He probably felt immense pressure to do it. Wasn't marrying a princess and raising an heir and a spare a crucial part of being a prince?

"There aren't that many children's parties on Friday nights," she said, failing to directly address the question. She wasn't sure she was ready to admit to making brownies from a box and binge-watching *Fairy Tale I Do* while he was probably waltzing his way across Europe. "What about you?"

She tried not to look at him, measuring the sugar with excruciating care so he wouldn't notice she was holding her breath.

"Oh, I'm never home alone on Friday nights," Nick said.

"Never?" Gracie's stomach clenched. "Wow."

He gave her a shoulder bump, prompting her to glance up and meet his gaze.

"I've got Mittens to keep me company." Nick winked.

Gracie couldn't stop the smile that came to her lips. Relief flowed through her, although she wasn't even sure why. Tomorrow was Christmas Eve. This would be the last Friday night she'd ever spend with His Royal Highness, Prince Nicolas of San Glacera. What he did with the rest of his Friday nights—the rest of his *life*, even—was none of her concern.

"Hey," Nick said softly. "You disappeared for a minute. Where'd you go?"

Gracie shrugged. "I guess I was just thinking about home."

He took the measuring cup from her hand and poured the sugar into the mixing bowl. "Do you miss it?"

"I kind of do." She felt bad admitting it. This week had been like a dream, and she didn't want him to think she wasn't grateful for the experience. "Not so much the place, though. I meant my family. This is the first Christmas I haven't spent with my mom and dad."

"I suppose that makes baking these cinnamon rolls bittersweet, then?"

"A little bit," she admitted. But if she was going to make them with anyone other than her family, she was glad it was with him. "I love that we're doing this, though. I wanted to do something special to help Ingrid and Max with Advent Night, and nothing's more special than this. Thank you for suggesting it."

"My pleasure. You spoke so fondly of the tradition. I

thought it would be nice to bring a little bit of a Clark family Christmas to San Glacera. You've been so gracious about taking part in our holiday customs." He pressed a hand to his heart. "I'm eager to experience one of yours."

"I hate to tell you this, but you're off to a messy start." She pointed at his chest, where he'd just left a perfect flour handprint on his fancy pressed dress shirt.

Nick looked down at it and laughed. "I'm committed to the process, no matter how terrible I am at it."

"You'll be fine. Just watch and learn."

He picked up Ingrid's rolling pin and inspected it as if he'd never set eyes on one before. "What is this thing, anyway?"

It was a good thing that their relationship had progressed far enough that she could laugh right in his face, because she did. The man seriously didn't know what a rolling pin was? She couldn't wait to introduce him to the wonders of a cookie sheet.

"It's a rolling pin. We don't need that until later. Right now, we're supposed to knead the dough." Gracie plunged her hands into the mixing bowl and started blending the ingredients together.

Nick peered into the bowl. "Aren't there mixers for that sort of thing?"

"Sure there are, but the Clarks do it the old-fashioned way."

"Just like your great-grandmother used to do?"

"Yep." Gracie's hands grew still. "Do you want to try?"

"I thought you'd never ask." He unfastened his silver cufflinks and began rolling up his sleeves, flashing a glimpse of his royal forearms.

Gracie did her best not to stare, redirecting her gaze to the mixing bowl. "Okay, just put your hands right into the dough and use your fingers to mix the ingredients."

"Here we go." He plunged his hands into the mixture and started working the dough—stretching and kneading it until it began to hold its shape. "Like this?"

"That's perfect." Gracie nodded.

He kept going until the dough was ready to be turned out onto the floured counter.

"Here's where things get a little trickier. Use the heel of your hand to push the dough away from you. Then you refold it and do it again." She grinned up at Nick, watching her intently. "And again. And again."

"And again?"

She nodded. "Yep. And then we place it back into a bowl to rise and we do it some more an hour or so later."

He gave the dough a tentative, wholly ineffectual nudge.

Gracie laughed. "You're going to have to use way more elbow grease than that, Your Royal Highness."

His eyes narrowed into a mock glare. "I thought I told you never to call me that."

"It just slipped out. I couldn't help it. You just look so—" She waved a hand at the flour covering his shirt. He'd somehow ended up with a smudge of it on his cheek and a generous dusting of white in his hair. "Majestic."

He puffed out his chest. "I do, don't I?"

Gracie swatted at him with a dish towel, and for a second, she thought the baking session was going to devolve into a battle, just like their snowball fight.

But it didn't. Instead, Nick winked at her and then turned his attention back to the dough, kneading it with care.

A lump formed in her throat.

Care. She turned the word over in her mind. *Nick really cares. He wants to get this right...for my family. For the Kriegs.*

For me.

She'd been wrong about Nick...so very wrong.

Gracie tried to swallow, but the lump in her throat grew threefold, just like the Grinch's heart did on Christmas Day. Because the prince she'd tried her best to resist had done the impossible—he'd stolen her heart, as surely as that famous green villain had snuck into Whoville and stolen the roast beast.

I'm in love with my Prince Charming.

The muscles in Nick's forearms flexed as he gathered the dough and started again—just like generations of her family had done for more Christmases than she could count. This was a man who valued family, valued the past, and was committed to building a future for the people in this winter wonderland that he called home.

And despite every effort not to, Gracie had fallen for him, head over her glass-slippered heels. She'd come to San Glacera to play the part of a snowflake princess and rule over a fantastical, frozen celebration carved from ice.

But what would happen once Christmas was over, the ice melted, and it was time to go home?

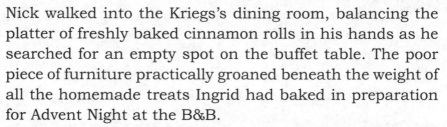

Nick walked into the Kriegs's dining room, balancing the platter of freshly baked cinnamon rolls in his hands as he searched for an empty spot on the buffet table. The poor piece of furniture practically groaned beneath the weight of all the homemade treats Ingrid had baked in preparation for Advent Night at the B&B.

"Can I help you find a spot for those, Prince Nicolas?" Ingrid swept into the room holding two slender silver candlesticks. Where she planned on putting them, Nick had no idea.

"It's Nick, remember?" He lifted an eyebrow. "Not Prince Nicolas. We talked about this."

Ingrid's eyes lit up. "That's right. Nick." She said his name like she was trying out a new word and grinned. "It's so nice having you here with us this evening."

"I wouldn't miss it. Gracie has really enjoyed her time here, and we both wanted to pitch in a little." As the words left his mouth, he realized how they sounded. He was talking about Gracie like they were a couple...like they had a future beyond Christmas.

The past week had been a whirlwind. In the span of just seven days, their lives had become so intertwined that Nick was only beginning to realize that after Christmas Eve, she'd be gone.

A weight settled on his heart as Ingrid shuffled a few things around, making space for the cinnamon rolls among all the other baked goods.

"Here you go, a nice spot in the center. We're all excited to try Gracie's family recipe. It's nice to add new traditions to the mix on occasion, isn't it?" Ingrid met his gaze and didn't say anything else.

Nick got her message, loud and clear. "It certainly is."

He'd been so wrong...about everything. Wrong about Princess Snowflake and wrong about his own kingdom. The presence of a party princess hadn't taken a thing away from the traditions his grandfather had started all those years ago. Rather, Gracie's participation had added fresh joy—and yes, more than a little sparkle—to San Glacera's rich history. In a way, she'd been like a bridge between the people and the monarchy, bringing them together. Just like she was doing here, tonight.

"Perhaps you'll come back and spend Advent Night with us next year, with or without Gracie?" Ingrid said as she took the platter from him and wedged it in place.

"I will." Nick nodded. "That's a promise."

"And now that you know how to make her family recipe, you can bring cinnamon rolls next year too." Ingrid nodded. "It's all settled."

He laughed. "It is, is it?"

"Absolutely. You know, if you don't mind my saying so, Your Royal Highness..." Ingrid offered him a meaningful smile, and her eyes shone with a sincerity that Nick didn't often see when he interacted with people outside the palace walls. At least not before this holiday season. "You're not all that abominable."

"Thank you, Ingrid." He was really going to end up making those cinnamon rolls next year, wasn't he? "Do you happen to know where Gracie is? She said she needed to check on something, but it's been a while and I haven't seen her."

"I don't know." Ingrid glanced through the stone archway, toward the reception area and shook her head. "I don't see her around. You might want to check upstairs in her room? It's the second door on the left."

"Thanks." He bent to kiss Ingrid's cheek and then headed for the stairs as she made a big show of fanning herself with her apron.

The old wooden steps creaked beneath his feet, and he had to duck to avoid hitting his head on one of the exposed wooden beams that added to the charm of the chalet-style building. When he got to the top of the staircase, he found most of the doors closed. The one that led to the room Ingrid had mentioned was open just a crack.

Nick lifted his hand to tap lightly on the door but grew still when he heard music coming from inside the room. He strained to hear, and soon, Gracie's lyrical voice washed over him. She sounded like an angel, just as she had the last time he'd stumbled upon her singing, but there was an ache in her tone that he'd never heard before—a longing sense of melancholy that wrenched his heart.

What song is this? He closed his eyes and gingerly leaned his forehead against the door as his throat closed up tight. *Blue Christmas.*

It was the old Elvis Presley song, but Gracie's version was far more poignant, more meaningful. Or maybe that was just Nick's interpretation because suddenly he'd stopped living and breathing in Christmas Present. He'd skipped straight to Christmas Future, imagining what the holidays would be like next year when he'd be facing them without Gracie by his side. It wouldn't be the same. None of it—the Christmas tree maze, the carriage ride and candy cane toss, the gondola, the party at the soup kitchen, caroling in the square, Advent Night.

Nick had been participating in most of those activities all his life. He thought he knew how Christmas was supposed to look; how it was supposed to feel. But this year, things had changed. They'd invited a party princess to their tiny kingdom—a woman who'd arrived with a flamboyant ballgown, paper snowflakes, and glitter fairy dust in her suitcase. But little had he known that she'd bring genuine magic to San Glacera. Christmas magic, the best sort of magic there was.

He couldn't imagine what the holidays would look like next year.

Blue Christmas, indeed.

"Prince Nick?" Someone behind him rested a hand on his shoulder.

Nick's eyes flew open and he turned around to find a very well-dressed, familiar-looking blonde woman watching him, forehead scrunched in concern. "Princess Alana?" he guessed, and she nodded in confirmation.

Finally.

"Just Alana," she said. "I'm so glad to see you. I feel terrible that we haven't connected all week. I'm sorry. It's all my fault."

"No apology needed. I just hope you've enjoyed your stay in San Glacera."

"Absolutely. It's been wonderful." She glanced over his shoulder toward the door to Gracie's room and smiled. "I would ask if you'd come looking for me, but you're here for

Gracie, aren't you?"

Was it that obvious? Could everyone in the kingdom tell that out of all the people who'd fallen for Gracie this week, Nick had been the one who'd fallen the hardest?

Probably. But for once, Nick didn't much care what everyone else thought.

"I am, yes." He gestured toward the door to Gracie's room. "But then I heard her singing, and I didn't want to interrupt."

Alana angled her head, straining to hear. Her eyes lit up. "She's singing to Gumdrop again. Isn't that sweet?"

"Gumdrop?" Who—or what—was that?

"She didn't tell you? Gracie sure knows how to keep a secret. I asked her to keep things quiet, but I was sure *you* knew about it. Everywhere I look, I see pictures of you two together." Alana pressed a finger to her lips as she pushed the door open a fraction further. Then she motioned for Nick to take a peek.

He hesitated, not wanting to invade Gracie's privacy more than he already had. Alana seemed so sure, though. When she prodded him a second time, he leaned to sneak a glance inside the room.

Gracie sat on the bed closest to the door with a quilt thrown over her lap and a small lump of fur nestled in her arms. Nick squinted and realized the furry lump was a puppy.

A smile tugged at his lips as he shifted his gaze back to Alana. "Gumdrop, I presume?"

She nodded, grinning from ear to ear. "Isn't she darling? My father lost his longtime canine companion a few months ago, and I wanted to surprise him for Christmas. I'm giving the puppy to him tonight at the Advent Night celebration. It seems like half the people in this B&B have been helping me keep Gumdrop a secret, so I thought it would be the perfect time for her unveiling. This Christmas gift has had me quite distracted in the past few days. I'm sincerely sorry I haven't been able to make it to dinner at the palace."

So this was the reason Alana hadn't seemed interested in spending time with Nick. It wasn't because of anything she'd read in the press about him. She'd simply been pre-occupied with trying to hide a Christmas puppy from her father.

He couldn't help but smile. "What a thoughtful gift. Where did you get her?"

"From that little animal shelter right here in San Glacera. I read about it before we arrived and made plans to visit and pick out a Christmas puppy for my father." Alana waved a hand in the direction of the village square. "I believe you're their patron?"

"I am, yes." Nick had thought the dog looked familiar. Now he realized Gumdrop was the puppy that had waved at him during the candy cane toss, albeit with a little as-sistance from one of the shelter volunteers.

"Gracie has been such a help with her. I would never have been able to pull this off without her. She's a very special woman." Alana narrowed her gaze at Nick. "Then again, I have a feeling you already know that."

"Indeed I do." Nick's eyes found Gracie again through the crack in the door. She was still singing to the dog in a quiet, peaceful voice. He wondered why she'd chosen such a sad Christmas song for a puppy lullaby.

He was probably reading too much into the song selec-tion. He hoped so, anyway. But the poignant lyrics kept spinning through his mind on repeat.

"You don't think Gracie had anything to do with the shelter's big donation, do you?" Alana asked, dragging him back to their conversation.

He blinked. "Big donation?"

"You haven't heard? I stopped by the shelter late this afternoon to deliver a batch of Ingrid's Christmas cookies to the volunteers. They'd just gotten news of an anonymous donation. The shelter staff was delighted. They were toasting with hot apple cider when I got there. It was an impromptu holiday party." Alana's eyebrows lifted. "Apparently, the donation is going to go a long way. It was quite a sum."

A warm, fuzzy feeling came over Nick, and he tried his best to push it away.

No. She wouldn't.

It couldn't have been Gracie. She had a business to run back home. Bills to pay. A whole staff of princesses to support.

But something in his heart stirred as he remembered how much she loved seeing the dogs at the candy cane toss. As soon as he'd mentioned the shelter's troubles, she'd asked how she could help.

He glanced at her now, tenderly running her fingertips across Gumdrop's tiny head and singing like an angel. "Do you know how much the donation was, Alana?"

His breath froze in his lungs while he waited for the answer.

"Thirty thousand dollars."

The exact amount of the Royal Winter Wonderland Contest's Grand Prize.

CHAPTER EIGHTEEN

They Say It's Tradition

G RACIE HAD PROMISED ALANA TO help keep an eye on Gumdrop until the big Christmas puppy reveal, but in truth, she'd also needed a moment to collect herself. Being in the kitchen with Nick had left her feeling all warm and gooey inside, and it had nothing to do with the cinnamon rolls they'd been making.

She couldn't be in love with Prince Nicolas of San Glacera. She just couldn't.

They hadn't known each other long enough for that... had they? And more importantly, they lived on opposite sides of the world, both literally and figuratively. He was *royal*. She was a party princess. He was going to be a king someday. Nick's public life was carefully controlled. He did his best to never put a foot wrong and was always thinking about how to properly represent the people of his kingdom. Gracie's job, on the other hand, was pure fantasy.

Sure, so far everything had gone splendidly. But what

would happen if the press and the people grew weary of her snow queen act? Or if she made a mistake? Would she end up on the front page of every newspaper and magazine in Europe, like Nick had, through no fault of his own?

What if she caused more bad press for *him*, when he deserved so much better?

Gracie had already had to pick up the pieces of her life after one public embarrassment. She wasn't sure she could do it again, especially if history repeated itself and she ended up with a broken heart.

"Hey, there." Alana poked her head in the door. "The party is about to start."

Gumdrop jumped out of Gracie's lap and romped toward the foot of the bed to greet Alana, while Gracie stopped singing and wiped a tear from her cheek. She hadn't even realized she'd started to cry.

"Is everything okay? You seem sad." Alana scooped Gumdrop into her arms and the sweet puppy licked the side of her face.

"No, of course not. I'm fine." Gracie pasted a picture-perfect smile on her face. She'd been doing it for so long that it had become second nature. "It's Christmas, the most wonderful time of the year."

"Good." Alana gave her a warm smile. Gracie could hardly believe she'd originally thought that the princess had been snubbing her. Alana was one of the kindest, most gracious people she'd ever come across. She embodied all the traits Gracie tried to emulate with her princess character. "You might want to come downstairs, though. Nick has been looking for you."

Gracie's stomach did a rebellious little flip.

"And I think it's time to finally unveil this furry sweetheart." Alana lifted Gumdrop in the air and touched noses with the tiny dog. Gumdrop's tail wagged so furiously that it looked like a black and white blur.

Gracie slid off of the bed and smoothed down the front of her red tartan dress. "That sounds perfect. I can't believe it's already almost Christmas Eve."

Just one more day. Tomorrow night she'd do what she came to San Glacera to do, and then she and Clara could pack up and go home. Life would return to normal, just as it was supposed to.

Gracie inhaled a steadying breath and went downstairs to make sure King Hans and Queen Sophia had already joined the partygoers in the sitting area of the lobby. She spotted the king's familiar profile right away and waved for Alana to come down with the puppy. As the princess descended the staircase with Gumdrop tucked neatly under her arm, Nick found Gracie.

His warm breath tickled her neck as he bent to whisper in her ear. "Here you are. For a minute there, I thought you'd gotten lost, like in the Christmas tree maze, Princess."

Princess.

The nickname had been funny at first—a sweet, tongue-in-cheek endearment, like when Gracie called him Prince Charming. Except there was one important difference: Gracie's nickname for him rang true, whereas hers was pure make-believe.

"I didn't get lost." She shook her head. Who was she kidding? She'd wandered so far out of her depth that she'd never been so lost in her life. "Just helping out with a Christmas surprise."

"Yes, I know all about your little secret," Nick said, and the sincerity in his expression told Gracie he wasn't just talking about Gumdrop.

His eyes locked onto hers, and Gracie's breath bottled up in her throat as he took hold of her hand and held it tight. "Gracie, I—"

A squeal pierced the air. "Oh my goodness, is that a puppy?" A woman Gracie recognized from the chocolate shop next door clasped her hands on either side of her face.

Every head in the sitting room swiveled toward the staircase, just as Alana reached the bottom step. Gumdrop wiggled like mad, delighted to be the center of attention.

"Sweetheart?" King Hans rose from the chair where he'd been sitting. He gave a slight headshake, then rubbed his brow, clearly trying to make sense of the sight before him.

"Merry Christmas, Dad." Alana beamed, and her eyes went shiny.

All the sneaking around the past few days was more than worth it to see the tender look exchanged between father and daughter right then. In that sweet moment, King Hans wasn't a monarch. He was a kid on Christmas morning, and when Alana set Gumdrop gently down on the Kriegs's wood plank floor, the puppy scrambled straight toward him.

It was a match made in heaven. Not technically speaking, of course. But from where Gracie was standing, San Glacera came awfully close.

Clara caught Gracie's gaze from across the crowded room and grinned as she snapped pictures of Gumdrop and the king. Her phone had practically been glued to her hand the past few days. It pinged with calls and messages almost nonstop. Demand for princesses had skyrocketed. Gracie wasn't sure she was prepared for whatever waited for her back in Denver.

Nick gave her hand a squeeze, anchoring her back to this moment, this place she couldn't quite imagine leaving behind. "Can we talk?"

Gracie smiled, but her mouth felt like it wasn't cooperating. Her lips trembled, and she almost wanted to press them still with her fingertips. "Sure, although it's a bit crowded. Advent Night seems to be a hit."

People poured through the red-wrapped front door. Ingrid and Max waved everyone inside, offering hot cocoa and warm, fragrant treats to their guests as they unwound scarves from their necks and shook off the chill of another snowy December night.

"Nothing gets a party started faster than a puppy with a red satin ribbon around its neck. I'm happy for the Kriegs. So many of the participants in the Advent Tour this year are visitors. This is going to be great for the B&B." Nick nodded as he scanned the bevy of merrymakers. So many happy faces.

Then he turned back to Gracie, as if he only had eyes for her. "I know the perfect place. Come on."

He led her through the crowd, never letting go of her hand. Every so often, one of the guests appeared to recognize him and blinked in disbelief. Each and every time, Nick smiled and welcomed them to San Glacera on behalf of the Crown.

Gracie felt a strange emptiness in the pit of her stomach. *The Crown.* To her, a crown had always been the flashy tiara she pinned to her head for parties, or the smaller, plastic versions she passed out to children to make them feel special and unique. But here, the word meant something different. It was even spelled with a capital *C* because in the context of real royalty, the Crown wasn't just an object. It was an idea, a concept. A living, breathing symbol—not just of power or sovereignty. It also stood for strength and the responsibility to always do what was best for the kingdom, to always stand up for the people and use the power of the monarchy for good.

The Crown wasn't just a word or an adornment. It was a commitment. Gracie would never look at her snowflake tiara the same way again.

"Here." Nick let go of her hand just long enough to place his palm on the small of her back and guide her toward a cozy nook in the back corner of Ingrid's kitchen.

The alcove was tucked beneath a stone archway like the ones in the lobby and the dining room, only on a much more diminutive scale. Nick had to duck to fit in the small space, and so did Gracie. Once inside, they sat facing each other on a narrow window seat with cushions and a faux fur throw covering the chiseled stone.

Nick took both of her hands in his, and when he spoke, the window overlooking the towering Christmas tree in the village square fogged over. "Gracie, I know about the donation to the animal shelter."

Honestly, you couldn't hide anything from a man with a title on his own turf, could you? It had taken a literal village just to keep a puppy under wraps from a visiting king.

Gracie bit her lip, fully intending on feigning innocence, but Nick ruled that out at once.

"Don't even think about pretending it wasn't you. I know for a fact that it was," he said.

She released a breath she didn't quite realize she'd been holding. "Who told you?"

"No one told me. I heard about the donation and had a hunch. Once I found out the exact amount, I just knew." He reached to tuck a stray lock of her hair behind her ear and as soon as his fingertips grazed her cheek, she felt like she was back in the palace courtyard the night of the carriage ride. It had been the first time he'd been tempted to kiss her. She'd seen the longing in his gaze, *felt* it in the way her lips tingled in anticipation.

It had been too soon then. They'd only been starting to get to know each other, but now...

Now things were different. Now, if Clara had jokingly called Nick *her* prince, Gracie wouldn't have protested.

He'd once told Gracie that he wanted to be her friend, not her prince. She knew what he'd been trying to say—he wanted them to be real with each other. He wanted to be able to trust her, and he wanted her to know that he didn't see her as a commoner or just as a party princess, but as a person. An equal.

It had meant the world to Gracie, especially after the dubious start to their relationship, but even then a part of her had wanted to disagree. It wasn't his title that she'd cared about, though. It had been that one small word, the one that made her heart beat fast as he'd said it.

Her prince.

Hers.

"Why did you do it?" he asked, eyes glittering in the dim light of the kitchen.

Moonlight streamed through the window, and a delicate pattern of frost had formed along the edge of the glass. It looked almost identical to the silver confetti in Gracie's magic snow queen dust.

"You need that money for your business. It's why you came here." Nick searched her face, as if all the complicated feelings she was experiencing were written across her features.

She hoped with everything she had in her that they weren't.

"You're right. The prize money was why I came to San Glacera, but things are different now. I've loved my time here, Nick. It's such a special place." And she'd experienced it with a special man. More special than she could have imagined. "It didn't feel right taking such a huge sum home with me when it could do more good here, where it belonged."

"But it was yours." Nick's grip on her hands tightened. "I want you to have it."

"It's okay, really. With all the publicity from the trip, business is booming back home. Clara is convinced we'll have bank officers lined up, waiting to fund our expansion. With all the events we've got coming up now, I don't think we'll even need a loan to give our princesses benefits. All because of you."

He shook his head. "Not me. *Us.*"

Nick's eyes grew soft, heavy-lidded. Gracie had to concentrate hard on simply breathing in and out, and when she did, she inhaled the lingering aroma of cinnamon rolls. Sticky sweet, with just a hint of oranges and cardamom. It was a fragrance she'd associated with Christmas all her life, but even more than that, it was the scent of home.

In a flash, so quick that Gracie almost missed it, Nick's gaze flitted upward. She glanced overhead and drew in a sharp breath.

Just like all the other stone archways in the chalet, this one was decorated with a small sprig of mistletoe. It hung from a red velvet ribbon like a timeless promise.

Gracie let her eyes drift back down until they met Nick's.

The corner of his lips quirked up. When he smiled at her, a question shone in his eyes. "They say it's tradition."

"Then I suppose we don't really have a choice," Gracie said, her voice dipping low and sweet. Barely a whisper.

Then he leaned forward and ever so gently touched his lips to hers, and Gracie saw stars. They exploded behind her eyes like tiny, crystalline snowflakes. She took a deep gulp of air to steady herself, but the heady scent of the cinnamon rolls was overwhelming. She'd come so far, only to find that San Glacera and Prince Nick—*her* prince—were beginning to feel like home, like the place she belonged more than anywhere else on earth.

And that's when she knew it was time to say goodbye.

CHAPTER NINETEEN

The Trouble With Mistletoe

"I CAN'T DO THIS, NICK."

It broke Gracie's heart to say it. She'd thought she could protect herself by ending things right here and now. She'd thought she could spare herself the awful feeling of being rejected. But somehow, choosing to be the one to say goodbye felt far more painful than she could've imagined.

"I just... I can't." She stood up, promptly hitting her head on the stone archway above the alcove.

"Gracie? Are you okay?" Nick reached for her, but then drew his hands back as if she'd suddenly changed the rules on him, which she supposed she had.

She stood in the center of the kitchen, away from their cozy little hideaway, wrapping her arms around herself. A shiver ran up and down her spine. She felt so cold all of a sudden, like she was standing on a snowy mountaintop without a thing to keep her safe and warm.

Nick dipped his head and stepped out of the stone nook. The mistletoe swayed behind him as he tucked his hands in his pockets and faced her. He didn't talk for a long while, instead choosing to give her the time and space to articulate her feelings.

"I don't live here," she finally blurted.

"I know that," Nick said quietly.

She threw her arms in the air. "And you're a prince."

"I know that too." He nodded with a calm that drove her nuts.

Was he really going to stand there and make her connect the dots for him?

"So." She cocked her head, as if that single word was a complete sentence.

"So. I have feelings for you, Gracie. I don't care about the rest. We can figure all of that out, just like we've been doing everything else all week." He gave her the tiniest shrug imaginable. "Together."

No. No, no, no. She couldn't let him distract her like this, no matter how wildly her heart started beating in her chest the moment he'd said he had feelings for her.

"Please don't say that." She shook her head. *"Please*, Nick."

His eyes flashed, even as his body remained perfectly still. It was the first hint that she'd managed to crack his regal composure. "Why not? It's true."

"Well, it might be true, but it's not...sustainable." Sustainable? Really? Was she giving a speech at a climate control conference or trying to break up with a prince?

You can't break up with someone who was never really yours to begin with.

"Everything we've done together this week was part of a PR stunt, as pretend as my royal credentials," she said.

A muscle in Nick's jaw ticked—the one that Gracie had gotten an eyeful of back when they truly disliked each other.

She hadn't seen it in days.

"Not for me," he said. "Not for a long, long while. Maybe not ever."

This was excruciating. She'd never wanted to believe anyone more in her entire life.

How could she trust that any of this was real? She'd been pretending for so many years that she wasn't sure she really knew how to stop.

And even if she could, it still wouldn't solve the problem—she was in love with him. The longer she stuck around and played at being princess with him, the harder it would be to walk away. If she didn't tell him goodbye now, she'd never be able to do it without breaking apart.

She was a snow princess frozen in time, and when ice was under pressure, it only did one thing. Shatter.

"Nick, you don't really want to be with me. You don't. You care too much about what people think of you to make this real between us. And that's okay. You care because you have to. It's not just your job. It's your birthright, and I don't want to mess that up," she said, because apparently if her heart was going to splinter into pieces, she was going to break his too.

What am I doing?

"That wouldn't happen," Nick said through gritted teeth, and Gracie had to give him credit. She was being unfair, and she knew it. And he was still standing there, still trying to help her believe they were real. "You're not going to mess up. You've done so well dealing with the public so far. Much better than I expected. Everyone *adores* you."

He meant it as a compliment, but Gracie couldn't quite grasp hold of it. She was only human. Eventually, she'd make a mistake. Everyone did. What happened when the public no longer adored her? Would Nick's feelings about her change too?

She wanted *unconditional* love, not to be put on a pedestal.

223

Not even by a prince.

Then, as if he could read her mind, Nick said, "I'm not him, Gracie. I'm not Philip. I'm not going to let you struggle all on your own, and I'm not going to blame you if something goes wrong. We're a team. You can trust me, Princess."

Tears pricked the backs of her eyes. She really wished he wouldn't call her that. Not now. "I'm not a princess, Nick, and I never will be. I'm just a girl who's really good at playing make-believe."

Then she closed the space between them, pressed a tender kiss to his cheek, and bid Prince Charming and his fairy tale life farewell.

"Happy Christmas Eve!" Emilie swung the door open to Nick's quarters the following morning and barged inside, still wearing the footie pajamas she favored during the holidays—red fleece, with flying reindeer zipping all over them.

Nick didn't bother lifting his head from his pillow. There wasn't an ounce of holiday spirit remaining in his body. Nor his soul. It was going to take a true Christmas miracle just to get him through the festivities later tonight in one piece.

"What's going on in here? You never sleep in." Emilie strolled toward the bed and plopped right down.

Nick was going to have to invest in a lock for his door. With any luck, there'd be one under the Christmas tree tomorrow morning, right next to the big box of dog treats that Jaron always bought for Mittens.

At least his dog was still curled against his side, making little snuffling noises in his sleep. Nick supposed this was why Cavaliers were so often called "comforter spaniels." They stuck right by you, both physically and emotionally, when you needed them most.

No sooner had Nick processed that idea than Mittens cracked his eyes open, let out a squeaky dog yawn, and shimmied toward Emilie. She ran her fingertips over his copper-colored ears, and he rolled onto his back and let out an obnoxious sigh.

Consider yourself comforted, Nick thought wryly. The dog had moved on.

Nick picked up one of the numerous pillows on his bed and plopped it over his face.

Emilie nudged his leg with her foot. "Seriously, what's with you? You're being all broody again."

"How can you tell? I'm not even awake yet," he said into the pillow.

Emilie snatched the pillow off him and tossed it toward the foot of the bed. Nick squinted against the ray of morning light drifting through the crack in the draperies.

"That's exactly how I can tell. You haven't slept this late in...well...ever. It's almost nine. You've been bouncing out of bed every morning, eager to get on with the Christmas tour. It's been rather annoying." Emilie sighed. "But not as annoying as this abominable act you've got going on. I thought you were finished with all of that. I can see the knot in your jaw from here."

Nick said nothing, but noted that his jaw was, in fact, tense.

"I kind of thought you'd want to spend the day with Gracie before her performance tonight. She's leaving to-morrow, isn't she?" Emilie stretched her legs out long and wiggled her toes.

Mittens went into a play bow in the middle of the bed before pouncing on one of the feet of her footie pajamas. The pup grabbed the tip of the material with his teeth and tugged. Emilie quite purposefully bent her knee, and thus commenced a ferocious game of Christmas pajama tug-of-war.

At least someone was enjoying Christmas Eve.

"She's planning on leaving tonight, actually. Right after the unveiling of the ice ballroom," he said tersely.

That's what she'd told him, anyway, before she'd left him standing alone in the kitchen at the Kriegs's B&B. Of course, Nick had planned a surprise for today—a surprise that might derail her plans for an early-as-possible departure from San Glacera. But now he wasn't so sure. Maybe she'd still want to go. She seemed awfully determined to get back to the States and put her time in San Glacera behind her.

"That can't be right. She's not leaving tonight." Emilie wiggled her toes again and Mittens attacked her foot with renewed vigor. "We talked about this when we planned the contest. She's definitely staying at least until Christmas morning."

Nick gritted his teeth. "Not anymore."

Emilie propped herself up on her elbows and narrowed her gaze at him. "What did you do?"

Nick threw the covers off and got out of bed. He'd already spent half the night turning everything he and Gracie had said to each other over and over in his mind. He didn't need to rehash it yet again with his younger sister. "Drop it, Emilie. Christmas is almost over."

Gracie had probably done him a favor by refusing to admit that she had feelings for him, even though he knew that it wasn't true. The very fact that she hadn't tried to say otherwise was a pretty good indication that the way he felt about her was mutual. It was always going to end this way, though. December couldn't last forever. It never did.

Except he'd sure wanted it to this year.

"Christmas is *not* over. It's only Christmas Eve, and San Glacera's biggest celebration is tonight. You have time to fix whatever went wrong," Emilie said.

She was still sprawled on top of his bed like she had no intention of leaving anytime soon. Maybe Nick could talk her into taking Mittens for a walk in the palace courtyard so he could get a sliver of peace.

He didn't want peace, though. He'd had enough decorum and serenity to last him a lifetime. For the past week, his life had been infused with unabashed joy. After spending the day with Gracie, he'd sometimes come home, look in the mirror, and spy a fleck of glitter on his face. The strange thing was, he didn't even mind.

"I told her I had feelings for her," he said quietly. His mouth went dry, so he turned his back to Emilie, pushed the curtains open, and pretended to be interested in the workers outside, busy constructing the skating rink for tonight's show.

"Whoa." Emilie jumped off the bed, shuffled over to him, and hugged him from behind. This is amazing. It's just like an episode of *Fairy Tale I Do*."

"No, it most definitely isn't like an episode of your favorite reality show," he said.

Although, she wasn't entirely wrong. He'd watched the show a few times with Emilie and teased her afterward that it had qualified him to win a brother of the year award. He knew enough about it, though, to appreciate the comparison.

Gracie was a party princess, and he was a prince. It was the stuff of theme park romance dreams, right up *Fairy Tale I Do*'s alley. Except for the part about Gracie not loving him back.

Nick's gut churned. *Who said anything about love?*

As everyone in the kingdom so famously knew, those words didn't come easily to Nick. More so now than ever before.

"Gracie doesn't think things could ever work between us." Nick disagreed, obviously. But he couldn't force her into a relationship. She had to want him as much as he wanted her.

Emilie's gaze narrowed. Mittens sat at her feet. Even

Nick's dog seemed to be eyeing him with judgment. "You told her how you felt though, right?"

"As I said. She knows I have feelings for her."

Emilie arched an impertinent brow. "But does she know that you *love* her?"

Nick stared at his sister, long and hard. She knew he didn't like to discuss the things Sarah Jane had said about him. People all over Europe had already talked about it ad nauseam.

Emilie had no intention of dropping the matter, though. "Fine. If you can't say it, you can still show it. That would probably mean more to her anyway."

Nick opened his mouth to ask what she meant, but then he remembered something Gracie had said last night and he promptly closed it.

You care too much about what people think of you to make this real between us.

It had been a difficult thing to hear, and Nick's first instinct had been to deny it. But he hadn't, because he did care about his public image. He had a responsibility to the monarchy to live his life in a way that honored the kingdom. He wanted to be a good king someday—a man who would've made his grandfather proud.

But what had his father tried to tell him?

You don't need to carry the weight of the kingdom entirely on your shoulders, son. Not yet—that's what I'm here for.

"You know I'm right, don't you?" Emilie said.

"You're letting a bunch of Instagram posts go to your head, Em. What Gracie and I had wasn't a romance," he said, but it felt like a lie. A whopper, in fact.

"Please tell me you don't actually believe that." Emilie shook her head. "No one told you to look at her the way you did, and no one told Gracie to light up every time you were around. Jaron and I were the ones writing the captions, but you and Gracie wrote the *story*."

"It's complicated," Nick said, but it sounded like little more than a weak excuse.

Emilie shook her head. "I can't believe this. You've been different since Gracie got here, and now you sound like the same old Nick."

He'd *felt* different. Getting to know Gracie had made him a better man, a better prince. His dad had been right. She'd taught him how to let go and live in the moment.

And now that moment was over.

"Look, Emilie. You were right about the contest. You were right about all of it. San Glacera and its traditions can change while still honoring the past. I realize that now. Just because Gracie is leaving doesn't mean I've changed my tune about any of that."

"But do you realize that kingdoms and traditions aren't the only things that can change? People can change too. Maybe what Gracie really wants is for you to put your heart on the line and make yourself vulnerable as a person, not just a prince." Emilie's brows crept all the way to her hairline. "You realize the reason Dad is always trying to get you to relax is because you're still just a prince, right? You've got the rest of your life to be king. The time to make mistakes is now. Be messy. Be real. The throne isn't going anywhere. Grandpa taught you how to be a monarch, but Dad is doing his best to teach you how to be human."

His father hadn't put things quite so brutally, but he'd told Nick pretty much the same thing. As had Jaron. He'd told Nick the reason he and Gracie were so good together was because she made him seem more accessible...more human.

How many times did he need to hear the same sentiment before he believed it?

"I miss him too, you know," Emilie said quietly. "Grandpa."

Nick's chest gave a pang. He'd been so caught up in his own grief for so long that he sometimes forgot Emilie had lost a grandparent too. "I know you do, Em."

"Did you know he loved ice cream sundaes as much as we do?" She flashed him a cheeky grin.

"Grandpa?" Nick had no recollection of King Noël eating an ice cream sundae. Ever. Sundaes were a secret treat that Nick and Emilie shared on late-night, sneaky trips to the palace kitchen. Nick wasn't sure his grandfather even knew where the kitchen was located.

"Yep. In fact, he's the one who first showed me where the chef kept the hot fudge and caramel sauce." Emilie gave Nick a meaningful head tilt. Caramel sauce had always been his favorite.

"Top back shelf of the walk-in refrigerator, all the way to the right." Nick let out a low laugh. "*Grandpa* knew about that?"

"He sure did. He was Grandpa. I'm pretty sure he knew about every single thing that happened in this castle," Emilie said. Her gaze slid toward Nick, eyes brimming with affection. "He probably still does. I like to think that he's up in heaven right now, watching over us. And if he could come down here and say just one thing to you, do you know what it would be?"

Nick swallowed hard. He couldn't begin to imagine what the late, great King Noël would have to say about the most recent mess he'd made of things.

"I'll tell you," Emilie said with a firm nod. "Grandpa would say he was proud of you. You were always the apple of his eye, Nick. Nothing you could ever do would change that."

Maybe that had been true for a while, but once King Noël had gotten sick and Nick's personal life had become front page news, he doubted that was the case.

Nick shook his head. "But..."

"But nothing. He told me so himself the night before he passed away." Emilie's smile went tender, and tears filled her eyes.

Nick just stared at her, not quite believing what he was hearing. He shook his head. "No."

It couldn't be true. Could it?

"I snuck into his bedroom to bring him a sundae. We talked late into the night—about all sorts of things. And then in the morning, he was gone." A tear slipped down Emilie's cheek, and Mittens let out a quiet whine.

Nick's sister wiped her face, and the dog curled into a ball in her lap.

"Anyway, he was very clear. He said he didn't care about Sarah Jane and the scandal she'd whipped up. In fact, he said that dealing with it would one day make you into a better leader. A better king." The corner of Emilie's mouth quirked into a smile. "He loved you, Nick. He was so proud of you. Always. He told me so himself, right at the end."

Nick's throat closed up tight. He could barely speak.

"Why did you wait so long to tell me this?" he finally asked.

"Grandpa asked me not to—not until the time was right. He said I'd know when." Emilie reached for his hand and squeezed it hard. So hard that Nick's knuckles turned white. "And that time is now."

Nick looked away, focusing intently on the village square and its transformation into a smooth sheet of ice. A chill came over him, from the inside out. He didn't want to end up like the snow maiden in the fairy tale Gracie had told him about. He didn't want to go through life worrying that love might warm his heart and make him melt. He wanted to once again be the man who'd made his grandfather proud.

He *wanted* to melt.

For Gracie.

He looked out the window again and let his gaze sweep over the skating rink. It shimmered like a glacier, with the grand Christmas tree rising from its center. A small stage shaped like a snowflake sat near the edge of the ice, ready and waiting for Princess Snowflake to appear alongside her Prince Charming. Not Nick this time, but someone else. An actor playing a part.

And then, all at once, Nick knew what he had to do. He didn't know if it would work or not, but he had to try. If he didn't, he'd regret it for the rest of his life.

He turned back toward Emilie, and a slow smile came to his lips. When had his kid sister gotten so wise? "Thank you. This conversation was the Christmas gift I didn't know I needed."

She beamed at him. "Happy Christmas Eve."

He flashed her a wink. "Happy Christmas Eve, kid."

Mittens's tail wagged a merry beat as the dog crept toward Nick and pawed at his foot. Nick bent to pick the spaniel up and held his soft, warm body close.

"Happy Christmas Eve to you too, Mittens," he murmured, pressing his cheek against the dog's sweet face.

It might just be time for both of them to come down from their tower.

CHAPTER TWENTY

Her Princess Heart

G RACIE GLANCED AT CLARA AS she slid the last bobby pin into her hair, securing her snowflake crown in place for her final appearance in San Glacera. "It doesn't feel like Christmas Eve."

Clara looked up from the open suitcase on her bed. "Maybe you should take a look out the window, then. It's like the North Pole out there. The skating rink is glorious. A sparkling, frozen mirror."

Gracie couldn't look. Not yet. If she did, her gaze would be immediately drawn to the castle, and she couldn't bear to see it knowing that Nick was somewhere inside those palace walls. This would be the first day since her arrival in San Glacera that she wouldn't be spending by his side. It felt so strange...so wrong.

She missed him. She missed *them*, even though practically every moment they'd spent together had been orchestrated to look like they were a happy couple enjoying the holidays in the most beautiful place she'd ever seen. Somewhere along the way, she'd forgotten it was an act. In her heart, it had been real. Every single moment. None of the things she'd said to Nick last night could change that.

You did the right thing. Maybe if she kept telling herself that, she'd eventually believe it.

But really, what had she thought would happen? That she might stay here, become Nick's real princess, and live happily ever after? Impossible.

The ache in her chest told her that it was exactly what she'd wanted, though. And for a bright, shining moment when Nick's lips touched hers, she'd believed.

"Have you heard from Jaron about changing our flight? I've checked my phone a million times and there hasn't been a single email or text from the palace." Clara folded her favorite Fair Isle sweater and tucked it neatly into her bag. "If we're really leaving tonight after the show, we're going to need an airline reservation."

"I haven't heard anything," Gracie said. She'd looked at her phone more times than she wanted to admit, and... nothing. "Jaron is great, though. I'm sure he'll get it taken care of."

"Unless a certain prince is hoping you change your mind?" Clara aimed a questioning glance in Gracie's direction.

She refocused her gaze on the mirror in front of her, pretending to check over the details of her costume so she wouldn't have to look her friend in the eye. Gracie had told Clara all about her painful goodbye with Nick after the Advent Night party. There was nothing more to talk about—not if Gracie was going to have to go out there in an hour, paste a smile on her face, and sing in front of the entire kingdom, Nick included.

"I'm sure that's not the case. Even if he wanted me to change my mind, it's not going to happen." She took a deep breath and pressed a hand to the lacy bodice of her princess gown in a lame attempt to somehow hold herself together.

Getting through a song seemed impossible, but so had saying goodbye to Nick. Maybe she was stronger than she thought she was.

"Are you sure about that?" Clara said with a sigh.

And then Gracie was saved from answering by a knock on the door of their bedroom. She and Clara exchanged a glance.

"I hope it's Alana. I miss Gumdrop. We're *so* getting a puppy when we get back to Denver," Clara whispered.

Gracie laughed. "Come in!"

The door creaked open, and Ingrid popped her head inside, meeting Gracie's gaze in the mirror. "So sorry to bother you, girls. I know you must be busy getting ready for the show. But Gracie, you have a visitor downstairs."

A visitor?

Gracie spun away from the mirror, heart thundering in her chest. *Calm down. It's probably just Jaron, dropping by to talk about travel logistics.* She swallowed, but her thoughts still ran wild. "Great. Thanks for letting me know. I'll be right down."

"Good." Ingrid gave her an appreciative once-over. "You look lovely, by the way. Like a real Christmas princess."

"Thank you, Ingrid," Gracie said, and her smile went wobbly. It was a sweet thing to say, but she wished Ingrid had chosen another way to put it. Nothing made her feel more like an imposter than the words *real* and *princess* strung together in the same sentence.

Her heartbeat slowed closer to normal. Of course Nick wasn't waiting for her downstairs. If it had been him, Ingrid would have simply said so, wouldn't she?

"Who do you think it is?" Clara said, eyes sparkling.

"Don't look at me like that. It's not him." Gracie gathered the puff of her gown in her hands and made her way to the door.

Clara dropped the pair of jeans she'd been folding. "Well, I'm following you anyway. I can't stand not knowing."

Gracie didn't protest. She liked knowing that Clara had her back, no matter what happened. That's what best friends did. They supported you, even when you did something monumentally stupid like running away after a prince kissed you under the mistletoe.

Butterflies swarmed in her belly as she descended the stairs. *It's not him,* she kept telling herself. *It's definitely not.* But no matter how many times she repeated it in her head, she still hoped. She couldn't help it, because that's what love did. It gave you hope, even when things seemed impossible.

So she kept her gaze fixed on the floor, careful not to trip over her yards and yards of snowy white tulle until she finally reached the bottom of the stairs. Then, with her heart in her throat, she lifted her head and scanned the lobby.

Just as Gracie thought, it wasn't him. But it was the next best thing. She wasn't home for Christmas, but to her complete and utter astonishment, home had come to San Glacera.

The knot in the pit of her stomach that had been there all night slowly unspooled, like a ribbon on a Christmas gift—the most perfect present imaginable.

"Mom and Dad. What are you doing here?"

Half an hour later, Gracie still couldn't believe her eyes. Her parents were here in San Glacera. As Ingrid fussed over her mom and dad, offering them hot cocoa and insisting they try the pistachio Bundt cake she'd just taken out of the oven—a Christmas dream of a dessert with delicate green sponge in the center and topped with a dusting of snowy powdered sugar—Gracie tried to make sense of how this had happened.

She was almost tempted to believe that the cinnamon rolls had magically summoned them, but she knew that couldn't be true. There were limits to what even party princesses could make themselves accept as fact.

Besides, this Christmas Eve surprise had Nick's fingerprints all over it. He knew how much her family meant to her, which was why he'd suggested making the traditional cinnamon roll recipe. He'd wanted her to have a little piece of home while she was here, far away from the only place where she'd ever celebrated Christmas. And then, just twenty-four hours ago, when Ingrid's kitchen had smelled so much like her grandmother's house did when she was a little girl, Gracie had told him she was thinking about her family. She'd stopped short of saying she wished they could come to San Glacera, but he'd known. He'd always been interested in what she was thinking and feeling—even back when they'd had their royally embarrassing misunderstanding about their true identities.

And now here her parents were, sitting in the wingback chairs that faced the Kriegs's big stone fireplace.

"I'm so excited to see both of you." Clara's eyes danced. She hadn't budged from the hearth since Mom and Dad sat down. "Now does it feel like Christmas Eve, Gracie?"

She nodded, not quite trusting herself to speak. Every time she tried to utter a word, she felt like she might burst into tears. "It really does."

"When did you make plans to come?" Clara asked, gaze flitting between Gracie's mom and dad.

Dad laughed and set down his empty dessert plate. "It's the funniest thing. We wanted to come, obviously. We looked into it, back when Gracie first found out she'd won the contest."

"But the flights were so expensive." Mom's eyes widened. "We just didn't know how we'd swing it."

"And then yesterday, someone from the palace called. What was his name again, dear?" Gracie's dad rested a hand on her mom's knee.

"Jacob." Mom frowned. "Or was it Jaden?"

"Jaron. He's the palace press officer," Gracie said as she tried to ignore a ridiculous stab of disappointment. Even if Nick was behind this surprise, he would've left the logistics to Jaron. It wasn't like princes went around making their own flight reservations.

Not even princes who kneaded dough by hand and spent eight hours on their feet in a soup kitchen?

When was she going to stop making assumptions about Nick? Had being on the receiving end of stereotypes about dress-up princesses taught her nothing?

"He was a tremendous help. He got us here overnight. Your dad didn't think it could be done," Mom said.

"I didn't. Christmas is the time for miracles, though." Dad's face split into a wide grin.

"It sure is," Gracie said and as her gaze drifted out the window toward the icy village square, she finally let herself look at the castle.

A wreath hung on every palace window, and the royal standard flag flew from the highest turret, indicating the royal family was in residence—home for Christmas. Snowflakes drifted gently through the air, frosty white. As crazy as it seemed, it felt like they were falling just for her.

And Gracie's princess heart couldn't help but hope that the season had just one more miracle in store.

CHAPTER TWENTY-ONE

The Empty Chair Beside the King

G RACIE STOOD BEHIND A CURTAIN covered in silver sequins, hidden from view of the crowd. The urge to sneak a peek of what was happening out on the ice was almost irresistible.

She'd seen skaters dressed in Victorian costumes lining up, ready to hit the ice ahead of her performance. They'd looked like they stepped straight out of a Dickensian Christmas village, with the women dressed in long velvet dresses and the men in black top hats. Now she couldn't see a thing, but the blades of their skates cut through the ice as they waltzed and spun. The music swelled, sending a shiver of anticipation up her spine.

This was a real performance—not a children's party, not a school or hospital visit, and definitely not a fun little Christmas tour. Gracie had forgotten what the electric moments just before stepping onstage felt like. It had been so long. *Too* long.

Back when she'd been at Juilliard, she'd always been afraid that her voice would fail onstage. She had the worst visions of her mouth opening and nothing coming out. Then one horrible day, that fear had come true. She hadn't known how to handle it. When she'd turned toward Philip for help, the only thing she'd seen in his eyes was the same stone-cold fear that had washed over her, staring right back at her like she'd been looking into a mirror.

Maybe it was the Christmas cheer, so thick in the air that she could feel it. Maybe it was knowing that her mom and dad had come to support her, and that Nick had been the one who'd brought them here. Or maybe it was years upon years of playing Princess Snowflake, a character who was so second nature to Gracie that the two of them felt like one and the same person. Perhaps it was all three of those things, wrapped into one beautiful package. Gracie couldn't say for sure, but the fears of yesterday seemed to melt away while she waited behind that silver curtain. A whisper of calm found its way into her soul, and it sounded like her own voice, her own words, spoken just for her.

Never be afraid to melt.

Gracie smiled to herself. She was the snow maiden, ready to melt to make her deepest dreams come true. She'd been doing nothing but melting since that first sip of San Glacera's legendary hot chocolate. If she could lose her heart to a prince and open herself to everything that came with loving someone—even if just for a week—she could do something as simple as sing. This was the easy part. The hard part would come later, when she stepped onto a plane bound for the States.

"Gracie, you're on in five. Are you ready?" Jaron slipped behind the curtain and flashed her a questioning look, along with a tentative thumbs up.

"As ready as I'll ever be."

"Good, good." Jaron nodded and a crease formed between

his eyebrows. "Listen, there's one small thing. Remember how the actor playing Prince Charming was supposed to join you on stage after your song?"

Gracie gasped. "Oh my goodness, I forgot all about that." Apparently, she only had room in her life for one prince at a time. "I haven't even met him yet. Where is he?"

Jaron winced. "That's the thing. He's not here."

She was getting stood up by Prince Charming. On Christmas Eve.

Perfect. Just perfect.

"I'm really sorry," Jaron said, but he stopped short of offering any sort of explanation.

Not that it mattered. It wasn't as if he could produce a Prince Charming out of thin air. Princess Snowflake had been a solo act for years—since the very beginning. She could handle things on her own.

"It's okay, Jaron," she said.

"Are you sure?"

She nodded. "It's fine, I promise. I've got this."

"There was never a doubt in my mind. The Crown has the utmost faith in you, Gracie." Jaron's smile went warm around the edges, and the air between them grew heavy with all the things he chose not to say. "We all do."

Joy warmed Gracie from within. "Merry Christmas, Jaron."

"Merry Christmas." He tipped his head in the direction of the ice. An announcer called Gracie's name, and the whole kingdom seemed to explode into cheers. "You're on."

And then she squared her shoulders, lifted her chin, and stepped out onto the frozen ballroom.

The snowflake-shaped platform was just a few steps away, and Gracie carefully navigated her way toward it, waving to the audience with her exaggerated party princess flourish. Everywhere she looked, she saw children wearing plastic snowflake crowns. Gracie did her best to soak it all in and bask in the sweet display of affection. She loved San Glacera, and San Glacera loved her right back, but no matter how hard she tried to avoid it, her gaze went straight to the royal box. She scanned the red velvet seats, searching for a glimpse of Nick. All she wanted was one last look, even if he glowered at her like he'd done on the opening night of the Ice Festival.

He's not there.

Reality crashed into her just as the opening bars of her song started. She was alone out here. Really and truly alone. She'd been so sure Nick would be there, watching. Once her parents had shown up, she'd even started to believe that somehow, some way, she and Nick could work things out before she left to go back home. They could start over and build something real. She could take back all the things she'd said the night before.

Gracie hadn't realized how much she'd hoped for a second chance until right then, as her eyes settled on the empty chair next to the king. Her gaze bore into it, and then the strangest thing happened. She spotted a flash of copper and white and then the tilt of a little spaniel's head.

Mittens? Gracie squinted to make sure she wasn't seeing things. Nope, the dog was really sitting proudly in Nick's seat.

She forced herself to look away. Clara stood right at the edge of the ice, smiling so wide that it almost felt like she knew something Gracie didn't—some wonderful Christmas secret. Gracie blinked. Her thoughts were spinning, and she needed to get them under control in three, two, one…

Then it was time. Gracie closed her eyes, took a deep breath, and remembered who she was. She was Princess Snowflake—winter royalty, friend of reindeer, daughter of Frost and Spring, granddaughter of Father Christmas. She was the girl who believed in love so much that she wasn't afraid of what it might do to her. Frozen, fearless…ready to melt if that's what it took to find her happy ending.

Her voice rang out, as clear as a bell.

The crowd clapped with such force that Gracie wasn't sure she could make herself heard above the cheers. But she kept on, her tone growing more rich and powerful with each line of the Christmas carol. When she reached the chorus, she pulled back, letting her voice go breathy and fragile, infused with the tender emotions that were so unique to this time of year. Before she knew it, she was halfway through the song, and she caught Clara's gaze again, fully expecting her friend to have her iPhone pointed in her direction.

It was, of course. But Clara was recording everything blind, not even paying attention to the screen. Instead, she cast a purposeful look to a spot just over Gracie's left shoulder and smiled. For a second, Gracie thought she might have seen tears glistening in Clara's eyes.

She turned to see what had captured Clara's attention just as she reached the song's chorus again, and this time, she didn't need to try to make her voice go tender. It went there all on its own as she took in an impossible sight.

Nick.

But was it really him? Instead of being clothed in his fancy military regalia, he wore what looked more like a costume than anything a Crown Prince would actually put on. The red trousers and white jacket didn't remotely resemble the exquisite ensemble he'd worn the night they met each other at the side castle gate, and the sash across his chest definitely looked a little wonky. As he drew closer, Gracie realized the medals attached to the sash weren't even real coins. They were just round cardboard cutouts that had been spray painted gold.

The truth hit her in the moment Nick's eyes found hers and he winked. It *was* a costume. Prince Charming hadn't stood her up, after all. He was right here, taking his place at her side.

Again, the audience cheered. The applause started as a roar and then, as the spectators recognized that Prince Charming was, in fact, the Crown Prince of San Glacera, they rose to their feet in a rousing standing ovation. Gracie finished the song with a smile in her voice and tears in her eyes. The microphone slipped from her hand, and she threw her arms around Nick as if no one was watching.

"What are you *doing?* Is this real?" she whispered into the crook of his neck.

He tipped her chin with a gentle touch of his fingertips so he could meet her gaze.

"It's always been real for me, Princess. As for what I'm doing?" He let out a laugh. "I'm trying to show you that I'm in love with you. Is it working?"

He'd said it. He'd actually said the words.

I'm in love with you.

Gracie's heart overflowed. "It's definitely working." She wrapped her arms around his neck and rose up on tiptoe to whisper in his ear. The cheers were so loud, she wanted to make sure he heard what she wanted—*needed*—to say. "And I love you, too, Prince Charming. Forget everything I said last night. I'm not going anywhere."

"Good, because I was going to ask you to stay through New Year's Eve. We'll spend the next few days with your family and then we can celebrate the new year together, just you and me. No more pretending, no cameras, no PR. Just us. How does that sound?" His voice rumbled through her.

She inched up closer, and closer still, breathing in his Christmas tree scent. And then she whispered one last thing before the Crown Prince kissed his party princess, right there, for all the world to see.

"Like a fairy tale come true."

EPILOGUE

One year later...

GRACIE GRINNED UP AT NICK as she smoothed down the blue sash stretched across the cheap white material of his Prince Charming jacket. "If we're going to do this every year, we're going to have to invest in a better costume for you."

Nick looked down and gave himself a once over. "What's wrong with this one?"

Gracie bit back a smile. "Nothing at all, if it's what you prefer. I'm just not sure it's going to last another decade of the two of us playing Prince Charming and Princess Snowflake on Christmas Eve."

"Only a decade? You know how I love my Christmas traditions, Princess. This could go on for twenty or thirty more years. Or possibly..." He reached for her hand, turned it over, and pressed a kiss to the emerald-cut diamond and platinum engagement ring that decorated the fourth finger of her left hand. "...for as long as we both shall live."

Joy sparkled inside Gracie. "In that case, you're definitely going to need a new costume. I can sew it myself if you like. Princess gowns are my specialty, but I'm sure I could manage."

"I have no doubt you could, since you seem to accomplish anything and everything you set your mind to, but I kind of like this one. It's special."

Special, indeed.

In the year since Nick surprised Gracie by showing up as Prince Charming during her performance on Christmas Eve, so much had changed. Gracie accepted Nick's invitation to stay in San Glacera through the start of the New Year, and they spent those precious, private days doing the things that normal people did when they'd just started dating.

They went for long walks in the quieter parts of the kingdom with Mittens romping ahead of them in the snow. They cooked together. They played board games, and every time one of Gracie's checkers landed on the back row of Nick's side of the board, she found great joy in yelling *king me*. They binge watched television, and it was revealed that not only was Nick familiar with the show *Fairy Tale I Do*, but he also had strong opinions about which theme parks were the best. Luckily, they both agreed that Once Upon a Time in Florida absolutely ruled, followed closely by Disneyland Paris.

Nick taught Gracie how to snowshoe, which she loved. He also taught her all about mountaineering and living in an ice cave on a jagged cliff for weeks at a time, which she decided might not be her thing. Most of all, they spent their time falling deeper and deeper in love. And on New Year's Day, when Nick went down on bended knee and asked Gracie to become his princess bride, she said yes.

She still wasn't willing to bend on the ice cave thing, though, which was perfectly fine. Even after he slipped the diamond on her finger, Nick still had his life, and she had hers. They decided that the next time Nick went on an extended mountaineering trip, Gracie and Mittens would spend those weeks in Denver helping Clara adjust to her new job as owner and director of Perfect Party Princesses.

That's right—Gracie had hung up her tiara.

Sort of.

Once a party princess, always a party princess. Gracie took a full-time job as the activities director at the San Glacera Children's Hospital, and on special occasions, she slipped back into her Princess Snowflake ballgown and performed for the kids. Even as San Glacera's future queen, Gracie still pulled the occasional snowflake out of her sleeve and wore glitter on her face while she taught children about bravery, kindness, and everything that made them unique and special—mostly, when a patient had a birthday. Or on special holidays, like Valentine's Day and Halloween.

But the entire kingdom had been holding its breath waiting for Christmas Eve when Gracie and Nick would repeat their appearance as Princess Snowflake and Prince Charming at the ice ballroom. And now the big event was only minutes away.

Gracie shivered beside the same silver curtain she'd hidden behind a year ago while the skaters glided and waltzed over the surface of the ice. San Glacera's snowfall this year had hit records numbers already and showed no signs of stopping. Emilie insisted it was because the kingdom had its own snow princess now.

"Cold?" Nick asked as he slid his hands inside Gracie's velvet cape. He rubbed her arms in an effort to keep her warm.

"Yes, but that's okay. The cold is kind of my thing, remember?" She grinned at him.

"Are you kidding? I remember every single minute spent with you, Princess. And I treasure them all." His gaze narrowed. "Even the one where you threw a snowball at my face and told me you didn't like me."

"I was lying about that, you know," she confessed.

Nick bent to kiss her and whispered softly against her lips. "I know."

Gracie let her eyes drift closed as she snuggled against his broad chest. "After this is over, do you want to sneak off to the Christmas market with me? We can share a waffle."

"Sorry, love. I can't." Nick ran his hand over her back in gentle circles. "I've got plans."

She opened her eyes and drew her head back to meet his gaze. "Do you, now?"

"I sure do." His eyes glittered as gray as the sky after an early morning snowfall. "Big ones."

She tilted her head. "And what might those big plans be, exactly?"

He smiled wide, like a kid on Christmas morning. "Marrying the love of my life."

Gracie winked. "Oh, that's today, isn't it?"

"It sure is. Meet you at the cathedral instead?" Nick took her hand, brushed a tender kiss just below her knuckles, and then pressed her palm to the sash draped across his chest.

She felt the pounding of his heart against her fingertips, ever true. The heart of a prince. *Her* prince.

"When the clock strikes seven," she said.

"Don't be late, Princess." He toyed with a lock of her hair, and a warm intimacy percolated between them.

Gracie hadn't realized she'd stopped shivering until right then. "I wouldn't dare."

She felt light on her feet, just thinking about it—as weightless as a snow flurry. They were getting married today. What could be dreamier than a royal wedding on Christmas Eve in the kingdom she now called home?

"We're in this together now. Nothing else matters—not the past and not the press. Just you and me. Are you ready?"

Nick whispered.

"Always," she said.

Then the music soared, the sparkly silver curtains parted, and with her prince by her side, Gracie Clark placed a glass slipper onto the ice and stepped into her future.

THE END

ROYAL HOT CHOCOLATE

Prep Time: 5 minutes
Cook Time: 3 minutes
Serves: 2

Ingredients
- 4 ounces bittersweet chocolate (at least 60 percent cacao), chopped
- 4 ounces brandy (optional)
- 1/2 cup heavy cream
- 1/2 cup whole milk

Preparation

1. In a small heavy saucepan, bring cream and milk to a simmer over medium-high heat.
2. Remove from heat and quickly add chocolate, stirring until melted and very smooth.
3. Return to medium-low heat and warm for 3 minutes or until a bubble or two form on the surface.
4. Pour the hot chocolate into espresso cups.
5. Serve immediately with a side of brandy or Kahlua —or the liqueur can be added to the hot chocolate.

Thanks so much for reading
Once Upon a Royal Christmas. We hope you enjoyed it!

You might like these other books
from Hallmark Publishing:

A Royal Christmas Wish
Christmas Charms
On Christmas Avenue
Mistletoe in Juneau
A Timeless Christmas

For information about our new releases and
exclusive offers, sign up for our free newsletter at
hallmarkchannel.com/hallmark-publishing-newsletter

You can also connect with us here:

Facebook.com/HallmarkPublishing

Twitter.com/HallmarkPublish

ABOUT THE AUTHOR

USA Today Bestselling Author Teri Wilson writes heart-warming contemporary romance with a touch of whimsy, including *Once Upon a Royal Summer* and *Christmas Charms* for Hallmark Publishing. Three of Teri's books have been adapted into Hallmark Channel Original Movies, including *Unleashing Mr. Darcy* (plus its sequel *Marrying Mr. Darcy*), *The Art of Us*, and *Northern Lights of Christmas*, based on her book *Sleigh Bell Sweethearts*. Teri has a major weakness for crowns, cute animals, and pretty dresses, and she loves ballet and Audrey Hepburn films. You can follow her on Instagram at instagram.com/teriwilsonauthor.

Turn the page for a sneak preview of

Christmas CHARMS

A small-town Christmas romance
from Hallmark Publishing

TERI WILSON

CHAPTER ONE

EVERYONE TALKS ABOUT CHRISTMAS MAGIC as if it's an actual, literal thing. As real as silver tinsel draped lovingly from the stiff pine needles of a blue spruce tree. As real as snow on Christmas morning. As real as the live toy soldiers who flank the entrance to FAO Schwartz, the famous toy store now situated in Rockefeller Plaza, right at the center of the bustling, beating heart of Manhattan.

But here's the truth—as authentic as those costumed soldiers seem, they're really just actors killing time until they land a role in an off-Broadway play. I know this because a pair of them stood in line behind me last week at Salads Salads Salads during the lunch rush. Dressed in their tall black hats and red uniforms with glossy gold buttons, they piled their bowls high with lettuce, cucumber slices and shredded carrots while discussing their audition monologues for the upcoming revival of *West Side Story*. It was all very surreal and not the least bit magical.

Genuinely magical or not, though, New York is undeniably lovely during the holidays. After four Christmases in Manhattan, I still go a little breathless every year when I catch my first glimpse of the grand Rockefeller Center

Christmas tree. Every time I stand on the frosty sidewalk in front of Saks Fifth Avenue for the unveiling of their big holiday light show, I feel my heart grow three sizes, just like a certain green you-know-who.

I love this time of year. I always have, but this particular December is special. This Christmas will be my best yet. I just have to make it through my last day at work before taking off on my first real vacation in eight years—to Paris! My boyfriend, Jeremy, has family there, and this year, he's invited me to spend the holidays with them. Christmas magic, indeed.

Oui, s'il vous plaît.

I pull my coat tighter and more snugly around my frame as I jostle for space on the busy midtown streets. The very second the floats in the Macy's Thanksgiving Day parade pack up and go home, Christmas shoppers and holiday tourists descend on Manhattan in droves. The switch is kind of jarring. One minute, a sixty-two-foot inflated turkey is looming over Central Park West, and the next, his giant, colorful plumage is nowhere to be seen. Swinging shopping bags are the only thing in sight, all the way from one end of 5th Avenue to the other.

The Christmas crowds are predictably terrible, so I always leave extra time during the holiday season for my walk to the upscale jewelry store where I work, just a few blocks from FAO Schwartz and its not-so-magical toy soldiers. A snowstorm blew in last night—the first of the Christmas season. And even though I'm in serious danger of being swallowed up by the crush of people headed toward the ice-skating rink at Rockefeller Center, I can't help but marvel at the beauty of the season's first snowfall.

Manhattan looks almost old-fashioned covered in a gentle layer of white. Frost clings to the cast iron streetlamps, and icicles drip from the stained-glass windows of St. Patrick's Cathedral. Huge Christmas wreaths have been placed around the necks of Patience and Fortitude, the massive stone lions that flank the main branch of the public library like bookends, and when a winter storm is sprinkled on top, the tips of their front paws and noses are the only visible glimpses of pale gray marble beneath a blanket of sparkling snow. I can almost picture them rising up to shake the snowflakes from their manes and prowling through Midtown, leaving a trail of paw prints in the fresh powder.

I smile to myself as I near the toy store. One of the actor soldiers out front pauses from saluting at passersby to pose for a selfie with a little girl bundled up in a bright red snowsuit. It's an adorable scene, and I let my gaze linger longer than I should. Before I register what's happening, I plow straight into a man exiting the store.

Oof.

We collide right at the edge of the red carpet stretched out beneath FAO Schwartz's fancy marquee. Technically, I'm only partly to blame. The man's arms are piled so high with gift-wrapped packages that I can't even see his face, so I doubt he can tell where he's going or who might be in his way. My gaze snags on the sight of his hands in the seconds just before impact. They're nice hands—strong, capable. The sort of hands that can probably steer a car using only two fingers. Cradle a sleepy puppy in a single palm. Loosen a necktie with one swift tug.

I blink, and then impact occurs and the packages scatter. The rattle of what sounds like airborne Lego bricks and who knows what else snaps me back to attention.

"I'm so sorry. I wasn't watching where I was going," I say. I drop to my knees on the sidewalk to try and collect as many of his gift-wrapped packages as I can before they get stepped on. "Here, let me help you."

We reach for the same box and when our fingertips collide, I realize there's something almost familiar about those nice hands of his. Something that makes my stomach do a little flip, even before I look up to meet his gaze. And when I finally stand and get a glimpse of his face, I'm more confused than ever.

Aidan? My arms go slack, and all the presents I've just scrambled to pick up tumble to the ground again. *Aidan Flynn?*

No. It can't be. Absolutely not.

One of his packages must have conked me on the head or something and made my vision go wonky, because there's no way my high school sweetheart just walked out of FAO Schwartz. The Aidan Flynn I used to know wouldn't be caught dead in New York City. He was a hometown boy, through and through—as much a part of Owl Lake as the snow-swept landscape. Hence, our awkward breakup.

"Ashley," Aidan says, and it's more a statement than a question. After all, he shouldn't be as surprised to see me. I'm the one who belongs here. This is my city, my home—the very same city I left him for all those years ago.

Still, he seems to be almost as stunned as I am, because he makes no immediate move to pick up the remaining gifts scattered at our feet.

"Aidan, what are you..." I clear my throat. Why is it so difficult to form words all of a sudden? "What are you doing here?"

This can't be real. It's definitely some sort of Christmas hallucination. Not magic, definitely not that. Even though I can't exactly deny that there's a pleasant zing coursing through me as we stare at each other through a swirl of snowflakes.

I shake my head. *Get ahold of yourself.* I've moved on since Aidan and I dated, obviously. Eight years have passed, and now I'm practically engaged...sort of.

In any case, I shouldn't be wondering why Aidan looks as if he's just bought out an entire toy store. Is he a father now? Is he *married*? Is he a married to a *New Yorker*? All of these possibilities leave me feeling a little squeamish. I wish I could blame my sudden discomfort on something gone off at Salads Salads Salads, but alas, I can't.

"I'm working," he says, which tells me absolutely nothing. He could be one of Santa's elves for all I know. Or a professional gift wrapper. Or a personal shopper for a wealthy Upper West Sider who has a dozen small children.

Somehow none of those seem like realistic possibilities. Against my better judgment, I sneak a glance at his ring finger.

No wedding ring. My gaze flits back to his face—his handsome, handsome face. Goodness, has his jaw always been that square?

"Oh," I say. Ordinarily, I'm a much better conversationalist. Truly. But I'm so befuddled at the moment that I can't think of anything else to say.

Plus, I'm pretty sure Aidan noticed my subtle perusal of his most important finger, because the corner of his mouth quirks into a tiny half smile.

My face goes instantly warm. If a snow flurry lands on my cheek, it will probably sizzle. When Aidan bends down to scoop up the packages I dropped, I take advantage of the moment to fan my face with my mittens. Out of the corner of my eye, I notice one of the toy soldiers smirk in my direction. As if I need this surprise encounter with my Christmas past to get any more awkward than it already is.

Aidan straightens, and I jam my mittens back into my coat pocket. I really should get going. My shift starts in less than ten minutes, and Windsor Fine Jewelry is still a good eight-minute walk this time of year.

But something keeps me rooted to the spot, and as much as I want to blame it on simple nostalgia, I'm not sure I can. Aidan is more than my high school sweetheart. He's the personification of another place and time. And every now and then, the memories sneak up on me when I least expect them—now, for instance. Whenever it happens, I feel strangely empty, like one of those chocolate Santas you don't realize are hollow until you bite into them and they break into a million pieces.

That's silly, though. I'm fine, and my life here in Manhattan is great. I'm certainly not on the verge of breaking.

I square my shoulders as if to prove it, but when I meet Aidan's soft blue gaze, my throat grows so thick that I can't speak. Not even to say goodbye.

"It was good to see you, Ashley," he says.

And then he's gone just as quickly as he appeared, and I'm once again standing alone in a crowd.

CHAPTER TWO

"IT'S MAGICAL!"

The little girl stands tippy-toe on the opposite side of the glass display case, beaming at me as she wiggles her hand to and fro. Six whimsical silver charms dangle from the bracelet on her wrist, glittering beneath the twinkle lights of the towering white Christmas trees that Windsor Fine Jewelry is famous for at this time of year.

I grin back at her. "I can't promise it's magical, but it's a beautiful bracelet. Perfect for Christmas in New York."

It's been hours since I ran into Aidan Flynn on the sidewalk, and I've just spent the past thirty minutes helping this sweet child and her father select half a dozen custom charms from Windsor's new holiday collection. I'm back in my element on the fourth floor of Manhattan's finest jewelry store, and I almost feel like myself again. Aidan is part of my past. Period.

After much deliberation, my young customer has settled on a silver candy cane with stripes in our store's signature blue, a Santa hat, a reindeer with a petite ruby nose, a gingerbread man with three Windsor-blue buttons and a snowflake sparkling with tiny diamonds. Upon my recommendation, they've also added a shiny silver apple charm to represent their holiday shopping trip to the Big Apple.

All in all, quite an extravagant Christmas gift for such a young shopper. But luxury is Windsor's specialty and the primary reason tourists flock to the store's flagship location on the corner of Madison Avenue and 57th Street, especially during the holidays. *Everyone* hopes to find one of Windsor's coveted royal blue boxes under their tree on Christmas morning. Locals and tourists alike.

It's one of the things that makes working at Windsor so exciting. Sometimes I have to pinch myself to make sure I'm not dreaming. Manhattan is only a six-hour train ride away from the small lakeside town where I grew up, but glamour-wise, it may as well be on another planet.

"Thank you, Daddy," the little girl says, turning wide blue eyes toward the man towering beside her. *Adorable.* My heart gives a little clench.

So do my feet, for less sentimental reasons. I've been positioned behind the charms counter for six hours straight with no opportunity to sit. As much as I love my job, the holiday hours are brutal, and with the crush of Christmas shoppers, sometimes it feels like there's no end in sight.

Except there *is* one in sight—the most dazzling, glamorous ending imaginable. And it's headed my way in less than twenty-four hours.

This time tomorrow, I'll be on a plane to the most gorgeous city in the world!

I bite the inside of my cheek to keep myself from squealing out loud.

Across from me, the little girl's father rests an affectionate hand on his daughter's shoulder. "You're welcome, pumpkin."

"Shall I wrap it for you, or would you like to go ahead and wear it?" I shift my weight from one throbbing foot to the other.

"I'd like it wrapped, please. In one of those pretty blue boxes tied with white ribbon?" The sweet child bounces up and down as she offers me her wrist so I can unfasten the bracelet.

"Of course." I wink at her as I release the tiny silver clasp. "I'll be right back. Have some hot cocoa while you wait."

I nod toward the wall of big picture windows overlooking snow-dusted Manhattan, where a gloved coworker dressed in a dark suit and blue silk tie serves hot chocolate from a silver tea service to waiting customers.

Read the rest!
Christmas Charms is available now.

Cozy Up & Enjoy More Hallmark!

Sit back, relax, and watch
Hallmark Channel!

Wine and a great book: a perfect pairing!
HallmarkChannelWines.com

Satisfy your sweet tooth
with **Hallmark Channel Chocolate**
at Bissingers.com

Get our official fan merchandise at
Hallmark.com

Never miss a premiere!
Download the **Hallmark Movie
Checklist App!**

Watch anytime & anywhere with
Hallmark Movies Now